Bird Summons

Leila Aboulela was born in Cairo and grew up in Khartoum. She has written four other novels: *The Translator, Minaret* and *Lyrics Alley*, all of which were longlisted for the Orange Prize, and *The Kindness of Enemies. Lyrics Alley* won Novel of the Year at the Scottish Book Awards and was shortlisted for the Commonwealth Writers' Prize. She was awarded the Caine Prize for her short story 'The Museum', which is included in her collection *Elsewhere, Home* – winner of the Saltire Fiction Book of the Year. She lives in Aberdeen.

Also by Leila Aboulela

NOVELS

The Translator
Minaret
Lyrics Alley
The Kindness of Enemies

SHORT STORY COLLECTIONS

Coloured Lights
Elsewhere, Home

Bird Summons

Leila Aboulela

WEIDENFELD & NICOLSON

First published in Great Britain in 2019
by Weidenfeld & Nicolson
an imprint of the Orion Publishing Group Ltd
Carmelite House, 50 Victoria Embankment,
London EC4Y 0DZ

An Hachette UK Company

1 3 5 7 9 10 8 6 4 2

A CIP catalogue record for this book
is available from the British Library.

ISBN (Hardback) 978 1 4746 0012 5
ISBN (Export Trade Paperback) 978 1 4746 0013 2
ISBN (eBook) 978 1 4746 0014 9

Typeset by Input Data Services Ltd, Somerset

Printed and bound in Great Britain by Clays Ltd, Elcograf S.p.A.

www.orionbooks.co.uk
www.weidenfeldandnicolson.co.uk

Assembly of birds, the Hoopoe spoke,
I am the Messenger Bird . . .

A bird who carries Bismillah in its beak
is never far from the wellspring of mysteries.

Farid'ud-Din Attar, *The Conference of the Birds*

It is travel which lifts up the curtain
hiding people's characters.

Al-Ghazali, *On Conduct in Travel*

Chapter One

She had hired a coach, then when the women started pulling out after the anger over the photo, a minibus, then when the numbers fell still further, a people carrier, then when there was just the three of them, Salma decided to take her own car. She had fought a battle and lost. The next time the Arabic Speaking Muslim Women's Group held their annual election, she would be voted out and someone else would be in charge. She had misjudged the situation. 'How was I meant to know that the grave had been defaced!' This was a lame defence. If her rivals in the group could find a news article and post it to the group chat, Salma hadn't done her research properly. But even if she had known, it wouldn't have deterred her. It certainly wasn't deterring her now. She still wanted to go and offer her respects. She still believed in the purpose of the visit – to honour Lady Evelyn Cobbold, the first British woman to perform the pilgrimage to Mecca, to educate themselves about the history of Islam in Britain, to integrate better by following the example of those who were of this soil and of their faith, those for whom this island was an inherited rather than adopted home.

Salma's determination stemmed from her recent restlessness. Ever since her last birthday, time seemed to be snagging. She would put her foot forward and find herself still in the same place, as if she were about to stumble. More than once, she found herself wondering, can I last till the end without giving up or making a fool of myself?

In her argument to the Arabic Speaking Muslim Women's Group, she said, 'We might never understand what it's like to be the eldest daughter of the seventh Earl of Dunmore or to have a town house in Mayfair and a 15,000-acre estate in the Highlands, but Lady Evelyn was a woman like us, a wife and a grandmother. She worshipped as we worshipped, though she kept her own culture, wore Edwardian fashion, shot deer and left instructions for bagpipes to be played at her funeral. She is the mother of Scottish Islam and we need her as our role model.'

The outrage had blown up right in her hands. One minute she was taking confirmations, collecting money, debating whether the cut-off age for including boys should be eight or ten, and the next, the photo was posted on the group page – a photo of the headstone broken off and the plaque bearing the Qur'anic verse of light crossed out. This was followed by a deluge of comments seemingly from all thirty-six members of the group. *Is this what u want our children to see? that u can be from the Scottish aristocracy, buried in the middle of nowhere and still the haters will get u.*

After the initial anger, further doubts surfaced and were posted – *Why didn't she wear hijab? Why wasn't she in touch with other Muslims? Sounds like an eccentric imperialist no offence* . . . Then women started dropping out of the trip because their friends were dropping out or because their husbands discouraged them. *Its 2 far away. Heard that some brothers from Glasgow tried to find it and got lost.* Apathy crept in too. *Khalas we know about her from what u said. We read the links u sent, no need to visit.* Even Salma's daughters refused to go because no one their age was going. And so, it now whittled down to the three of them – Salma, Moni and Iman.

Salma's refusal to abandon her much-diminished trip stemmed from her insistence not to be stopped or cowed by the Arabic Speaking Muslim Women's Group and her assumption that a true leader forged ahead without need of followers. She was, though, grateful for the company of the other two and adjusted the journey with them in mind. Instead of an overnight visit to Lady Evelyn's grave they would stay a week at the loch, a resort on the grounds of a converted monastery, then make their leisurely way to visit the grave.

'Why so long?' Moni had asked.

'Because you of all people need a break.'

Moni didn't think she needed a break, but she did feel beholden to Salma for all her help with Adam's condition, and when the other women in the group had started pulling out of the trip, she had decided to express solidarity with her friend.

It surprised Salma that, out of all the women in the group, Moni was the one who ended up coming. They were not particularly close. As for Iman, she went everywhere with Salma, sitting next to her in the front seat. If you wanted to be mean, you would say that Iman was Salma's sidekick. If you wanted to be nice, you would say she was like a devoted, much younger sister.

Iman was beautiful. Old-fashioned eyes and sulky lips, the dip of her head and husky voice. Even with her hijab, men smelt her from afar, looked longer at her, exerted themselves to make her smile. She was in her twenties but on her third marriage. Once widowed, and once divorced. When Moni had first met Iman at Salma's house, she was kept amused listening to Iman's tales of prospective suitors. She seemed to have an unlimited supply – of both tales and suitors. Yet she narrated her stories in a flat voice, as if it was boring, after all, to be stunning. Moni would never know. She had, at certain times of her life, with the help of expensive attention and good taste, pulled off looking attractive. Her wedding photos, professional and stylish, were widely admired. These days she looked nothing like she had done at her wedding.

Salma, Moni and Iman – travelling companions. Escaping the stuck-together buildings of the city, the regenerated Waterfront, the Jute Museum, the busy Tay Road Bridge and the pretty park overlooking the estuary; distancing themselves from the coffee-scented malls, the kebab restaurants and the trapezoid mosque; getting away from the scheduled rubbish collections and the weekly meeting of the Arabic Speaking Muslim Women's Group. The three of them moving together and alone.

On the morning of their departure, Moni needed to settle her son first at the nursing home. Salma and Iman waited for her in the car. Moni had never been separated from Adam. She sat on the bed that had been assigned to him, holding him up on her lap, manoeuvring him out of his jacket. She was used to doing this, his head lolling if she didn't support it, his arms flopping wide. Five-year-olds his age would be tying up their own shoelaces, but Adam had severe cerebral palsy. Looking around her, Moni approved of the small ward, it's cleanliness and order, and she had been given a tour of the dining room, the recreation room full of toys and a television, the garden for regular fresh air. 'It's Adam's first time with us, right?' the nurse had asked her. Moni liked the direct use of his name, the dignity of it. Moni had often been encouraged to take a respite, and Adam's health visitor outlined the length of time and kind of relief that the services offered for carers of profoundly disabled children. But it had taken Salma's insistence to get Moni to take up the opportunity.

Moni felt soothed by the soft colours of the walls, the cartoon decorations, the tunes of a childish song coming from the next room. Once his jacket was removed, Moni placed Adam on the bed, folded his wheelchair and started putting his things away in the bedside chest of drawers. Another nurse came to talk to her, though when she introduced herself, she said she was a student volunteer. The girl, with angelic eyes and braces, smiled and chatted to Adam as if he could understand all that she was saying. It made Moni smile and pitch in for him, venturing answers as if speaking on his behalf. She glanced at the other children, some in wheelchairs and some in bed. A few were even more disabled than Adam and that made her feel better.

The real nurse came back and explained how Moni in the next few days could phone in to check up on Adam. 'Anytime is fine, but please avoid calling during mealtimes when the staff are busy with the children.' The sentence startled Moni. She wasn't really going to leave him to be fed by strangers, was she? Strangers who might need to answer the phone calls of inconsiderate parents. Adam started to cry and fidget, his right leg jerked. She sat down on the bed and pulled him onto her lap. She gathered the expanse of his limbs, the awkward angles of his body, his spread-out weight and smoothed him to a centre. He fretted while she rocked and soothed him, her chin on his curls, his saliva dripping on her wrist. When contentment settled on him, he became less stiff and she felt settled too. With him was total belonging and peace. She didn't want to leave, neither to take him back home nor to travel with Salma and Moni. She was happy like this, her lap full of his closeness, his smell, his sounds. She had given him a bath this morning, dressed him in his best clothes so that he would make a good impression. This was a special outing for him. The nursing home was a nice place and the nurses were kind. She would stay with him, why not? Yes, that was the best idea, she would help the nurses by looking after Adam while they concentrated on the other children. It would be a change for her, all the change she needed. Never mind about the trip to the Highlands.

From outside, the nursing home looked like any ordinary bungalow in a residential area, perhaps a little bigger, but it blended with its surroundings. Iman opened her door and undid her seat belt. The weather was pleasant, a late summer that was hitting its stride rather than giving in to the cold winds of autumn. 'Moni will take for ever. The meat will thaw,' she said. They were carrying frozen halal chicken and minced beef in the boot, knowing they would not find any in the shops near the loch.

'No, it won't,' said Salma. 'I wrapped it in aluminium foil.' She strummed her fingers on the steering wheel, already thinking of how to utilise the time. Nip inside to use the toilet, check her phone for messages or chat to Iman? She reached into her bag and felt something square and hard. She pulled out a gift-wrapped box. There was a note attached to it from her husband, David. *Happy Journey, my love.*

She tore through the wrapping, tossing it on Iman's lap, and gasped when she saw the new smartphone.

'Ooh, you're lucky,' said Iman, starting to fold up the paper.

The screen was larger than Salma's two-year-old one, the whole phone slimmer, its back a pure creamy white. She switched it on straight away, the button only needing the slightest touch, the lights flaring towards her in a swarm of colours.

'He's so sweet,' she said, almost to herself. Last night, he had hugged her as she was packing her suitcase, pressed his palm against her lower stomach and she had felt pleased that it was flat (well, almost flat) even after four pregnancies, her pelvic floor muscles in excellent condition.

On the dashboard she placed her old phone and the new one next to each other and started the smart switch. She must phone him to say thank you. Once she put in her SIM card, he would be the first one she would call. She noted the time on the screen. 'I'll give Moni an extra ten minutes before I go in and get her.'

Iman said, 'When I see what Moni goes through, when I see Adam, I'm glad I don't have any children.'

'You're just saying that. You don't mean it. Most children are healthy. Yours will be too, inshallah.'

7

Salma's four children were burly and good at everything: school, sports, hobbies. She was often anxious that the evil eye would smite them. Perhaps it already had. Her quarrel with her daughter still blazed in her ears. Free to study what she wants, to turn down an offer to medical school, after all the private tutoring and the gruelling interview. To get that far then cop out for something easier. Sports science! 'What would you become?' Salma had reasoned with her. 'A fitness trainer? That's not much better than me!' Ungrateful, lacking ambition. And David's laissez-faire attitude towards this issue was infuriating too. Just thinking about the whole thing made her feel betrayed – the daughter she had fed through cracked nipples, taught how to belly dance, worked extra hours so that she could afford to give her the best of everything. But a girl backed by her father could not lose a fight. Salma instead was the one left smarting. Which was why this holiday was a good idea. She must forget the anxiety about her daughter's future and focus on Iman instead, the one who was always there for her, never thwarting or challenging. The more Salma's children grew away from her, became more British and less a piece of her, the more she found herself relying on Iman. She didn't need to justify herself to Iman, or feel self-conscious about her accent, or put up with the roll of the eyes and accusations that she just 'didn't get it'. Iman was easy to talk to, easy to understand. 'Your children will be in the best of health,' she now said to her friend.

Iman sighed. Husband after husband and they had given her nothing. Not even a miscarriage to kindle some 'nearly there' hope. She had done the tests and they were all inconclusive.

Salma began her pep talk – a mixture of religion and popular psychology. Iman fidgeted with the contents of her handbag, but she was listening. She didn't disagree with Salma but a sense of resignation was creeping in. Was that what life was about? Trotting after the carrot, if you were lucky enough to escape the stick. Fighting for what could be got by fighting. Otherwise waiting your turn with a smile. There were things she wanted – to be queen of her own household, to bring her mother over from Syria, to walk in expensive shoes. She listened to Salma's words, which were intended to soothe and brighten but instead stoked a steady hunger. What if she never ever had a child? What would the future look like?

Salma was moved by Iman's anxiety, the dip in Iman's head, the darkening of her eyes. At the same time, a side of her could not help but admire the aesthetics. Sadness on Iman was like dark eyeshadow, like good mascara or smudged kohl. There was a cosmetic veneer about it that rendered Iman photogenic. Iman now took out an emery board from her handbag and started filing her nails. Only then did Salma stop talking.

Salma removed her SIM card from her old phone and put it in the new one. She called David and, when he didn't pick up, left him a voice message, saying she was speaking from her beautiful new phone, laughing through her thanks and goodbyes. She checked for new messages. It was now lunchtime in Egypt and Amir would have had time to answer her text. But there was nothing new. 'Remember,' she said to Iman, speaking as if she had to choose every word with care, 'some time back I told you about an old colleague from university who contacted me via social media?'

'The one you were engaged to?'

'We never did get officially engaged. But yes, him. You told me not to accept his friend request.'

'Of course. Most people are desperate to unfriend, block and avoid seeing news of their exes, let alone adding them as friends. Don't tell me you did?'

Salma made a face.

Iman laughed. 'Well, I warned you, didn't I? What happened?'

'Nothing.' What could possibly happen when they were in totally different countries, when they were both happily married – at least she was, she wasn't sure about him. They were both tied down by children and jobs, continents apart. It was this sense of safety that allowed her to correspond with him. A confidence in herself. Now in the car, she said to Iman, 'Strange thoughts and dreams of a parallel life I could have had, if I hadn't left him.'

'It wouldn't have been a better life,' said Iman. Her tone was careless, like tossing back her hair or flopping onto a sofa. 'You have a good life, Salma. A lot of people envy you.'

The word 'envy' irritated Salma. Roused her anxiety for her children, and for her successful life too. David was a Scottish convert and that meant she was treated better by him than her friends were who were married to Arab, African or Asian men. David gave her all the freedom she wanted. He respected her opinions. He shared all the household tasks. She had nothing, not a grievance small or large, unless you counted the latest quarrel, to complain about. Only perhaps the occasional feeling of greed, of wanting more, more of David's time and touch. More of his undivided attention. But surely that didn't count. Perhaps she should have listened to Iman, who had more experience with discarded partners. A mixture of curiosity and feigned innocence had made her accept that friend request.

Salma said, wanting to be clear, wanting to justify herself, 'Maybe not a better life. But completely different.'

'So what?' said Iman.

Salma was disappointed. There was an intellectual satisfaction in pursuing that 'what if' parallel scenario. Why was Iman so pedantic and literal? But she regarded her younger friend as a useful sounding board. She said, 'I've started to imagine that other life clearly, like I'm watching a film. A film about myself.' The other Salma would have been Dr Salma for a start. Not a massage therapist. When Salma had first come to Britain, she found that her medical degree was not sufficient. After failing her qualifying exams twice, she had sat herself down firmly and taken stock of the situation. Not enough money, baby on the way and David, himself the first in his family to go to university, was not exerting undue pressure on her to practise as a doctor. It was time to pursue other alternatives. Changing sheets and bedpans would have been too much of a blow to her ego. She said no to nursing. The qualifications and training to become a massage therapist were affordable and accessible. She surged ahead. She didn't look back. Until last month when, in their very first exchanges, Amir addressed her as Dr Salma and she had to say, 'I'm not a doctor.' And because he wasn't as polite as David, he contradicted her and said, 'Nonsense. You are. We graduated in the same year and you got better grades in the exams than I did.'

'Told you Moni would take ages,' Iman drawled. 'Bet you,

she'll now say she doesn't want to go on this trip at all. It won't be easy for her to leave Adam.'

Salma hadn't thought of this. Surely Moni couldn't back out now, not after all the preparations. Not after having got this far. She hurried into the nursing home.

Iman stepped out of the car. She walked a few steps and stood under a tree. The tree hid her from the road. She took off her coat and felt the breeze through her clothes. She felt submission wafting towards her from the nursing home, as if it were tangible and elemental. The submission to imperfection, to illness, to fate. It didn't make her sad. Instead she understood it as if it were an old language she had practised, as if it were as basic and solid as the ground beneath her feet. She closed her eyes and heard the distant traffic, a few soft sounds coming from inside the home, then the caw of seagulls. The sunlight played on her closed eyelids, she smelt the leaves of the tree and the fresh air. Existence without feelings or desires – nothing to complain or brag about. She smelt the grass and heard a bird sing *hoo poo hoo poo* again and again. She opened her eyes and saw it on a branch of the tree. Gold necklace around its neck, a delicate crown. There was something reassuring about it, a weight and a balance. Iman reached up her hand as if she wanted it to settle on her wrist. Instead it fluttered and hopped further away up the branch. 'Come back,' she said in Arabic, her voice sounding foreign in her ears. But would the bird understand English better? What language was the speech of birds?

Moni was sniffling into a tissue when she and Salma walked out of the nursing home. Iman took up her place in the front

12

passenger seat and pretended not to notice. She didn't want to embarrass Moni. It was a shame, but what was the right thing to say in such a situation? It was obvious that Salma had pulled off a miracle in persuading Moni to leave Adam. Iman admired Salma's perseverance, her confidence in doing the right thing. This was why she felt safe with Salma. Someone who knew all the answers, who filled in the gaps for older cousins and young aunties left behind. Last year, when Iman married Ibrahim, Salma had helped her with all the preparations, hosting the henna party at her house and even sugaring Iman's legs for her.

Salma led Moni into the back seat behind Iman. She buckled up the belt for her. Moni started saying the travel prayer even before Salma got into the driver's seat, '. . . *we are returning* . . .' Spread out in the back, she could see Salma skirting the bonnet of the car, the definitive bounce in her step, the way she sat up straight and punched in the destination on the GPS.

Iman answered a text from her husband. All her husbands, one after the other, were possessive. Even Salma was a possessive friend. Iman, surrounded by this tight grip of adulation and comfort, didn't long to escape; like a pet, she neither bristled nor rebelled. She did, though, see herself growing up, becoming more independent. She was not sure how this independence would come about. It would not take the shape of aloneness, she was sure. Always, Iman was surrounded by others. She was sought after because she was decorative and enhancing. If she felt hemmed in, it was because she was popular and in high demand. Everything has a cost. Whenever she turned, there would be someone to guide her, adopt

13

and sponsor her. In return, they owned her one way or the other. She tolerated all this for the time being. She took it for granted. It was bearable and not altogether unpleasant. Deep down she knew that when the right time came to exit, she could slip out and no one would be able to hold her back.

Moni prayed that she would return safely to her son. She prayed that he would be all right while she was away. Through her tears, she saw the familiar orange sign of Sainsbury's. It had been a long time since she was in a supermarket. She ordered everything online and had it delivered. Weeks passed in which all she did was take Adam back and forth to the doctor, to the district nurse and to Salma, his massage therapist. It got harder, not easier. And she needed every cell in her brain and every ounce of energy to look after him.

Salma drove fast, out of the city. She had chosen to take the longer route because it afforded the better road. The speed made her aggressive. 'The loch is a great place, Moni. Beautiful scenery. There are forest trails where we can go for walks. We can go on a boat. You'll love it. And then, inshallah, we will accomplish our goal and read Fatiha at Lady Evelyn's grave. There'll be a selfie of us stuck online showing everyone that, yes, we've done it!'

Through her sobs, Moni managed to say, 'Thanks, Salma.' When Salma had found her telling the baffled nurses that she wanted to stay, she had, to Moni's relief, taken control of the situation. Gentle and firm, she had eased Adam out of her arms and reassured her yet again that he would be in the best of care. Adam had not understood that she was leaving him, and she was grateful for that. She now wondered if he cared that he was the only black child. If he even noticed.

Sometimes at home, looking into his eyes, she searched for things other than the dull pain, other than the acceptance. The staff had been kind and patient with her. Every medical establishment Moni had encountered through the NHS was full of sympathy and understanding. While all Murtada could say was: We must behave normally. Life goes on. He said this when she was still refusing to have sex three whole months after the birth. When she did not want to go back home on holiday. Eventually they did go to Sudan for Murtada's brother's wedding, but people were so unkind about Adam, so blatantly curious, at turns blaming her (it had to be someone's fault) and pitying her, that she was miserable. She began to keep Adam not only indoors but in her room, away from the prying visitors, who seemed to be attracted to him as a grotesque curiosity.

Before his birth, Moni had been active, positive and smiling, with her high-powered bank job and independence. Murtada had courted her for years before she succumbed. At first, she had not judged him good enough for her and assumed she could do better. It was his own matter-of-fact awareness of this which caught her attention, his blunt, 'I know your family is better off than mine, I know that you are socially higher, but I will not take a penny from you because that's not why I want you,' which roused her admiration. He was a chartered accountant specialising in corporate finance and they had met when he was securing a loan through her bank. She was impressed and humbled by his dedication to his career and perseverance; his efforts at improving himself touched her, his ambitions for gaining international experience captured her imagination. She wanted a large family and his instinct to provide – 'I will pamper you even more than your family pampered you. I will do anything for you' – won her over. She loved how he described his very first impression of her on the day they met – bust straining against the tailored jacket she was wearing, her hijab tied slick, the ruthless way she questioned his proposal. This truly was how she had been. Then Adam's birth bulldozed her. After that failed visit back home, she stood up to Murtada. 'I will not take Adam there again. I will not take him to those backward fools.' Murtada had replied, 'These fools are our flesh and blood.' But she didn't care. She became one of those women to whom things were clear-cut. Everything back there was bad, and everything here was good.

The more they slept apart – she with Adam and Murtada on his own – the more they disliked each other. Murtada was not comfortable with Adam and she could not forgive him for this. Just the sight of Adam depressed Murtada. He would gaze at him with bewilderment and dismay. Murtada wanted a cure, he wanted state-of-the-art surgery and strong medication. It took him time to accept that nothing could be done. When he did accept this fact, after an inner tussle and genuine agony, he wrote Adam off. He shelved him. We must go on and live our lives as fully as possible, he said to Moni. We must have other children. We must be happy. We cannot let his condition rule us. All this fell on deaf ears. Moni was busy. Busier than she had ever been in her life, and more important. You're a good mum, the nurses said. You're doing a brilliant job. A job that was hard but encompassing and all-absorbing, rousing all her sincerity and resilience. Looking after Adam, Moni became stronger. Father of a disabled son,

Murtada became weaker. He was in Saudi Arabia now, in a new job, still on probation. He wanted Moni and Adam to join him but wasn't yet in a position to bring them over. This distance apart suited Moni.

'So many trucks,' Iman was saying. She was watching the road as if she herself were driving. She could neither drive nor afford to take lessons and admired Salma's flair in over-taking the slower vehicles. 'Even if I ever get my licence, I won't drive on these big roads. I'll stick to the city.'

'*When* you get your licence,' Salma corrected her. 'Say inshallah.'

'Inshallah.'

'It's you, Moni, who really needs to drive.' Salma glanced up at the mirror. 'It will help you with Adam. Make taking up lessons your resolution after we get back from this holi-day. Honestly, it will change your life.'

Moni smiled but didn't reply. Salma was right of course, but she had no energy for self-improvement. Nor could she be bothered to explain to Salma that she used to drive before she moved to Scotland. All she needed were a few refresher lessons and to study the British Highway Code, then take the test. Perhaps. The old Moni wouldn't have hesitated. Before his birth and after his birth. That was her life, split right in the middle. Adam was her first baby and she didn't know what to expect. When he was born he looked odd and couldn't feed, but she wasn't sure what was wrong. She had no one to compare him with. Then it was one hammer blow after the other, extra days in the hospital, the doctors not sure what was wrong. Denial, clutching at straws, the minute-by-minute challenge to cope. A long time, or so it felt, before the correct diagnosis, the reality check, the sinking in of the truth that Adam was not a healthy, normal baby.

She rallied and did her best, ears alert when the doctor spoke. The urgency of it all. The steepest learning curve. Oh yes, getting an MBA had been much easier, standing up to male colleagues at work a doddle in comparison. All her resources, all her intelligence, were needed to be a mother to Adam and not let that role floor her. And in the meantime, she let herself go. Weight gain and no time to cut her toenails, to moisturise her elbows or buy deodorant when it ran out. Sleep became a treat. A nap the only gift she wanted. The news on the television screens burnt past her throughout each hectic day and meant nothing. The world could go to hell for all she cared. No one on the whole of planet Earth could possibly be suffering more than her.

Sitting in the back seat of Salma's car, soothed by the rain and the rhythmic swipe of the wipers, tired from crying and the stress of leaving Adam for the first time, Moni allowed herself to fall asleep.

Iman looked out of the window. Green fields swept past her, hay rolled up in stacks, cows with their heads sloped down as if they were praying. She could hear the wind outside the closed window, beneath the sound of the traffic. Again, I am disappointed, she thought. Last night she had dared to hope and at first not even packed any sanitary towels. Then when she got up for the dawn prayer, there was the tangible failure. I am still young, she told herself. Everyone says so. Still plenty of time. Young women my age aren't even thinking of settling down, let alone having children.

Iman had been first married off at the age of fifteen. She had walked home from school and just as she rested her bag on the floor, standing in her school uniform, was told that there was a suitor waiting to see her in the living room. 'Hurry and change,' her mother had said in a voice that meant there would be no negotiation. 'I took a dress out for you.' In the bedroom that she shared with her four younger sisters, Iman found the dress laid out on the bed, one that she didn't particularly like, and there was no time to bathe. It was a hasty marriage, for no good reason, except that a year later her new husband died at the hands of government forces in the very first uprising against Assad. People said, 'It was as if he knew he didn't have a long time to live, that's why he was so keen to get married.' Iman cried theatrically, then grumbled at the restrictions of the mourning period, then, once it was over, started to enjoy her 'young widow' status. Among her still unmarried friends, she became not only the most beautiful but the one with the sad tale and the experience. She could hold court if she wanted to, or drape her long black hair over a cushion during a sleepover and, while the others twittered away, hold back her secret knowledge. For her second marriage, she inspected and rejected one suitor after the other, annoying her family and providing material for plenty of gossip. Out of the many, she cherry-picked the most ambitious. He was the one who brought her to Britain.

Salma, Moni and Iman heading out. Salma was the oldest but not the tallest. Moni was the tallest and the fattest. Iman had the best hair, Moni the best teeth, Salma was the most stylish. Moni had a postgraduate degree but no job. Salma's rate for a full-body sports massage had doubled since she first started out. There was little that Iman was qualified for.

Salma still spoke English with an accent, Iman's English was poor, and Moni spoke English well but most of the time she couldn't be bothered to speak at all. Iman could recite the Qur'an better than the other two could, Salma knew more of it by heart, it was only after giving birth that Moni had become religious. Moni could bake anything, Salma stuck to her national dishes and Iman made the best pickled aubergines. When Salma spoke people listened, when Iman spoke it brought attention to her looks, when Moni spoke she sounded highly strung. Salma, Moni and Iman together but not together, fellow travellers, summoned by Fate. Salma wanted to visit Lady Evelyn's grave, Iman wanted to be with Salma, Moni was worried about the amount of walking involved.

Chapter Two

After driving for an hour, Salma couldn't resist the need to check her phone. She stopped at a motorway service point after Forfar. Iman got out to use the toilet, but this did not wake up Moni. Salma reached into her handbag. She found that her phone had slipped between the pages of Lady Evelyn's book, *Pilgrimage to Mecca*. The book had an introduction about Lady Evelyn's life with plenty of photographs. As Salma pulled out her phone, she caught a quick look at the hunting lodge beneath the dark slope of a mountain on the Glencarron estate. How exciting that they were heading there now! And it would not be in black and white like in the photo. It would be spread out in late-summer colours.

The feel of the phone in her hand was a welcome relief from the waiting. Again she admired it and smiled. Checking messages had become a reflex. Her excuse was the children. They might need something. She was good at organising things from a distance. She had even set up a group page so that the six of them could circulate their whereabouts and news. At first, David had thought it unnecessary. But it did turn out to be useful when Daughter No. 2 missed her bus coming back home from school and Son No. 1 broke his arm at judo. Diligently, Salma checked the family group and sent an update of her whereabouts with a 'miss you already'. There were no phone messages for her and only a few inconsequential emails.

On social media, there was no message from Amir either, and he hadn't updated his status. Instead of feeling disappointed, she felt calm. It was the need to check that was becoming more and more urgent rather than the communication itself. In his last message, sent yesterday when it was late at night for him and teatime for her, he had asked her to phone him. It thrilled her of course, this request to move the relationship up a gear. They would talk properly, hear each other's voices, maybe even use the camera and see each other. It was flattering and intriguing, but his request also flustered her. Receiving it, she skirted past David setting the table and went to check on the bubbling pasta. Phone in hand, feeling the slightest bit uncomfortable.

So she had lowered the volume of the television set, examined her youngest child's hand to see if it needed washing – annoying him because it interrupted his homework – and told David the truth. Not the whole truth, but no lies either. A segment of the truth, that a former university friend had contacted her. She had said his name out loud – Amir Elhassan – a blast from the past with links to other old friends. Photos she couldn't even remember having been taken popping up on screen. She started to rattle on a bit as she stirred the pasta. Updates about people that David had not heard her talk about since their time in Egypt. The one-time firebrand head of the students' union now working for an insurance company and driving a Mercedes; the handsome swimming champion bald and overweight; so-and-so at her daughter's graduation. David only half listened and she was glad of that, as if his indifference was lifting a weight off her conscience. He looked up to swear at the television, where a politician was saying that anyone not born in the country should be deported.

'Mama, out of all of us that's only you!' Such a clever thing for her youngest to point out. But despite his calm tone, she knew that an anxiety could start to lurk. This was how childhood fears began, beneath the surface of the everyday. She gave him a hug to reassure him.

While Moni was yawning herself awake in the back, Salma stared at the screen in case a message popped up there and then. She reread her last message, sent as a response to Amir's 'let's talk' request. Neither a yes nor a no but, 'Away for a few days, out of reach of internet.' Not that she really believed that there wouldn't be any internet access at the loch. Surely there would be free wi-fi and she could use her data, but she was buying time, sidestepping out of his reach before he came too close.

It was Moni, instead, who received a phone call. Struggling to wake herself up, she had decided to get a coffee from the service station café and was standing in line waiting for her order of three lattes to take back to the car when Murtada called from Saudi. 'I need you to send me a photocopy of your passport,' he said. 'The boy's too. It's good news. I've passed my probation. The job is mine now permanently and I can start to apply for you two to join me here.'

Moni turned away from the counter. Everything he said

was wrong. Every single sentence. She didn't know where to start, so she said, 'No.'

'No what?'

'I am not sending you the passports.'

'Photocopies,' he said with deliberate patience. 'Not the passports themselves. Haven't you been listening? I said copies, not the original documents. For me to apply for your visas, I need the copies. Then, afterwards, we'd need to send in the originals.'

'I'm not going, Murtada. I am not going anywhere.'

'Just send me the copies, Moni, and we can discuss all that later. A step at a time.' He spoke as if all she needed was for him to jolly her along.

'I can't,' she said. 'I'm not at home. I told you all this. I told you about the respite for Adam and the trip with Salma.'

'Ah yes, I remember now. How inconvenient! When will you get back? Can't you cut your visit short for this?'

'That's not the point,' she said, her voice rising. 'I told you a thousand times. Here is the best place for Adam. Here is where he's getting the right treatment, he might even go to a special school. He—'

'But I am not there, Moni. I am here, and I want my wife and son with me. It's as simple as that.'

She became angry now, but still she was conscious of her surroundings, the lunchtime restaurant, people coming in and leaving while she argued out loud in Arabic. 'You don't even say his name,' she said, and that was a mistake because it brought tears to her eyes. 'You don't even say Adam. You can't bring yourself to say it.' She did not want to sob in public, so she hung up.

He immediately called her back. 'Adam. There, I'm saying his name. Adam. Happy? Listen, I'm earning well here. I don't pay a penny in taxes. If you expect me to give this up and come back to you, then you're dreaming. We need to move on, Moni.'

No, it was not enough.

'You need to get back on track, Moni. Be fair to yourself. Get this through your head, Adam isn't going to get better—'

'He *is* getting better. Not cured. But the massage therapy and the cognitive therapy are helping. In little ways. In Saudi there will be nothing for him. He'll be stuck at home all day, every day.'

'I'll get help. I promise you. I'll get you a Filipina.'

'I don't want a Filipina!' People looked up from their plates as she shouted into her phone.

'Moni, you're being unreasonable. This isn't how we imagined our future. This isn't what we planned.'

He was right: the togetherness, the love, her banking career were all expendable. Life was about getting through each day; it was no longer about futures. 'It's fine that you come back for holidays,' she said.

'A month,' he snorted. 'Out of the twelve. One month in which you get to play the part of a wife. That sounds fair to you?'

'No one is stopping you from coming back. Get a job here.'

'It's that easy, is it? And even if I do get a job as I had before, why live where I'm not wanted? Here I come and go as I like without ever having to justify myself. On Fridays I wear my jellabiya and saunter to the mosque in my slippers.

There is no pressure to prove anything. I do my work and get paid. No nonsense.'

'How dare you talk like this! You aren't thinking about Adam. You want to pretend he doesn't exist. But he does.'

'Actually, I am thinking about him growing up where he's seen as a burden. Where's your pride, Moni? You're not wanted in Britain. People see you as a leech benefiting from the free health system.'

'I don't care what anyone thinks as long as it's good for Adam. You just don't get it.' She sensed the disapproval of the restaurant gathering around her. Her coffees getting cold. When Murtada started to protest, she said, 'I can't talk now, I have to go.'

With trembling hands, she carried the lattes back to the car. She had bought some shortbread too. Salma started to make her way through it, in no great hurry to start driving. Iman didn't want to eat. She had cramps and the hot drink was comfort enough. Moni felt congested as if the sob threatening to rise from her was a tangible object, stuck in her throat. Even sipping the sweet milky coffee was an effort. Her phone rang. Her first thought was that it was Adam's nursing home, but it was Murtada again. She rejected the call.

'Let's play a game,' said Salma, enlivened by caffeine and sugar. 'Just for fun, let's imagine a hypothetical situation.' Iman turned to her with a smile. She would play along with her friend. For Moni, though, the delight in Salma's voice sounded foreign. She craned her head forward to understand.

Salma said, 'Imagine a hypothetical situation in which you are allowed to commit one sin and get away with it. Only one major sin. It would be wiped clean straight afterwards and would never count against you in this life or the next. What would you do?'

Kill Murtada, thought Moni. No, kill myself. No, kill both Adam and myself. Her eyes filled with tears. She had been counselled once and was told that these fantasies of self-harm were signals that she was exhausted, highly stressed, on the verge of not coping. This was the sort of professional guidance Moni appreciated. No one in Saudi would give her that. Instead she would sit in her nightdress with the air conditioner on full blast watching television while the Filipina maid fetched and carried. Whenever she wanted to go out she would put on her black abaya on top of her nightdress and for many reasons, ranging from lack of wheelchair access to intrusive do-gooders and fools, she would not be able to take Adam with her.

Salma was oblivious to Moni's mood. She sipped her coffee and mimicked the voice of a TV game show, 'One chance to do whatever haram you've always wanted to do. Free without repercussion. What would it be?' She turned to look at Iman and said gleefully, 'I know what I would do. But you say first, Iman.'

Salma was visualising this as a fun activity. Each of them would say something outrageous followed by peals of laughter.

Iman considered Salma's question. Already every minute of every day, the angel on her left shoulder was writing down her minor and not so minor sins. But Salma wanted a major sin.

'I don't know,' said Iman. 'I can't think of anything.'

'Champagne?' said Salma.

Iman imagined it to be like 7UP but pink, fizzy on her

tongue, the taste a blend between perfume and overripe fruit. She shrugged.

'Model a bikini?'

'Maybe.'

Salma laughed. She could imagine Iman on the cover of a magazine. Long hair cascading down to her hips. But she was too beautiful to be a model. Whatever piece of clothing she was modelling would be overshadowed by herself. But then maybe not. Maybe as soon as she uncovered herself, all the mystique would be swept away, the spell broken. Iman would become another pretty face, another great body. One more woman on a screen.

'No.' Iman made a face. She shook her head and said, 'Nothing. There is no sin that I *want* to do.'

'Oh, you are a spoilsport,' said Salma.

'Wait,' said Iman. 'There is something I want. To be completely alone.'

'But you love having people take care of you.'

'I mean not be accountable to others.' Her voice was soft. 'Free as a fish.'

'I have no idea what you're talking about. Besides, how is that a sin!' Salma turned her head towards Moni, who was still only halfway through her coffee. 'Moni?'

'You're too optimistic, Salma,' Moni said. 'What if the sin doesn't get wiped away, instead it manifests itself physically and we are stuck with it? If you punch someone, your arm gets twisted round your back and you can't move it. Or if you abuse someone, your tongue hangs out of your mouth.'

'Like Pinocchio,' said Iman. 'When he lies, his nose gets long.'

'Oh come on,' Salma laughed. 'Moni, play the game. What would you do if you could get away with it?'

'I would kill someone,' Moni's voice was flat. 'More than one.'

'Who?'

Moni didn't answer.

It wasn't funny. 'Well,' said Salma. 'This isn't how I thought this would turn out. Neither of you are any fun. So I will keep my secret to myself.' She spoke lightly but she was irritated with them both. They had let her down. She sent a message to Amir asking him the same question. It had been her intention all along, hadn't it? The reason she had come up with the game. He replied immediately, 'I would steal.'

'What would you steal?' she typed, the smile stretched across her face. Here was someone on the same wavelength. Someone with a sense of humour.

'What was once mine and then got taken away from me,' he replied.

She almost laughed out loud. Yes, it would be stealing. What she wanted to do with him (in theory, of course, definitely in theory) was also a kind of theft. She started the engine.

Sometimes Moni found Salma and Iman juvenile. *Imagine you were allowed one major sin . . .* Did this not sound like some game teenagers would play? Iman was in her twenties, so she could be forgiven. But Salma was older than Moni, over forty, even if she did look younger. The first time they met, Moni thought they were the same age. It was just another massage therapy appointment for Adam, but instead of Kathy or Anne, there was Salma in a plain navy headscarf that matched her uniform. When she spoke Arabic, Moni was won over, though she had to admit that, at first, she doubted Salma's abilities. Surely, Moni thought, Salma would neither be as professional nor as qualified as her white British counterparts. But Salma was even better with Adam. She was patient and interested. She made Moni feel that Adam was more to her than just a client. Once, during the Christmas break when the clinic was closed, Salma came over to Moni's flat and gave Adam a session free of charge, a session that made all the difference to those long days when Moni had nowhere to take him. Salma made him relax and when he relaxed he ate and slept better.

Moni and Salma became friends after that day, with Moni feeling a little beholden. She often brought Salma gifts, or cooked falafel for her. Salma adored the way Moni cooked falafel. There were variations to the recipe across the Arab world and Salma acquired a taste for Moni's version with crisp chickpeas and dill. It gratified Moni that she could please Salma. Her admiration of her friend was so great that she elevated her to a special status. Salma belonged to the healthcare establishment on which Adam was dependent, and she was trained as a doctor. She was someone Moni could consult on every large and small detail.

Moni's self-conscious appreciation of Salma was coloured by her own privileged upbringing. One in which women were gracious and men lauded for their largesse. One in which useful connections were cultivated and favours reciprocated. Compared to Salma and Iman, but not too blatantly,

Moni was the one most financially secure. Wealthy parents, Murtada's salary and her own prudent savings had resulted in this enviable position. Yet it hardly showed on her. She was unkempt and repetitive in her choice of shoes and handbags. An expensive piece of jewellery looked odd against the sunglasses she picked up from Primark.

To Iman, all this reeked of miserliness. Iman had known a wide spectrum of poverty, from scrambling for the next meal to ultra-careful rationing to tremendous efforts to keep up appearances, all glued together by insecurity. So it made no sense to her at all that someone as loaded as Moni could see beauty through a shop window and pass it by. To Iman's dismay, Moni's spacious flat was sparsely furnished, with Adam's paraphernalia taking centre stage. When Iman brought this to Salma's attention, she was surprised at how staunchly Salma had defended Moni, pointing out the generous gifts she had given her and how she spared no expense on Adam's treatment. Iman was unconvinced but her own lack of confidence made it difficult for her to argue with Salma. Growing up in a family in which her opinion never mattered, she found that her thoughts only developed up to a certain point before the argument aborted or disintegrated. She sensed without having proof; she saw in Moni a supressed meanness and a deep-set strictness.

'Iman, sing for us,' said Salma, still in a good mood despite not being able to drive as she wanted to because of roadworks blocking one side of the motorway. Iman started to sing. There was a yearning in her voice for a home that would be more than a physical space, carried in the ancient words and melodies all the way from the Euphrates. Usually this familiar song brought tears to Salma's eyes but today she was carefree, heedless of the words, distracted by the other cars on the road.

It was Moni who suddenly felt choked. The longing in the song was spiritual but it manifested itself to her as a drowning person's gasp for air. A necessity, a grab for freedom from pain. It reminded her of the times she had prayed for a miracle. The kind of miracle that would have Adam standing up on his feet. His illness was a test of her faith, but sometimes she indulged in fantasies. Fantasies of him doing well in school, opening a gift she had wrapped up for him, laughing out loud while watching cartoons or stomping off in a huff when she rebuked him. 'Stop it,' she snapped at Iman. 'Stop singing.'

Iman stopped singing. Salma looked up at the mirror. Moni's breathing returned to normal. An apology was due, or at least an explanation. She told them about how Murtada wanted her and Adam to join him. Iman said, 'You must obey your husband.' She tossed this sentence without the slightest turn in her seat, in the flattest of tones.

At first, Moni was too stunned to reply. The cheek of the girl! She thought Salma would say something, explain or take her side. But Salma was watching the road, acting as if she hadn't heard. Moni took a deep breath in and started to speak. She outlined the complexity of the situation and the practicalities. She explained that 'obedience' was not a blind imperative; it was an acknowledgement of leadership, but still leadership could be challenged and interrogated. It had been a long time since she had talked at such length. Iman yawned and Salma didn't comment. It suddenly made

Moni feel lonely. They couldn't possibly understand her situation.

Iman was distracted by a text from her husband. *Where exactly are you? I could catch up with you. How far did you go? Perhaps there is somewhere nearby where we could have some privacy.*

She texted back, *I can't ask Salma to stop.* She added a sad face to the message and settled herself comfortably in her seat. Ibrahim had been opposed to this trip. Three women on their own gallivanting across Scotland – it was wrong and unnecessary. Iman had pleaded, pouted and sulked until he gave way. 'I can't bear you out of my sight,' he said the night before she left. 'What am I going to do?' he wailed in his boxer shorts, punching pillows and slamming doors.

Iman's husband was a young student from a conservative family. His scholarship, paid for by his home country's government, was ample and reliable. Ibrahim had suffered from homesickness and culture shock when he first arrived and the imam of the mosque prescribed marriage. Ibrahim's family back home disagreed and so, with neither their consent nor knowledge, he took as his wife the most beautiful divorcee in the local Muslim community. He left the student halls, which – with girls in close physical proximity to beds they should not, would not and did not share with him – were a source of torment, and moved with Iman into a small flat near the university. She was his saviour. The one who met all his needs so that he could settle and study. And he was her saviour too. Dumped by the husband who had brought her to Britain (not exactly dumped, but he had ended up in prison and divorced her as a courtesy), she had been unsure what to do next, how to proceed. 'Do anything but don't come back,' her family told her. Because of the war, home was neither safe nor prosperous. Those who were lucky to be out stayed out.

Her ex-husband's lengthy sentence was for grievous bodily harm after losing his temper with a fellow Syrian. Asked if he had beaten her now that his violent credentials were proven without doubt, Iman shook her head and answered no, but the truth was he hadn't got around to it yet. So, she opted next for the peaceful, gentle Ibrahim. Of the string of suitors, he was the one least likely to lift a finger against her. Besides, when he said the magic words, 'I will do everything I can to unite you with your mother,' she was won over. His immaturity was endearing, his consistent lust for her reassuring. He rescued her from homelessness and from aimlessness. Closer to her in age than her previous husbands, she found herself loving him as a friend, someone she could cuddle on the sofa and play games with on the PlayStation.

Every morsel she put in her mouth, every piece of clothing, was provided for her by Ibrahim. The rent, the gas, the internet. She did not have to beg, borrow or steal. She did not need to get up at the crack of dawn, take orders from a line manager or clean up other people's homes. Instead, she was as pampered as a racehorse and as busy as a geisha.

To what extent is marriage religiously sanctioned prostitution? Iman sometimes pondered this question. She had even discussed it with Salma on more than one occasion – as much as she was capable of discussion. Salma of course had been adamant that the two were completely different. Iman wasn't sure, and the arguments Salma used didn't fully convince her. Prostitution and marriage. Man pays and woman serves. He houses, clothes and feeds her to get something in return. So what was the difference between the two?

Iman's phone rang. It was Ibrahim, insistent that they turn around so that he could speak to her. 'Give me Salma,' he said.

'She's driving. She can't speak to you.'

Salma turned to look at Iman. 'What does he want?'

Iman moved the phone away from her face. 'He wants you to stop somewhere so he can catch up with us. He says he needs to give me something and it's urgent.'

'I've already left Dundee,' Ibrahim was now shouting through the phone. 'I'm making my way towards you. Stay at Finavon. Just stay there and wait for me.'

Iman brought the phone back to her face. 'We've already left.'

'Let me speak to Salma.'

'I told you she's driving.'

'Put me on speaker mode.'

His voice was now in the car with them. 'Salma, turn back,' he shouted. 'I'll meet you at the service coffee shop.'

Salma made a face.

'Just ignore him,' Iman whispered.

Salma shook her head. 'Ibrahim, not Finavon. I'll turn into Stonehaven and we'll wait for you at the castle.'

'Are you sure?' The relief was obvious in Iman's voice.

'Yes.' Salma was made generous by the sense of holiday. They had time, so why not dawdle a little. 'It's beautiful

35

there. We'll enjoy it especially now that it's stopped raining.'
Getting away from it all. Away from responsibility, away
from authority, bodies set free from routines, perspectives
altered, distances distracting. Every holiday was a test. Every
holiday was a risk.

Chapter Three

The visitors' car park was separated from the castle by a narrow winding footpath. The three had to walk in single file. Salma and Iman walked faster than Moni. Moni dragged her heels. She was not interested in seeing any castles. But Salma had refused to let her wait in the car.

The path sloped downward, which made the walk pleasant for Salma and Iman but only made Moni worry about the upward return. She began to perspire. She took off her coat, draped it across her arm and walked on with the belt dragging on the ground. There were now steps and a railing she could hold on to, but still she struggled. The distance between her and the other two grew until it became too large for any meaningful conversation. She would have to shout if she wanted them to hear her. It was as if they were trying to shrug her off. Moni stopped making an effort to catch up and slowed down further. She could make out Iman's figure ahead and, beneath her on the slope, Salma's wide bouncy strides. Then the track flattened again, and she lost sight of them.

Moni was now out of breath, sighing noisily and feeling faint. Her thighs rubbed against each other. She prayed for a bench and then, like a miracle, spotted one on the side of the path where the steps twisted into a right angle. She sat down, but sitting made her feel worse. She began to sweat and black blotches floated in front of her face. She needed to take in big gulps of air.

Iman forgot about Moni and felt that Salma was chatting too much. The sea was calling her and she speeded effortlessly towards it. She wanted to laugh out loud as she skipped down the grassy slope. It was as if she were a child again, before her body became a responsibility, before she understood how her beauty could be of value and of interest. She was carefree in those days, snotty and bare-footed, wild in the fields and the alleys of her Euphrates village. She had played and skipped and run, feeling the wind against her face, the animal smell of the grass and her voice humming in her ear. A song that no one else could hear.

Salma, who had been looking back expecting Moni to catch up with them, stopped. She grabbed Iman's arm. Now that she was standing still, Iman heard her phone ring. Ibrahim's voice sounded faint but persistent. She hardly paid attention; what she wanted was the sea. There it was, spectacular beneath her, and all she had to do was sing in order to reach it. Yes, she said to him, they had stopped at Dunnottar and she would wait for him down at the beach.

Next to her, Salma raised her eyebrows at the mention of the beach. She wanted to go inside the castle. 'I'll go back and see what's wrong with Moni. Wait for me.'

'*You* sort out Moni, I'll catch up with you later.' She ducked past her surprised friend and ran down straight for the cove. Seagulls circled above her.

Salma climbed back up the slope. Since when did Iman do her own thing? 'Yalla, Moni, get up. You're still not upset about leaving Adam, are you?'

Moni shook her head.

'You know, don't you, that to visit Lady Evelyn's grave we need to walk four miles up a hill? Only a four-by-four can reach there, or a coach, which was my original idea when the entire group was going. Now how are you ever going to manage that!'

'I guess I won't then.' Moni held her arms against her chest as if she was protecting her body.

Salma softened her tone, 'If you practise walking now, then that would be good training for you. You can build up some stamina.'

'You are forever planning ahead! I need to get myself back up to the car before worrying about anything else!'

Salma sighed. 'Don't you want to come in and see inside the castle?'

'It's a ruin, Salma. There's nothing to see. You go ahead. Personally, I think seven pounds is a swindle.'

Salma paid for her ticket and entered the grounds of the castle. Lawns and clusters of ruined buildings. A map marked out the area: first on the right was the tower, strategically placed to survey all access to the castle by land, behind it were the smithy and the stables. Further inwards towards the sea and beyond the bowling green were the living quarters, the suites, dining and drawing rooms. Salma wandered around, the grass a bright green beneath her, the derelict buildings humble in their simplicity, solemn in their inner darkness.

From the tourists around her, she caught the tones of foreign languages, a softness surrounded the place and the wind blew gently. From a porthole of stone, she looked down over the water. It was more purple than the sky, the waves uneven frills. To the left were high fields where bales of rolled hay looked like barrels laid down on their sides. This was the same view the inhabitants of the castle had gazed at long ago. The workers and ladies; the gardeners and stable boys. It struck her that Lady Evelyn must have come here as a girl in the late nineteenth century, as an adult in the twentieth. The woman who travelled in the Sahara and in Kenya would not have failed to visit the east coast of her own country. Once again Salma felt a closeness to her, an awareness that was more than curiosity.

In the chapel, she stood on consecrated ground, the sky above her withholding rain. In 1276, people knelt here and worshipped. They were not her ancestors and she did not share their religion, but she understood them because she herself believed and she herself lived each day knowing she would, after she died, be held to account. It suddenly dawned on her that this chapel perched on the edge of the sea was facing south-east, the direction of Mecca. It was parallel to every purpose-built mosque in the country! Lady Evelyn, who left instructions to be buried facing Mecca, would have delighted in this coincidence. Salma smiled, imagining bringing it to Lady Evelyn's notice. The one to hear back, 'Really?' in a posh Scottish accent.

In the nearby kitchen, indicated by the wide arch of the fireplace, she heard the word 'Really?' in Arabic. Clear and intimate, a snap into her consciousness, coming after a lag in the conversation she had been imagining, a delay in reply like on a poor long-distance line. There was no one near Salma and she was sure, as she could ever be sure, that it was Lady Evelyn's voice speaking to her in the Arabic she learnt from her nannies when she was a child growing up in Cairo and Algiers. Hearing the dead? Imagining, more likely. She knew what Lady Evelyn looked like from the photos — like Gertrude Bell, someone had described her, slim, active, snobbish and chatty with scrunched-up hair under a desert hat — and now Salma had her voice too. She looked up and saw a formation of grey clouds surrounding a sky-blue body of water. The loch was in her mind, where they were heading. How odd it had been to organise and reorganise this trip. The way it evolved from a day trip for the whole of the women's group, to only the three of them but with the addition of the stay at the loch. She could not give up the visit to Lady Evelyn just because the majority were against it. Many of these women lulled themselves into believing they were in Britain temporarily; that somehow, someday, they would return 'home'. Moni and Iman were different; they wanted to be here for the long haul. And Salma was the one with the Scottish husband, she was the one who must always be making the effort to belong. Digging deeper all the time, craving connections, self-conscious that her roots, despite the children, might not be strong enough.

Sometimes she would walk into a room to find them with David and she would have no clue what they were saying even though she could understand every single word. She would then feel that they were his children and not hers. She was the outsider, the foreign wife, and they were one unit.

She had believed foolishly that they would be born with a hard drive of her memories. That they would know Egypt as she had known it, the crowded bus to Saint Catherine on the trip she had organised for the student club – Egypt, the Beloved – and how they stopped on the way for breakfast. Foul and tamiyah and tea with mint, Amir shouting at the waiters, in truth abusing them to make everyone laugh. And she had laughed too though she wouldn't now, but still she noted with bitterness that her children lived in a world where it was okay to be rude to their parents but to a waiter they must be very polite.

She used to love a good argument but not with them. Despite all their bravado and independence, children growing up here needed to be handled delicately. One thwack with the hairbrush, only one, but the teacher saw the bruise and she and David were called in. The child was sticking a pencil in her ear and refusing to listen to warnings that she could puncture her eardrum. But no matter. Salma felt that she was embarrassing David in front of his own people, though he never reproached her except to say that when he was growing up plenty of children were given a good hiding, but no one did that any more. She didn't want him to be ashamed of her, to feel that he had picked her up from the back of beyond, and so she became more careful, often not at ease. No matter how many clients she massaged and no matter that she had given birth to children with Scottish blood, deep down his people would think that she was not really one of them, that she was not British enough.

A message flashed on her phone. It was from Amir: *I am listening*. If he was listening, what should she be saying?

Complaints and the luxury of regrets. She did not reply and instead wandered back to the tower and climbed to the top. This space still had a ceiling and the light was dim. Looking out through a cavity that must have been at some point a window, she saw miles of uneven land spread before her, green grass inland and, on the left, the steep edge of the cliffs into the sea. She looked out for the bench where she had left Moni sitting, but it was hidden from view. She could see a cove, but it was on the other side of the castle, it was not the one where Iman was now.

The castle was above Iman, its walls casting a shadow over the rocks and the sand. She wandered about the cove aimlessly, humming and singing, bending down to pick up rocks and examine them in her palms. At this close range, the sea was a moving world; the water cold and grand. Iman felt small in front of it. Not weak but limited. What did she know? She knew that every creature came from water, she knew that rivers poured into seas but never, in turn, became salty. She knew that fishes spoke. In their own language, they praised and glorified their Creator, they gave thanks and their hummed prayers were a blessing to the world.

Pearls, corals, rubies, emeralds. She picked up small stones, balanced them on the back of her hand and they became jewels. Traces of moss and glints of red caught the sun. Some of the rocks were as large as ostrich eggs, the discarded jewellery of a giantess, strewn in delicate colours. The lightest amethyst, cloudy grey, duck-egg blue. Above her, tourists and visitors walked up the steps to enter the castle. Their voices drifted down to her, as did the shuffle of their shoes. She felt a surge of goodwill towards them.

There was a cave beneath the castle and she had to scramble over a pile of rocks to reach it. The outer walls were covered in grass, but the interior was barren. She stared into the secret darkness, the moist, bulbous walls, growth ridged and uneven. A path worn by erosion where the seawater flowed up into the cave and down out again. It was like being inside a body's cavity. But how would she know? The air was cool in the cave, the smell marine-dank. She hummed the same song that she had sung in the car. Yearning, the lyrics of the song said. Yearning to live alone on an island and give up on the world, let it go, let it drop. But that would be lonely. A waste of her beauty. She felt the walls closing in around her, turned and made her way down the rocks to the flat part of the cove.

She put her hand in her pocket and found a date that had dried up and shrivelled. She popped it into her mouth and chewed for a long time, savouring what remained of its sweetness, before she swallowed. She bent down and buried the date stone in the sand. 'I am planting a date tree,' she said out loud. Maybe it will grow, maybe by Allah's will it can grow in this cold climate and be a little miracle. She smiled at her foolishness, her childlike arrogance. But it gave her great satisfaction to plant that palm tree. A palm tree that would hang forlornly in the snow, buffeted by gales and waves, clinging to the weakest form of life and yet, against the odds, still bearing fruit.

It was not difficult for Iman to imagine new life emerging from what was fragile and doomed. The way a grandmother

44

could give birth to her grandson's aunt. Iman's mother had one child after the other every eighteen months. Sometimes every two years. All in all there were twelve of them – boys and girls. Scattered now all over the place by the war and the ambition to live. Iman felt sorry for her mother, but her pity was tempered with anger. Anger at her and anger for her. If having all these children was an investment for old age, then it was an investment that had backfired. Iman was unable to bring her mother to live in Britain. She was often unable to send her money. One mother could look after twelve children and decades later these twelve adults would fidget and struggle to look after that one mother.

Moni continued to sit on the bench even though she was feeling much better. Her breathing steadied and she no longer perspired. Her vision, too, was free of the black floating jellyfish that had troubled her before. The path dipped down ahead and then rose again between two massive cliffs. Almost hidden behind the rocks was the castle and she could only see the highest point of the ruins, grey and white. The castle seemed protected and out of reach to her, but she acknowledged its beauty, accepted that this was as much of a glimpse as she was entitled to. She took out her phone and clicked open her Qur'an app. Every day she read a section of the Qur'an, or at least tried to. Sometimes, subject to Adam's needs, she could only read one or two pages. On bad days, she could read none. Now when she finished one page and started the next, it occurred to her that she was free to read as many pages as she wanted. His voice would not call her. His needs would not interrupt. The more she read, the more she zoned out. Her ability to concentrate had deteriorated of late. Her mind flitted from here to there. Images of Adam, his eyes, his hands; she could hear his grunts and unformed words, smell him, but he did not interrupt the flow of her reading. Silly thoughts wound their way through her head even though her tongue was reciting sacred words. She knew that this wasn't good enough. She knew that she should be reading with her heart and mind clear; she knew that she needed to transcend her circumstances, her daily anxieties and her issues with Murtada. She knew all this – that she was worshipping inadequately – and yet she did not stop. She kept reciting, absorbed in the process. She kept trying with neither hope of success, nor despair. This was because she was drawing support, gaining nourishment and she could do that precisely because she did not rate herself highly as a worshipper. She was inadequate, she fell short. But she was enjoying herself, especially now that her breathing had re-turned to normal. She gave in to the rhythm and the sounds.

In the back of her mind, she wondered if she was making history. Perhaps for the first time ever, the words of the Qur'an were reaching this particular part of the earth. Per-haps one day, to her credit, coastline, machair and sandstone would bear witness to what they had heard her recite. Long after Moni, with her faults and story, was gone and forgotten.

Submerged in the text, it was only when he came quite close to her and directly passed her that she looked up and saw him. Iman's husband. Ridiculously young, scurrying down the path towards the castle. He kept his head down and didn't greet Moni. He knew who she was and yet he

46

did not stop and greet her. He did not greet women he was unrelated to. He did not speak to them unless he had no choice. With a mobile phone in his pocket, he did not need to ask Moni about the whereabouts of his wife. Therefore, he did not need to speak to her.

Moni smiled. She had always moved in fairly liberal circles and Ibrahim's strictness amused her. There was something ridiculous about it, over the top. It almost flattered her. Since the birth of Adam, her self-esteem had hit rock bottom and never recovered. She no long considered herself attractive or even thought of herself as feminine. And yet Ibrahim, married to a beauty, would not look her in the face lest she tempted him with impure thoughts. She laughed out loud.

Her laughter and a glance upwards made her notice the catering van. It was near the car park, but she must have missed it when they got out of the car. The walk up the steps was not as gruelling as she had feared, now that her spirits were higher, and the reward of a meal was awaiting her. Slowly, at her own pace, she made it to the top. The smell of burgers and soup made her feel hungry. She stood in front of the van and looked at the menu. There was no point in texting Iman with an invitation for lunch. Iman was with her husband. As for Salma, she might as well make the most of the entrance ticket she had paid for. Moni would eat all by herself.

She had never done that. Never sat in a café alone. Back home, lone women eating in public were inviting attention, exposing themselves to trouble. She studied the menu, needing time to figure out what she wanted, what she could realistically finish, what would be good to eat.

Eventually she ordered the Scotch broth. Originally served in winter, the sign said, but now can be enjoyed all year. When it came, she poured salt and pepper onto it and appreciated the accompanying piece of bread. Picnic benches were arranged around the catering van and Moni found an empty one. She always found it easy to ignore her surroundings. Cracks in the wall or paintings were one and the same. This lost her plenty of experiences but at times was a useful asset. A place could be ugly, noisy and smelly and she would be oblivious. Awareness was not her strong point. When people were rude to her, she simply didn't notice.

So she continued to sit at the table, even after she finished her soup, dessert and coffee. She continued to sit even as others joined her at the table, expecting her to make way. She was thinking about Adam, imagining being with him. A queue formed of people waiting to be served and then waiting to be seated and still she sat staring straight ahead at them without feeling the need to move. It was the children who caught her eye. A toddler held by a harness. Two little girls holding hands. Healthy, moving, standing, talking to their parents. They were the same age as Adam, but they had swept past him, developed and progressed. For Adam, time was different. For Adam, time did not bring new skills or better understanding. She had forgotten what was natural, forgotten what normal children were like, what they were capable of doing and saying outside of the cocoon of Adam's world. Moni sat and stared at a little boy in a green rain jacket pulling at his father's hand. At the girl in flowery jeans, hopping from foot to foot, asking to be taken to the toilet.

Moni stared at them as if they were strange and it was Adam who was normal.

Iman was down in the cove when Ibrahim found her. She had spread out her coat on the sand and was lying on it. Above her, the jutting stone was like a ceiling. She thought Ibrahim would lie down next to her. She wanted him to, but he was flustered, obviously upset. She sat up and crossed her legs. He refused to sit down and instead paced to and fro, kicking pebbles out of his way.

'My father is here,' he said. 'He is here with my mother and older brother . . .'

She knew about this. It was why Ibrahim had changed his mind at the last minute and allowed her to go on this trip with Salma. At first, he had said no, three women travelling on their own was not a good idea. Normally, he was possessive about her, wanting her with him, near him, at home when he came back from university, always within reach. Not this time, though. As soon as he had heard that his parents were coming, he said she could, after all, with his full approval, join Salma and Moni. He had wanted her out of the way when his family came. They didn't know about their marriage. And he had wanted to keep it that way.

'They found out about us,' he said. 'They heard about it. I don't know how. Don't know who told them. But that's why they're here. That's why they came.'

Iman's first thought was that he had come to fetch her, to take her back so that she could meet them. No need to hide. No need to be tucked away at the loch with Salma and Moni.

'My father is furious,' Ibrahim said.

She was taken aback but still hopeful. 'He'll come round. Give him time. If he meets me—'

'No, you don't know him. He won't give you a chance. He's going to cut me off.'

'But you have a scholarship,' she said. 'The government pays for your studies.'

'They were, but when I failed and had to repeat the year, they stopped the grant and my father started paying—'

'Why didn't you tell me?' She hadn't even guessed. He had been as generous as ever.

'I was ashamed to tell you.'

'But I tell you everything.'

'The point is my father is now saying he'll cut me off. I have no choice. I have to divorce you.'

'You can't . . .'

'My father is ordering me to do so. I have no choice. Don't cry. Please.'

'You don't mean it,' she shouted. 'He can't force you. You don't have to listen to him.'

'I will send you money. As soon as he's back giving me my allowance. I'll put money in your account.'

But for how long? Until she remarries? Would it always be like this, from one husband to another? She stood up and grabbed him by the shoulders. His arms dangled by his side. Helpless and furtive, he didn't want to meet her eyes. 'You can't do this. It's wrong.' She shook him and struggled for the right words. The argument that would convince him, pull the brakes before everything crashed.

'They're all against me – my mother, my brother. There's no point talking to them. They don't understand. Otherwise, they say, I will have to abandon my studies and go back home. No degree. I don't have a choice. We will be separated either way.'

'No, we won't, because you're going to stand up to them.'

'I told them.' He shook his head. 'I told them that all I wanted was to live without sin. That's all. That's why I married you.' He shrugged off her hands and moved away.

'They'll come round. We just need to stick it out.'

'They said I should have asked their permission. But they would have said no, of course. That's why I didn't tell them. They're forcing me to divorce you. I brought all your things. They're in the car.'

'You're throwing me out! Out of my own home?'

'It's finished, Iman. I'll transfer your stuff to Salma's car.'

'Where am I meant to go?' She picked up small rocks and started to stone him.

'Stop it.' He blocked a stone with his arm, but the next one hit him on the forehead. 'You mad bitch,' he yelled, crouching on the ground and covering his face with his arms.

'Coward,' she shouted. She scrabbled on her knees in the dirt. 'Eunuch. Sissy!' Swear words in Kurdish that he couldn't understand, insults in Arabic which he could. 'Mummy's boy,' she screamed. 'You're not a man. I'm hitting you and you're not hitting me back. Hit me back!' She stood up and dropped the stone in her hand, launched at him, punching his shoulders and slapping his ears.

He let her kick him and he let her pull his hair and then they both cried.

Afterwards, they did not walk amiably back to his car, fetch her things and transfer them to Salma's car. Ibrahim did this by himself. And Iman, drained after her outburst, lay down on her coat on the sand. When her phone rang, she saw it was Salma, but she didn't pick up. The pain was in her torso and her head. Her legs and arms felt light and distant. Instead of Ibrahim, she found herself thinking of her siblings and her village, the way it changed during the war. Indoors, the women kept their homes clean, washed and ironed their family's clothes. Men went to the barber even when the children couldn't go to school. Women sugared the excess hair from their legs and armpits, even after the rationing started. 'Don't come back,' that's what they said to her whenever she phoned. 'You're envied,' her mother said. 'You're lucky,' her cousin said. So did her neighbour and her best friend. None of them wanted her back. For her own good, of course. But still, it felt, at times, like a rejection. She wanted them to say the opposite: come back, we need you, we miss you, we are waiting for you with open arms. Instead, they said, stay where you are, and with time a coolness grew in these conversations. Her family had less and less patience for her trials or complaints, and to mask jealousy there was now a faint contempt. A refusal to listen or understand. 'Stay put, my girl. Don't come back.'

Iman's anger ebbed away as her tears flowed. I am watering the date seed I planted, watering it with my tears, she told herself. It sounded like words from a song.

You're beautiful, Ibrahim had said. So had the husband before him and the one before him. Other men too, behind her back. And yet it wasn't a guarantee; not much of a safety net. She sat up and stared at the sea. Her feet were cold. She put her coat back on and stood up. She could walk straight into the sea. She could keep stomping the cold water until the final crush. Or she could drag herself up the slope. Salma would look after her. Salma would know what to do.

Salma, summoned by phone, was struggling to find room in the boot for all of Iman's stuff, which Ibrahim was intent on inflicting upon her. 'You can't just throw her out. She has rights. What you're doing is against the sharia.'

He shrugged, too miserable to care.

'And you just left her on the beach! Shame on you. I should be there with her, not dealing with this.' Where was Moni now when she could be of help? 'I will speak to your father,' she said. 'Give me his number. I will go back to town and speak to him.'

Ibrahim flinched at the suggestion. 'There's no point.'

Salma wanted to sound reasonable. She had warned Iman against this kind of paperless marriage. One that was solely religious and not recognised under British law. Mosques were forbidden to carry out marriage ceremonies without a civil marriage certificate. Iman and Ibrahim had been married privately by a transient Arab scholar who reinforced Ibrahim's view that such a ramshackle agreement, devoid even of the couple's parents' blessing, was preferable to living in sin. Not that Salma disagreed on that last point, but a token, casual marriage was not the solution. And now this was the result. A divorce on the beach!

Ibrahim tipped into the car boot a carton box filled with an assortment of clothes, a hairdryer, a shower cap, jars of spices, clothes hangers, a pair of sandals and a pregnancy kit. The poignancy of this last item made Salma raise her voice.

'Listen, I don't have space for all these things. I really don't. Not on top of our own luggage. Enough. Don't put in any more.'

'So what shall I do?' He had that sullen look her teenage children had when they were set chores, when they were forced away from their PlayStations, Netflix and phones.

'Take them to my house,' said Salma. 'I'll call David and he'll put them in the garage.' She thought ahead. After the holiday at the loch, Iman would have to move in with her. Daughter Number 1 would have to share her room. There would be tantrums and coaxing. But there was no alternative. Iman did not have anywhere else to go. Apart from the Woman's Shelter, that is, and Salma would not do that to her friend.

After Ibrahim drove off, Salma set out to look for Iman but found her already on her way to the car. Iman got into the back seat and started to cry when she saw her things. So many things that there wasn't any room for Salma to squeeze in to sit next to her. With the door open, she crouched instead on the ground and comforted Iman until Moni appeared.

'I have to phone David,' she told them and walked away from the car in the opposite direction to the catering van. It was past his lunch break. He didn't pick up and she messaged him, telling him about Ibrahim breaking it off with Iman. She suddenly wished they were lying in bed, talking in the dark. She typed, *You don't mind, do you, that Iman moves in with us?*

He wouldn't mind. She could rely on him to be supportive and, what was even more impressive, David was the only man Salma knew who was immune to Iman's beauty. This anomaly fascinated her and boosted her self-esteem. 'Iman needs to become more independent,' he texted back straight away. 'She needs to get a job or else a reliable husband. Someone who can be trusted.'

Salma had both these things. She knew she was lucky but, somehow, now David's decency made her feel uncomfortable. Why had she accepted Amir's friend request? And she had messaged him today flirting about one hypothetical haram thing that wouldn't be counted on Judgement Day. *I'm loving my new phone*, she wrote in another message to her husband. *I miss you.* She was missing how she was before Amir and the thoughts of Amir came back into her life.

Turn back, David replied.

She smiled and wrote, *Too late for that.* She was not one to give up. She would visit Lady Evelyn's grave no matter what. Moni badly needed this break, and now poor Iman could do with a few days off to get over her shock.

Amir,
Didn't want to drop off your radar without a goodbye or an
explanation. The latter is obvious and this is the goodbye.

Dear Amir,
To you this might be all harmless and well intentioned and
I'm probably making a big deal out of nothing. Call me old-
fashioned. But I say better safe than sorry. I'm too old for a
flirtation and too serious for a fling. Let's stop before we start.

Salma deleted the first message and did not send the second one because her phone rang. It was her mother-in-law, Norma.

'Hi Mum.' She called her Mum because David called her Mum. And also because the word 'mum' to Salma did not have the same meaning as 'mother'. It was like 'babe' and 'hubby'; endearments that could not be translated.

Norma wanted her to come over and give her a massage. Her left shoulder was so stiff, she could hardly move it. It was something that Salma did for her regularly and she was happy to be of help. Given a choice between the grocery shopping, cleaning up Norma's flat and a free treatment, Salma always opted for the latter and left David to do the other chores. They regularly visited Norma once a fortnight and spent almost the whole day with her. There was a time when Norma had enjoyed going out, when she was happy to be brought over to their place so that she could spend time with the children. But more recently she preferred the company of her own television and she contacted them less and less as the months went past. The rarity of her request made Salma want to comply. She was sincere when she said, 'I wish I could, Mum. But I'm away this week.' She explained to Norma about the trip to the loch. 'Use a heating pad,' she said. 'It doesn't have to be too hot. Just warm and comfortable.'

She continued to talk to her as she walked back to the car, got in and fastened her seat belt. Slowly, she drove out of the car park, sliding into the road, then turning on to the dual carriageway, picking up speed. *Glory be to Him who has given us control over this . . .*

'Sorry, sweetie, there's no room and you have to keep your seat belt on,' Salma said when Iman said she wanted to stretch

out in the back. Iman did not want to sleep but she was finding it an effort to hold herself upright. Plastic bags containing
her belongings were on the seat next to her and on the floor.
This was what Ibrahim had used to pack up her life and wipe
all trace of her from his rented flat. She rummaged through
the bags and felt a sense of surprise as if she were seeing her
possessions for the first time. They were all hers. Some of
them were presents from Ibrahim, like the skimpy nightdress
with the matching fluffy slippers, the purple headphones and
the Hello Kitty calendar. She loved calendars. The act of
matching dates with the day of the week enchanted her. She
was delighted the day she found out, online, that she had
been born on a Thursday. Her mother had told her she was
born on a Wednesday, but her mother must have got muddled up because of all the children she'd had. Iman flipped
open the Hello Kitty calendar. She had marked the days of
her period and the possible days of ovulation. Looking back
now, she wondered whether Ibrahim had ever been sincere
in wanting to have a baby.

Iman opened her mouth to stifle a sob. A funny sound
came out of her in between a hiccup and a croak.

'Are you all right?' Moni turned to look at her.

Iman nodded and closed her eyes. She did not want to talk
about Ibrahim any more. Enough for now.

Moni, upgraded to the front next to Salma, felt that she
was in a position of strength. She turned and chided Iman
while addressing Salma, 'She ran off down that slope as if
she was chasing something. And I saw him come down after
her. He didn't say hello, but he knew very well who I was. I
never thought well of him!'

When Salma didn't reply, Moni felt she could not go on. She checked her watch and saw that it was teatime now at the nursing home. That's what they called dinner. Adam would be eating food that she hadn't cooked. She felt guilty, but she also felt restless and empty-handed. Iman's predicament had been a distraction. It had taken her away from herself.

Iman heard a sound and sat up. It could not be the sea because they were no longer near the sea. It could be a song or a chant. A movement caught her eyes; it was as if something was skidding or flying alongside the car, like a shadow or a reflection. Perhaps it was only the car's silhouette on the moss-covered cliffs. But the shadow did have wings and at times it slithered nearer, then seemingly lost the connection, disappeared, then became visible again as if it was a struggle for it to catch up. Iman felt comforted by the shape and the sound it was making: soothing, not exactly urgent but with a forward lift. She opened her window and the sound became clearer, lilting and twittering. Opposite to the cliffs were fields and trees of rough beauty. Iman wished she was not cooped up in the car. She pictured herself a Disney princess, in one of the many films she had watched with Salma's children, walking between the rowan trees, surrounded by small creatures whose role was to protect her from harm and keep her company.

Today, at the beach, when she had planted the date tree and watered it with her tears, a connection to the land had begun. At first gentle and overpowered by Ibrahim barging in to hurt her and throw back her things, but now as she looked out at the countryside, it was reaffirmed. This could be his replacement, she thought. Not another man but a place made up of heather and hawthorn, wild cherry and birch. It was the strangest and most muddled of thoughts, but it had a zest to it.

Moni started to complain about the draught. Iman ignored her until Salma said, 'Iman, close the window.' She obeyed with a scowl on her face.

Chapter Four

It was time to leave the car and cross the water. They were all, in different ways, thrown by this. Moni had no idea that they needed to cross by ferry, Iman had misunderstood the word 'ferry' to mean bridge and Salma assumed that she would drive the car onto the ferry. But the ferry itself was small, a rugged smelly boat just enough for them and their things. Mullin, the man who steered it, wasn't interested in their misunderstandings. He shrugged when Salma wanted reassurance about the safety of her car and he didn't care that Moni nearly slipped on the wet gangplank. 'Are there monsters in the water?' Iman asked him (she had been primed by Salma's children). 'Yes, lassie,' he said. 'Selkies too. Do you ken that word?' Salma noted the softening Iman induced in him, her usual effect on men. She wasn't jealous. It wasn't worth it. Mullin was small and solidly built, with white stubble that grew on his scalp and chin. His clothes were dirty and his mood disagreeable. Afterwards, when Moni gave him a tip for helping them with their things, he looked at the coin with disgust as if he was about to toss it away.

The boat was unpleasant, but they were surrounded by

beauty. A glory that made Salma feel light-headed. Leaving the car behind meant that she lost one of her capabilities, a bit of her authority, and now instead there was a strange freedom from bulk, the necessary space ready to take in a blast of visual stimulation enough to make her unsteady. Iman, the only one of them who didn't cringe from Mullin's proximity and stood near him, began to hear more clearly than ever the vibration of water, the timbre of white, notes for purple, green, grey and the constant low pitch of the mountains. Even Moni, who was never moved by nature, felt grateful that she wasn't blind.

Disembarking, Salma had to concentrate on Mullin's voice as he gave them information about their accommodation and the loch in general. His voice was low and she struggled with his accent, too intimidated to ask him to repeat himself. The nearest shops were seven miles away. From the outside, their stone-built cottage looked very much like the picture she had seen online, red sloping roof and green door. Inside, it had low ceilings and pine furniture, chequered curtains and a bright kitchen. It was even prettier than expected. She was relieved. Moni, the hardest one of them to impress, smiled with approval. Mullin showed them how to use the wood-burning stove. He answered their questions. Yes, the mobile phone signal should be okay. Yes, there were other families staying on the estate. In turn, he did not seem curious about them except to assume that Iman was Salma's daughter.

That's new, thought Salma, slamming the door of the cottage after him. I look that old! She found that the other two had already chosen their rooms. There were only two. The downstairs one was larger with twin beds. Up in the attic was a smaller single room. Salma assumed that she would share with Iman and Moni would be alone upstairs, but it turned out that Iman had fallen in love with the attic. Besides, as she explained to Salma, with a completely straight face, no hint of mockery, the room was so narrow that Moni would hardly be able to squeeze into the doorway.

Usually Moni did not like new places. Change and different scents disrupted her equilibrium. She protected herself by ignoring her surroundings as much as possible, but moving to a new place had forced her to adjust. The surprise of having to share with Salma made her more energetic than she would have normally been. She set about unpacking, but not before running her fingers over the shelves and hangers in the cupboard. Not a speck of dust or grime. The sheets on the bed smelt fresh and clean. There was a rough woollen rug on the floor, which she suspected of not being hygienic enough. She moved it to Salma's side of the room. If they were going to be here a whole week, then it was important that she make herself comfortable. She was marking her territory. Her bed, her side of the cupboard; prayer clothes and mat on top of the one chair in the room. Prayer clothes and mats were communal property, borrowed without permission or hesitation, but still Moni preferred to have her own. She kept them spotlessly clean and regularly rubbed a solid perfume cube on her mat on the spot where her nose touched the ground. It was always pleasant to touch down to fragrance, to rise up with the lingering scent of musk.

Iman could not believe how perfect her room was, as if it were specially made for her. The size of it, the sloping protective roof, the way the window was just over the bed so that she could lie down and see not just the sky but everything else – the hills and the water, a path that led to the forest and, far away, more sky and the tips of mountains. There was a dressing table and over it an old-fashioned pitcher and basin, both painted with the same scene of a princess – Iman assumed she was a princess or at the very least a noble lady – standing under a tree. She was surrounded by flowers bigger than the tree. Long flowing skirt and curled hair piled on top. A bird was perched on her wrist, wings spread out as if it was ready to take flight.

There was a small cupboard in the room and when Iman opened it she found it full of clothes. But these weren't ordinary clothes, they were costumes. A nurse, a witch, a kimono, Batgirl complete with cape and mask and, best of all, a princess. The princess gown was sky-blue, and it had silver gloves to match. The gloves were long, reaching up to the elbow. The skirt of the gown took up most of the space in the cupboard. At the bottom were packets of dried fruit and nuts and biscuits labelled 'Meal Replacement'. They came in chocolate, banana, vanilla and orange flavour. Suddenly hungry, she ate one of them. It was chewy and satisfying. The pain Ibrahim had caused her was a small black tangle inside, undigested, like something she shouldn't have eaten. But as she lay back, she found the soft mushy biscuit covered the black tangle so that it no longer touched the walls of her stomach. The biscuit was therapeutic, it was on her side against the pain. It was there to help her.

Salma went for a walk. She wanted to see where the phone signal was strongest. Despite what Mullin had said, it was weak in the cottage. She walked towards the water, finding the air warmer the further she went along the path. It was smooth at first and then became twisted and unclear, and she kept looking behind her every once in a while to memorise the route so that she could find her way back. It felt good to walk after sitting in the car for so long. Her body, inherently athletic, needed movement. She used to play tennis with Amir, making sure that she never beat him but at the same time keeping him challenged so that he would not be bored. At times she wondered if he suspected that she was deliberately missing shots, slowing down in her reflexes, not running towards the net fast enough. His ego always needed massaging and she must have been good at massage, even then. Now it was her bread and butter.

She smiled to herself and walked faster, enjoying how her body warmed up. Tomorrow she would wear her trainers and go for a run. It would be great to thrash through these trees, to smell the earth and her own sweat. Normally, she would now be bustling back in the cottage, putting away all the groceries in the kitchen, deciding whether the meat they had been carrying had defrosted or not and to what extent. Let Moni deal with it. Besides, she needed a decent phone signal to send a message to David, reassuring him of their safe arrival.

Moni changed into a comfortable green jellabiya and set about organising the kitchen. Finding out where everything was, teaching herself how to use the cooker, absorbed her; each simple task a challenge she could overcome and feel proud that she had overcome. The meat they had been carrying – portions covered in aluminium foil – was impossible to tell apart. Was this chicken or beef cubes or mince? She chose the softest packet, which turned out to be the mince. It had defrosted quicker than the others. She started to make kofta, seasoning the meat and then rolling it into balls, which she coated with eggs and flour. She looked up in surprise when Iman came in dressed in costume. 'That turquoise belt is something,' she said.

'Cleopatra,' said Iman. She stretched up her neck, balancing an imaginary crown.

'What?'

Iman explained about the costumes in the cupboard. 'There is a matching wig too,' she said and complimented Moni on her jellabiya.

Moni was surprised and flattered. She sliced tomatoes to make a sauce for the kofta, searched for the black pepper. She knew why she was beginning to relax. It was because the phone signal was poor. Murtada could not call her now. All he did was put pressure on her. Send me a scan of your passport. Pack up and take your son to his father, that's where you belong.

'Moni isn't your real name, is it?'

'Manahil is my real name.' But to her family and friends she was Moni.

Iman walked around the kitchen, touching things, opening cupboards out of curiosity, peering into the fridge. She was absent-minded, not really watching what Moni was doing or even offering to help. 'Do you think marriage is religiously sanctioned prostitution?' she said it as if she was wondering out loud.

Moni glanced up but didn't immediately reply. She tested

66

the oil in the pan. If it wasn't hot enough, the kofta fingers would disintegrate and make a mess. When she finally spoke, her voice was calm, without protest and this surprised Iman. 'If a woman doesn't have her own means, it could feel that way. If she is passed from one husband to the next without choice, if there is no love or understanding, it could feel that way. But one is halal and the other haram. One is blessed, and the other isn't; that should be a sufficient difference.'

Iman could not think of a reply or a further question. She opened the door to the back garden and stepped out, trying to act regal but not pulling it off.

Moni was going to say, you forgot your scarf, but the garden seemed sheltered enough. She watched Iman through the kitchen window. The Cleopatra dress was see-through, it fell to the grass but did not cover Iman's arms. Iman's long black hair fell over her shoulders. She swayed when she walked, dragged down by the long dress and the weight of the padded gold collar. Such a pleasing image, almost detached from time and space. Youth and beauty in a garden. The perfect ingredients, a hint of paradise with Iman as a houri. As Iman bent her head and fiddled with the sash around her waist, her hair cascaded over a bush. Midges haloed her upper body. The garden was rich with colours: the pink of Himalayan rose, mauve delphinium, flowers that were white, yellow and blue. There was the movement of birds and insects and now Iman enhancing and being enhanced.

Religion is the recognition of beauty. Moni had read this some-where and, if it was true, then she possessed it now, looking through a windowpane. It was unusual for her to be visually moved, to notice, to see. And she could go out there too.

She could be part of it. All that separated her was the kitchen door. Iman turned towards her. The usual slightly bored look was softened but her rounded shoulders, which earlier conveyed amiability, now spoke of pain. Another time, Moni thought. It was a shame about Ibrahim. Another trauma in addition to the civil war she had experienced. Poor girl.

In the garden, a bee buzzed in front of Iman's face. The buzz spoke of anxiety for sweetness. It made Iman crave honey. Honey was a cure for burns. She remembered her mother using it when she scalded her hand while cooking. Village life, the clamour of children playing in the alleys, then the war changing everything. The war made her despise her elders. Suddenly, they who knew everything, they who had to be consulted and obeyed, were rendered stumbling and helpless. Frightened too. And when they became frightened, they became aggressive, lashing out at whoever was weaker and younger. Parents, uncles, teachers – sometimes they terrified her more than the planes and the bombs. When the war started, she was the wrong age: too young to assume responsibility and too old to receive the precious, precarious care reserved for children. She was in the way: unnecessary. Only her beauty was valuable. Hence the marrying off, hence the flight out of the country. If you were useful and necessary to your people, you would not leave all that and become a refugee. You would stay put.

But Iman did not want the flickering images of the past to be part of the garden. War should stay out of here. Shaking windows, wailing women, burnt skin, the terrifying gleam in the whites of a young man's eyes. Blood that was not menstrual, softness that was damaged flesh, stillness that was not sleep but death. She wished she could wash her mind of all these things. She breathed in the smell of the garden, touched the flowers. This was the present, and she was here inside it.

Salma felt light-hearted, confident that the holiday would be a success. When she was young, holidays had meant days on the beach, sticky sand and the roar of the Mediterranean. They also meant increased parental interference and telling off, tantrums caused by exhaustion and too much sun. Then, in university, there were trips with the Beloved club. Sometimes she would be so involved in the organisation that the trip itself would pass her by. Afterwards, she could not remember what they had seen or experienced exactly; she had been too busy, caught up with assessing whether her authority had been challenged or whether she had taken the correct decisions. It was meeting David that changed her. He took away most, if not all, of her anxieties, her sporadic harshness towards others and towards herself. With him she softened and learnt to enjoy those things that were essentially meant to be pleasurable but had descended into sources of stress.

When the signal on her phone improved, she sent a message to David. She did not phone the children. Instead she kept walking and the more she walked, the healthier and stronger she felt. Too warm now for a jacket, she took it off and tied it around her waist. She walked towards the sound of running water and when she reached the stream, she washed her face and then, on the spur of the moment, decided to take off her shoes and socks, make wudu and pray. The grass was her prayer mat, the wind a protector, her knees felt grounded to this particular piece of earth. She spoke to it and said, 'Bear witness for me on the day I will need you to. On the day you will be able to speak and I will not. Say that I prayed here in this very spot and nowhere else.' The sound of her voice, urgent and pleading, made her smile. She was acting out of character. Usually when it came to matters of faith, she was pragmatic and mild. But this place was something else.

She took out her phone. *Amir, this is the last time I will write to you. This might sound lame, but I have come to my senses. It is not healthy to poke into decisions taken twenty years ago.*

She was interrupted by the sounds of people talking as they walked through the forest behind her. She stopped and turned. There was the blur of red from a rucksack or a T-shirt, accompanied by a man's short laugh. She waited for them to appear, prepared herself to smile and say a friendly hello. Instead the group passed along and when she picked up her phone again, she could not find a trace of what she had written. All the words had been swallowed up and disappeared.

She lay back on the grass. The sun shone directly above her and she covered her eyes with her arm. The sweat on her T-shirt started to cool, her skin permeated by the breeze. She pulled her jacket over her and that simple action, of drawing a cover over her arms, reminded her of bed sheets, the lightest of materials on a sultry night that was too hot for duvet or quilt. She closed her eyes and the darkness was not black. It had moving colours like running water. Her weight was on the ground, she wanted to roll over onto her side but felt she couldn't. When she asked her clients to lie on their sides, she slipped a small pillow under their heads. But she was not at work; she was free to rest, to squander time, to let her mind run loose. If she opened her eyes now, she would see the sky through the trees, but she did not want to open her eyes. Later she would, but now she could not open her eyes. She dreamt that he found her lying down, that he left the group he had been walking with in the forest and found her ready, waiting for him. In the dream she is impatient, hardly needing encouragement or preamble, and pulls him to her in a hurry, desperate because there is only a short time, only a small chance, before the feeling is lost and everything else with it. Better this rush, better this grabbing, assertive and direct, linear without games, triumphant without strategy. There is more of her in this shadowy world, with more skin and stronger depths; she is not held back by mind or matter. Everything is permitted, there are no boundaries. It is one and the same between her and him, between who he is, familiar and unfamiliar, knowing her, but the end is up to her. Opening her eyes before it was completely over, she was wide awake to the last motion of her body, the surprise that was not a surprise but still out of her control.

Slowly, she sat up and looked around. Her phone made a sound. She picked it up. It was a message from Amir. *I can smell you.* She smelt of sweat and of wanting a shower. She started to walk back to the cottage.

Iman wandered into the room Salma and Moni would be sharing. She guessed which bed was Salma's and sat on it. The room, furnished for a couple on holiday, highlighted her failure. Another marriage ending. After all the times Ibrahim had kissed her feet and said he was devoted to her. The little gifts, when he had been at her beck and call – running to

71

McDonald's at 2 a. m. because she wanted a strawberry milk-shake, holding the hand shower so that she could wash her hair over the bath, borrowing money so she could send it, through Western Union, to her mother. All this had ended or been a mirage.

And what lies ahead for her, how will she live? Everyone had predicted she would marry a rich man and never have to lift a finger. Her beauty had pointed towards this. Marriage versus prostitution. Marriage a way to legitimise the oldest profession? It need not be like this. She knew this, glimpsed it in the lives of other couples. Two things could look alike and feel alike and seem alike yet be profoundly different. One was blessed and the other doomed. The intentions that led to each were different. The resemblance was superficial but understandable. Man pays and woman serves. He houses, clothes and feeds her to get something in return. Put love in the equation. He gives because he loves her and would give regardless of whether services were rendered or not; she gives because she loves him and would keep giving even if he didn't pay. Or they both give and receive in a flow generated by love with neither one keeping tabs, with neither one viewing the relationship as a transaction.

She looked up when her friend walked into the room. 'What am I going to do, Salma?' Tears started rolling down her face.

Salma sat next to her. 'You'll be fine. He isn't worth it. And how can you possibly cry when you're wearing this amazing outfit. Look at you, a queen!'

Iman rested her forehead on her knees and Salma continued talking. 'Everything happens for a reason. Earlier today, you were upset that you weren't pregnant. Imagine if you were, it would have been an added complication.'

'Ibrahim wouldn't have left me if I was pregnant.'

'Really?' said Salma with sarcasm. 'He wasn't up to the responsibility of a wife, let alone a child. Don't fool yourself.'

'You warned me against him,' said Iman, looking up and wiping her face.

Salma was pleased to hear this. She had been restraining herself from saying, 'I told you so.'

'You insisted on him,' she said gently.

'He was so nice to me, I can't believe it.' She remembered how he could scarcely keep his hands off her during the day-light hours of Ramadan, how he gave her everything she wanted – a Netflix subscription, a new coat, a weekend away in London. 'His parents are to blame.' She was musing now, looking for justification.

'You deserve better than him. Mark my words. This time next year, inshallah, you will be married to the right man and with a baby on the way.'

Iman shook her head. 'I want to depend on myself. To work, like you.'

Salma tried not to laugh. Iman's greatest asset was her looks, her finest skill was in drawing men to her; zero qualifications, English language minimal. What sort of job could she do? Iman was lazy too. With Salma's children, she watched chil-dren's TV and never got bored. Imagine being told, you're too beautiful to ever toil, you're to be kept home in a fine state, you're created to be pampered and adored – all that Iman heard as she was growing up. Salma said, 'I'll make you hot chocolate and you'll tell me the kinds of jobs you can see yourself doing.'

Iman perked up. The two of them sat side by side, their backs resting on the headrest, drinking the chocolate and Iman rambled on about work. Maybe she should have stuck to that job at the supermarket. Maybe improving her English was the way forward. Salma listened, indulging her from time to time, challenging her with questions or suggestions to help her formulate more realistic goals. Then Iman lurched back to talking about Ibrahim, reminiscing. 'Once, he had a friend over, spending the night on the sofa. In the morning I got to the shower first and washed my hair. As soon as I came out, Ibrahim said I had to go back in there and make sure I hadn't left a single stray hair down the plughole. He wasn't worried about the plug being blocked. He didn't want his friend seeing a strand of my hair.'

'You're joking!'

'No, I'm not. He was that possessive about me!'

'That's daft, Iman.'

'He said one single strand was enough to determine the length of my hair, its colour and texture.'

Salma burst out laughing and Iman said, 'It's true. I'm not making this up.'

Outside, dusk was gathering and although the ground was dark and hidden, there were still dabs of orange and pink high in the western sky. I am happy, thought Salma, sitting here with my friend. I am happy being of use to her, being needed. Already Iman was in a more settled if not cheerful mood. When she slid down and stretched out on the bed, Salma felt free to leave her.

At last, after running around all day, she could take off her scarf and shower. In the bathroom she combed her wet hair. She was conscious of its thinness compared to Iman's luxuriant tresses. In terms of looks, there was no point in competing. Enjoying Iman's beauty without succumbing to envy was the only sensible thing to do. But a month ago, at Salma's house, Iman had said with genuine surprise, 'Your hair is getting so thin, Salma!' Salma was not prone to overreacting, but from that day on she had become self-conscious about her hair. She started using an expensive scalp foam, volumisers and fillers. She topped up her supplements. Now, gazing into the mirror, she fancied she saw an improvement. Her hair was in better condition even if it was not any thicker. Turning sideways, she glimpsed a diagonal roll of fat above her waist. Where had that come from? Pilates twice a week, regular walks and eating more or less the same. Her bathroom scales back home had failed to flag this up. She put on her pyjama top and started to make wudu.

Stepping out of the bathroom, she asked Iman, 'Do you think I've put on weight?' Iman's eyes flickered over her friend, noticed the wet hair. It distracted her from answering Salma's question. Instead she said, 'How come you washed your hair?'

Silence is a sign of agreement, as the Arabic saying went. So, I am getting fat, Salma thought, I am spreading out, this is exactly what they call middle-age spread. 'I felt sweaty from my walk.'

'You just washed it yesterday. You told me so.'

When Salma confessed about the dream, they both laughed. It felt like a true holiday then. The setting sun shining on furniture that didn't belong to them, the smell of cooking from the kitchen. A meal they hadn't taken the trouble to cook. Iman in clothes that didn't belong to her. Salma's face as hot as a teenager's.

'You miss your husband.' This was Iman's verdict. 'Send him a message. Tell him you wish he was here.'

'I will,' she said. It was the generous thing to do, the right thing to do.

When Moni finished cooking, she called out for the other two. She could hear them talking in low voices in the bedroom and, guessing that Iman was upset, did not want to intrude. No doubt the hot chocolate had dented their appetite. She left the kitchen and wandered into the sitting room. Salma had put Lady Evelyn's book on the coffee table. Making herself comfortable on the sofa, Moni picked it up and started to read.

As a child I spent the winter months in a Moorish villa on a hill outside Algiers, where my parents went in search of sunshine. There I learnt to speak Arabic and my delight was to escape my governess and visit the Mosques with my Algerian friends, and unconsciously I was a little Moslem at heart. After three years' wintering at Mustapha Superieur we left the villa for good, much to my despair, but in time I forgot my Arab friends, my prayers in the Mosque and even the Arabic language. Some years went by and I happened to be in Rome staying with some Italian friends, when my host asked me if I would like to visit the Pope. Of course, I was thrilled, and, clad all in black with a long veil, I was admitted into the august presence in company with my host and his sister. When His Holiness suddenly addressed me, asking if I was a Catholic, I was taken aback for a moment and then replied that I was a Moslem. What possessed me I don't pretend to know, as I had not given a thought to Islam for many years. A match was lit and I then and there determined to read up and study the Faith.

Later when Salma and Iman complimented her on her cooking, Moni was pleased. She explained her cooking methods and told them about how she had found mint leaves in the garden. Mint in the kofta mixture enhanced the flavour and looked pretty too, all those specks of green that matched the jellabiya she was wearing.

After they ate, Salma washed the dishes. The cottage felt colder, and Iman abandoned the Cleopatra outfit for the witch costume. She looked dramatic, but at least she was warm. She brewed tea for the three of them using the rest of the mint leaves Moni had picked.

They played board games. A pile of them were on the shelves that lined one wall of the sitting room. Another pile was on top of the television. It was Salma's idea, something she and David did with the children when they went on holiday. If she was honest with herself, she was carrying out this holiday, the idea of it and the execution, with what he had taught her over the years. A British holiday. Needing a holiday. Going on holiday. All of these were expressions she had learnt from him and her co-workers over the years. The sense of entitlement. And now extending it to her two friends, who on their own would not have gone on any holiday and did not believe that they even needed a holiday without family members, especially without men. Serving our children, our husbands, our parents – that's how our lives revolve. Once in a while, though, we need our own space, our own break. Just once in a while. Watching Moni in the dim light of the cottage winning at Monopoly, Salma felt good. She had taken Moni out of herself.

Iman was not a natural at board games. The rules confused her, and she was a poor loser, huffing and grumpy. Salma allowed her to win, but Moni didn't. Moni played aggressively and played to win. It was getting her to play in the first place that had been difficult. Iman threw down the dice and threatened to go to bed. Frowning in her witch costume, flapping its matching silver wand, it was as if she was cursing the other two. 'We will stop playing,' laughed Salma. 'We will, dear Iman. We will put all these games away, sit quietly and hear you sing.' Iman pretended to be petulant while Salma pleaded and coaxed.

Moni left them and went into the kitchen for a glass of water. There was no need to switch the light on. None of them had pulled down the blind in the kitchen and the gloaming was enough for Moni to make her way towards the sink. The gush of water from the tap sounded excessively loud. It sounded like a child's cry. Not one of distress but of a child playing outside, calling out to one of his friends. Moni filled her glass and closed the tap. She imagined a group of young boys kicking a ball, playing five-a-side. But they wouldn't be playing now, not so late at night. Mullin had said there were others here at the loch, other holidaymakers, presumably families. Their children would play throughout the grounds.

Moni, well travelled, had lived in parts of the world where children stayed up past midnight when the schools were closed, where there was no concept of bedtime. Often this was because it was too hot to play during the day. So, at night, boys played football in the street until they were tired out. Girls watched television with their mothers and all these children slept till noon. She peered out through the window but all she saw was her own reflection. Of course, there were no children out and about.

She sat at the kitchen table and gulped down the cool, soft water. Even after finishing the whole glass, she still felt thirsty. I must have put a lot of salt in the food, she thought. Good thing the others didn't complain. She got up and re-filled her glass, caught the sound of playing children again. Joyful, passionate in its own way. It made her smile to think of them, their enjoyments and little triumphs, free from re-sponsibilities and worries.

When she joined the others in the living room, she found that Iman had finally agreed to sing. At first, she sang grudg-ingly, but then she let the beauty slide through. Outside the cottage, her voice could be heard, the foreign words landing on the grass, picked up by the ears of djinns and those with wings, who understood even more than all three women did what Iman's song was saying, who she was describing, for whom the longing was due.

Chapter Five

Later, lying in her narrow bed underneath the open window, Iman could see the night sky. It would never be completely dark, they were too far north for that. Instead, pink twilight glowed over the western horizon. There were clouds that looked round and full like candyfloss and ones that were as flat as milk stains. Low streaks of light touched the ground as if there would never be a deep dark night. In the east there was a crescent – low, orange and perfect. The stars were distant, much more distant than she could remember seeing before.

Back home, her family slept outdoors in the summer and indoors in the winter. The desert gave them scorching heat and bitter cold. Hers were a hardy people, able to adjust and pickle and organise. But it was not memories of home that Iman embraced, not memories of walks along the Euphrates or vendors selling grilled corn. Instead her ears caught the sound of wings, a rustle of movement, sounds that were at first gentle but then became distinct. Through the window, a shy creature hesitated, asked permission to come in and speak to her. I am dreaming, she thought. I am dreaming, and this is a good dream.

The creature was a bird, but it belonged to the night. The creature could be a bat, but it had feathers. It spoke a language that she could understand. It knew her from long ago, it had travelled with her all those miles, never left her side, was always there but only here, in this special place, could it make itself known. Yet it was not entirely visible, not exactly, for when she looked at it directly it disappeared. She had to pretend she was looking in another direction or at something else for the orange, black and white to materialise again. But this was not a problem, Iman wanted to listen to it and talk to it more than she wanted to look at it. The creature had a name. Hoopoe, it said, named after the bird in the Qur'an. You are too big for a hoopoe, said Iman. You are fat. She was not afraid to tease it.

He said, 'You are bigger than me, but I know more. I can find hidden sources of water. You are stronger, but I have flown further. I have seen east and west, north and south. Inhuman creatures that trail purple clouds. Remote forests, trapped people, animals as big as giants, humans as small as plants. I've seen surplus, building and tearing down. At times, I've seen nothing because in some places there was nothing, nothing alive. But all things submit to the rule of time. We can't stop it moving, it pulls us forwards; it takes us away. There is no escape. I am here to warn you. Do not stay here in this cottage, at this loch, for too long.'

'Oh, I love it here,' she said. 'A room all to myself and the cupboard full of clothes. I don't want to leave.'

'This is not a destination but a stage. The stage of consequence where what you do and what you want and what you secretly think will take a tangible shape. Things you will see and experience. Leave before this happens. Continue.'

'We are going,' she said, 'to visit Lady Evelyn's grave. The three of us.'

'Only one of you will get there,' the Hoopoe said. 'The one who is least distracted. The one who has learnt that to keep going it's best not to look right or left.'

This confused her, and she started asking why, how come, how did he know? When she got no reply, she wanted to know which one of them it would be. Moni? Salma? Herself? Which one of them would visit that difficult-to-reach place? Say Iman, she begged.

Instead the Hoopoe told her a story. 'This story is about a landowner from here, from the loch, long before it was called the loch. His name was Nathan and he was a Christian at a time when most people were still pagans. Nathan was hard-working and charitable. He was rich too. His farmlands extended all the way to the river. At one time there was a severe drought, which almost led to famine. Nathan distributed his stored grain to his villagers until he had none for himself. But winter was coming to an end and it was obvious that spring this time would not bring the usual crop of corn. So Nathan turned to the Almighty for help. He fasted and prayed continuously. What can I do? What should I do? These were his questions. The answer came. He must sprinkle the sand of the riverbank on the desolate fields. Nathan ordered that wicker baskets be filled with sand and brought back to the farms. The soft fine sand sank into the earth and everyone witnessed a miracle. They saw the sand germinate and oat and barley start to emerge. In time, the stalks grew and swayed in the wind. Everyone expected a rich harvest and Nathan was a happy man.

'His standing grew among the villagers. Not the usual respect granted by tenants to their landlords but something else, personal and rare – the awe and reverence that mystics and miracle workers evoke. Nathan began to preach to the villagers. Leave your pagan ways behind. Worship the one true Lord, the Creator, the Sustainer, the Giver. For Nathan, the miracle of the growing crops was proof not only of the truth of what he was saying but of his own elevated, special station in the eyes of the Lord. You should have seen his face the day he set out for the harvest. Flushed with happiness, the eager villagers surrounded him, scythes in hands, already visualising the riches to come, the meals, the celebrations, the overflowing stores. But suddenly the sky darkened, the heavens cleaved open and the river broke its bank in a flash flood. Before their very eyes, the crop was completely destroyed.

'Let us pause here for a minute, young lady. Tell me which is more difficult and more painful – to be deprived altogether or to reach out for your prize, it is there so close, within reach, already yours it seems, and then have it, at the very last minute, snatched away from you? Which is the greatest trial?'

'The second,' said Iman, but she wasn't sure if this was the correct answer.

It must have been because the Hoopoe continued, 'Nathan was distraught. He lost his composure and his good sense. He did the worst thing ever. He raised his fist up in anger against Heaven. He spoke words he would spend the rest of his life regretting. Suddenly, the river water receded, the sky cleared and the sun broke over the destroyed crops. Oh the guilt, deep and wretched. More so than the loss of the harvest. If it were not another sin, he would have thrown himself in the river. But he threw something else instead. A key. And where did this key come from? Let me tell you.

'Nathan ordered the blacksmith to forge large heavy chains. Standing in front of the villagers, he wrapped the chains around his ankles and up over his shoulders, tight around his waist. "I am going away," he said out loud. "I will walk to Jerusalem to seek forgiveness for the crime I've committed. That will be my penance." He secured the chains with a heavy lock and twisted the key into the lock. Then he threw the key into the river and set off.

'A young lad hurried after him, "I'll come with you. I will serve you and keep you company on the way." Nathan welcomed his company, someone familiar on a journey to unknown places with new languages. The two walked and walked. It is always a longer road than one thinks; even after you start walking and cover considerable distance, it stretches further. The chains dragged Nathan, but he pushed to catch up with the brisker strides of his young companion. Whenever they came upon other travellers on the road, the lad would explain Nathan's chains. He was talkative and often, to Nathan's embarrassment, boasted about Nathan's wealth and nobility. "All sorts of people travel on these roads – criminals, thieves and those desperate enough to do anything," said Nathan. "It is not right that you boast to the likes of them." As a result, one day Nathan and the lad were attacked and robbed. All the money Nathan was carrying to fund the journey was stolen.

'Arriving at the next village, they decided that the best strategy was to split up. Individually, it would be easier to find work and shelter, or beg for food. Nathan was welcomed into the workshop of a carpenter and given food. Curious about Nathan's chains, he drew him into conversation. When he heard all about Nathan's predicament, the carpenter said, "If you are travelling to find redemption, I would advise you to travel alone. Have you not heard the story of the brave hunter and the bear? Let me tell it to you."

'The carpenter took away the empty dish in front of Nathan, sat down and said, "A brave hunter once rescued a bear from the jaws of a mighty dragon. The bear was filled with gratitude and followed the hunter with devotion. The two became companions, sharing meals and hunting together. In town, when the hunter went to sell his wares and buy sugar, bread and tobacco, people marvelled at how docile the bear was, as faithful to the hunter as a dog would be. However, some of them warned him, saying, the fondness of fools – meaning the bear – is deceiving. He dismissed these words as envy. On a particularly hot night when many flies were buzzing around, the hunter lay down to sleep in a clearing in the forest. The flies annoyed him, fluttering around his nostrils and disturbing his sleep. Seeing this, the faithful bear sat next to the hunter and swatted the flies away. He would not let a single fly settle on the hunter's face. He waved his paws, but one fly was particularly persistent. No matter how many times he swiped at it, it buzzed and ducked down to the hunter's face. The bear became more and more angry. That wretched fly! If only he could be rid of it once and for all. He picked up a rock and brought it down on the fly. The rock smashed the hunter's face into pulp."

'Nathan pondered this advice from the carpenter and on

the following morning sent the lad back to the village. From now on, he would travel to Jerusalem alone. When he reached the sea, Nathan began to search for a ship on which he could set sail. He found that he would have to wait. This delay gave him time to work as a porter and earn more money for the journey. It was not easy to work while dragging around his heavy chains. Often, the snippets of stories he heard among the sailors and other porters distracted him from his struggles.

'Once, he overheard an elderly sailor say to another, "When I say island, you no doubt imagine solid land, surrounded by water, but this place was not like that. It was soppy like snow, the air as thick as fog, the vegetation brittle and sparse. On that island, a giant ape was trapped and its cries were as eerie as the blowing wind. They pierced the heart of anyone who heard them. But instead of invoking terror, these screams sounded like convoluted laments, the anguish in them was such that anyone who heard them was struck down with a broken heart. Grown men would sob like babes and collapse utterly helpless. Too smitten to feel hunger or thirst, many eventually perished. The island was sloppy and airy, neither water nor solid, the only hard objects were the human skulls and bones strewn about. The few who escaped this island could not talk for three months. They could only weep with a sense of terrible loss. It was the sound of the trapped ape they kept hearing. It echoed in their ears for the rest of their lives."

'From a fellow porter, Nathan heard about an island in which the trees bore women as their fruit. The women dangled off the branches, ripe and ready for plucking. But these women were poisonous, the slightest bit of their saliva or sweat could cause instantaneous death. Nathan heard about places where death couldn't reach, where crops didn't need to be planted or watered, where the barks of trees were made of cloths. Mountains could be smooth as enamel, sparrows could be larger than oxen and antelopes as small as mice. Places in which there was never day and places in which there was never night. Nathan heard that a captain seeking fur seals landed on the back of a whale, mistaking it for an island. Another captain, chasing an octopus, found the island of smoke and fire. Creation indeed was a wide and wonderful space where Nathan was but only a fleck.'

'I know I'm a fleck,' Iman interrupted. 'It is men who have the largest egos, the biggest heads, the delusions of grandeur. They're the ones who need these lessons, not me. There's no pride in me.'

The Hoopoe did not reply. Her words dissolved in the air . . . there is no pride in me, no pride in me, no pride . . .

He then said, 'A poor, helpless woman can have a higher spiritual standing than the mightiest of kings.'

She knew this, but she had forgotten it, laid it aside like any other ideal. 'What about Nathan? Did he get on the ship?'

'Yes,' the Hoopoe replied. 'On the ship to Jerusalem, his chains scraped across the wooden planks and the sounds disturbed the crew. They were jittery because of the bad weather they were encountering and their fear of pirates. A superstitious lot, they regarded Nathan as bad luck. It did not help that he introduced himself as a sinner in need of redemption, someone who had locked himself up in chains and thrown away the key. He was weighing down the ship. Dislike towards Nathan grew even more when the captain befriended him. This happened when the captain discovered that Nathan could read, write and, more importantly, play a good game of chess. It pleased the captain to find learned company, someone he could talk to about a diverse range of subjects, from monarchs to agriculture, from map making to astronomy.

'The first mate became jealous of Nathan's friendship with the captain. He mistreated Nathan by setting harder tasks for him on the ship and by giving him little or no food. Nathan accepted this as part of his penance. Wasn't this why he had set out on this journey? He knew it would be a road littered with tricks. No matter how strong he was, or how weak, there would always be something heavy to carry. There would always be a puzzle that was hard to solve. Everything was mixed or running in parallel – the gains and the losses, the lies with the truth. Nathan did not report the first mate to the captain, but he did his best to remain in the captain's company for as long as possible.

'To do this, he told him stories from his native home. The story of the selkie very much captivated the captain. It went like this. Once, a fisherman heard singing at night. He waded in the river until he came upon a small island and beheld a magnificent sight. Three maidens naked under the moon-light were singing and dancing. The fisherman had never seen anything more beautiful. When the moon hid behind a cloud, the girls picked up what looked like fur coats from the ground and started to put them on. They were sealskins and, on wearing them, the girls transformed back into seals, lowered themselves into the water and swam away. On the following night, the fisherman was waiting for them. The seals swam ashore, shed their skins and became women. This time the fisherman was prepared. He crept with care, unseen, and stole one of the skins. Quickly, he took it home and hid it in his house.

'When the moon disappeared behind the cloud, the maidens put on their sealskins and slipped back into the water. All except one. She could not find her skin. No matter how hard she searched, it was not there. She called to her sisters, but they were already out of earshot. Frightened and forlorn, she sat shivering on the rocks. The fisherman made his approach. He appeared as her kind and gallant saviour. Gently, he coaxed her back to his hut. She went with him.

'The fisherman was patient and cautious in his seduction. He provided her with clothes and as much jewellery as he could afford, he taught her to speak his language and to cook his food. Soon he had her as he wanted her to be: loving, grateful and dependent on no one in the world except him. But she did not like staying indoors and she did not stop searching for her sealskin. In all kinds of weather, she would be at the shore singing to her sisters. They would swim to her, bob their heads out of the water and look at her with sad eyes. How could she return to their world without her skin?

'It became known in the village that the fisherman had taken a foreign wife. The villagers did not warm to her, but neither were they unkind. She remained a lonely figure, taking her daily walks to the sea, where she would sit on the rock and sing her strange song. The years passed, and she gave birth to two boys and two girls. They were beautiful children, free-spirited and healthy. Everyone was particularly impressed by how well they swam. Although they occupied her time and alleviated her homesickness, there was still an inner sadness in her, a restlessness for the life in the sea she had known, a longing for her sisters and cousins.

'One rainy day as the children were playing in the attic, they came across a brown, furry bundle and took it down to their mother. She cried out when she saw her sealskin and understood immediately her husband's treachery. The skin was glossy and alive, inviting her to step into it, to pick up the past where she had left off. But how could she abandon her children! She was distraught with indecision and anger. When her husband came home there was a big row while the children cowered with fear and confusion.

'She was determined to leave. She would not stay. The fisherman pleaded. He was a man in love and she was a mother. This was a happy home. "No," she said. "You are all happy, but I am out of place. I belong in the water." "You are my wife," he said. And so it went on until he shouted, "I should have burnt that skin, destroyed it once and for all, instead of hiding it. I will burn it now."

'She fought him for the skin. They tugged and tussled, but he was stronger, and the skin fell with a thud into the fire. She dived after it and, although he pulled her out, much damage was done. Her skin was badly scorched, her beautiful face deformed and ugly. Watching her sealskin burn to ashes, she screamed in anguish as if she were the one dying.

'From that day onwards, the fisherman no longer had a beautiful wife. Instead he had a bitter, ugly presence in his home, one that forever wished him ill and brought him bad luck.

'After Nathan finished telling the captain the story of the

selkie, he crept into his bedding below deck with thoughts
of that beautiful woman who was on the land human and in
the water seal. He was woken in the middle of the night by a
warm, soft creature who put her arms around him and pressed
her breasts against his body. She was molten and her heated
breath was what had first woken him. She promised him that
if he gave her his body, she would melt his chains. She was
fire, she explained, and iron was hers to shape and to break;
she was a flame and wood was hers to crush into ash. Did he
not want to give up his chains, did he not want to abandon
what was dragging and holding him back? She tempted and
cajoled him; she mocked his reluctance and sneered at his
indecision. Did he not believe in her power? She blew on
the iron chain that was looped around his neck. He watched
it glow in the dark, he felt it soften and scald his skin. With
one more breath it would melt and his freedom would be
complete. He swayed towards her and then suddenly tugged
his chains away from her grasp. He wrestled and pushed
her with all his strength. He turned away. The breath of a
genie – because this was who she was, a shape-shifter, a half-
demon – was not the way to his salvation. It could not be his
just end. There was another way.

'The ship arrived on shore and Nathan was on the road
again. He was weaker but lighter on his feet, less healthy but
quicker. How familiar these chains were to him now! They
were almost a part of him. For hours, for days, he would
forgot all about them until people pointed them out and
asked for an explanation. What he did not forget, however,
were his sins and the particular sin that had brought him all
this way. He asked forgiveness at every step, under every tree,

past every field. At every shrine he came upon, he would kneel and pray. One day, sudden acute hunger distracted him from his prayers. Leaving the shrine, he found a little boy selling fish. The fish were raw and not gutted, but they were available for the meagre sum Nathan could afford. He bought two fish and immediately gave one away to the leper who was always sitting at the entrance to the shrine. Nathan took his fish to a nearby trough of water. He washed it and split it open down the middle. Inside the body of the fish was the sign of his forgiveness.'

'What was it?' Iman interrupted.

'The key, the very same key Nathan had locked his chains with and thrown in the river.'

Before she could speak again, the Hoopoe was gone. When she looked outside the window, there was a speck flying towards the moon.

Chapter Six

Moni vowed not to leave the cottage. Not out of anger or any desire to make a statement. It was just that she was fulfilled in the cottage. Unlike Salma and Iman, she was not curious to explore the area. Very early in the morning, the phone signal was strong, and she managed to call the nursing home and speak to the night nurse just before she came off shift. Adam had had a fairly good night given that he was in new surroundings. This reassured Moni and cancelled the need to venture out in search of a stronger phone signal. She found a deckchair and when she was not busy in the kitchen, she sat in the garden, content to read Lady Evelyn's book or doze. There were magazines in the cottage, but she avoided them. They were parenting magazines, *Mother&Baby*, *The Green Parent*. They did pique her interest, but she was worried that they might distress her and aggravate confused feelings about Adam. Since seeing him last, he had not stopped being at the forefront of her mind, between every thought, but her thoughts were becoming genial, uncomplicated memories of his nearness and voice. If she picked up a parenting magazine, a photograph, some words or an ad might disturb this tranquillity and plunge her back into the usual negativity. So, she stayed away from the magazines and from the television too. She made breakfast, washed the dishes and tided up. Then she sat in the garden and, after a while, especially because it wasn't cold, she forgot where she was. Place wasn't important any more. She could have been anywhere nice.

She heard a thump and a ball hit her left shoulder and rolled onto the grass. The pain – sudden and sharp – shot through to her neck. She rubbed her shoulder and rolled her head from side to side, then stood and picked up the ball. She went to the front of the cottage and looked around. At first she couldn't see him, but then she did. He was a beautiful little boy, with lively eyes and a mixture of chubby cheeks and loose, thin limbs that made him even more endearing. There was an energy in him, a friendly glow.

'Is this your ball?' she asked. It was a yellow football, hard under her fingers. It gave off a specific rubber smell. Perhaps it was new.

He nodded, but instead of coming near her, he opened his arms. She tossed the ball to him and he caught it. It made her smile that she was able to throw the ball in the correct way. A way in which he could easily catch it. It would have been embarrassing if she had thrown it into the bushes or thrown it with too much force or too little. Then it would have hit him on the chest or even failed to traverse the distance between them.

She thought he would say thank you and run off, maybe even just smile his appreciation. Instead he threw the ball back at her. She didn't catch it and it rolled back towards the gate of the cottage. She lumbered towards it, thinking how long it had been since she had run or even gone for a brisk walk, if you didn't count yesterday at the castle. Her body was an instrument for tending Adam, a piece of equipment for carrying, feeding and bathing him. She bent down to pick up the ball, stood up again and tossed it.

This time she was ready when he threw the ball back. She caught it in time. They continued to throw the ball back and forth. She noticed that his blue T-shirt had a small logo that she couldn't recognise. His shorts looked like they were too big for him – they reached his knees and once or twice he had to hitch them up as if they were sliding down. His feet were in canvas shoes that had most likely been white but were now streaked green and black with dirt. She tossed the ball and he reached out to catch it. He pitched the ball and she cradled it on her stomach, holding it while she asked him his name and if his family were staying at a nearby cottage. He seemed not to understand what she was asking. She threw the ball back at him and then found herself chatting to him, talking about their surroundings. He listened, his facial expressions responding to her words. When he started to show off his skills – how he could balance on a ledge or jump over a bush – she clapped and said, 'Wow, how clever you are, how strong, how quick,' which seemed to please him no end. After some time, without a goodbye, he picked up his ball and, carrying it under his arm, turned around and broke into a run. She wanted to shout after him, 'Wait,' but there was no reason to do so. She went back to her seat in the garden.

★

Salma jogged after the man because he cleared a path for her. He was the leader, the one showing her the way. But he himself wasn't clear. He wasn't near enough, and this was part of the incentive to keep running, to try and minimise the distance between them so that she could see who he was, maybe even catch a glimpse of his face. Right now, he was a blur of brown hair and red T-shirt, long black running shorts. The only thing about him that was tangible and near was the imprint of his trainers. They were the evidence, the clues she could follow. She brought her feet down on each print and pushed through woodland park and in between trees. Sometimes she heard a twig snap, the thud of his shoes, a gravel swish when he skidded down a slope covered in leaves. Sometimes she heard birds screeching his presence, ruffled, and taking flight because of his advance. He kept running and she kept following. She thought she was catching up with him only to find that he was further away.

It was her own breathing she was hearing, the contrast of cold wind on her face and her hot body breaking into sweat. She was no longer watching the time, measuring how long she had been running. It was as if she had broken through a barrier, leapt over a hurdle and entered another zone where she had extra strength and a longer wind. She opened her mouth and let the air touch her dry tongue. Sweat dropped into her eyes, the salt stinging and blurring her vision. She blinked and nearly tripped over the raised roots of a yew. When she collected herself and again broke into a run, she couldn't make him out any more. Did he go left towards the water or did he head towards the monastery? She wasn't sure. The uncertainty made her slow down. And when she slowed down, she came to her senses. It was like surfacing from cloudy water to normal air and breath. What made her do this, run after a total stranger, chasing a man and most likely giving him the wrong impression? Her behaviour embarrassed her. Usually she was reserved, not prone to silliness. Did she think he was Amir? But how would Amir be here. Holiday silliness. Daytime fantasies. She was suddenly conscious of how thirsty she was. She had forgotten to bring her water bottle, but she found a few coins in the zipped-up pocket of her jogging pants. Instead of walking further to look at the boathouse, she took the path that led to the monastery.

The monastery had been converted into luxury holiday flats. A placard said that up until 1983 one of the wings had been a boarding school for boys. The monks taught in the school and tended their vegetable garden and fished. With time, the number of priests dropped, the school shut down and hundreds of years of dedicated worship came to an end. Salma walked past a cemetery where the priests were buried. She tried to imagine their daily life: worship, work, fasting, fishing. It was a way of living that her own religion condemned. Instead men should love women, have children, beat the dusty track of work, profit and loss. It was an indulgence to give all that up, ungrateful to disdain the messiness and hide in this beautiful spot. They called it austerity and sacrifice, but she wasn't fooled.

Gothic architecture, long stained-glass windows, even a gargoyle. She stepped into the cloister. Tranquil deep purple and a sudden coolness so that she shivered in her sweat-soaked clothes. She had read about the converted monastery online and expected to find a café where she could get a bottle of water and maybe a coffee. The stone walls made the atmosphere solemn, arches after arches. But there were people around. A man and his daughter played ping-pong on a table placed under the columns. Salma wandered around and read the signs. The chapel pool. The church atrium ideal for weddings and concerts. What she knew about Christianity she had learnt from the Qur'an. Sometimes David explained things, or Norma, his mother, would answer one of her questions. Norma usually went to church on Christmas Eve but not every Sunday. When David converted to Islam, she neither opposed nor joined him, but it seemed to have dented her confidence in some way. That was how she came across to Salma, at any rate, as if she was not confident in her religious beliefs. Her answers to Salma's questions were often tentative. Words like 'scriptorium' and 'sacristy' meant nothing to Salma. She walked through the arches until she reached a grand staircase. Upstairs presumably would be the flats.

She was searching for drinking water and coffee, but she found something else. On the door it said Monks' Refectory. She pushed open the door. A big wide space, wood panelling along all the walls, red paint all the way up to the high ceiling, stained-glass windows. When the door closed behind her, she saw a sign with information about the room. Here was where the monks had their meals. This had been their dining room. A pulpit protruded from one end of the room. There, during mealtimes, one of the monks would stand and read from the Holy Scripture. The room was now a comfortable lounge, furnished in tartan with a billiards table and armchairs. There was no one using it, but Salma felt a thickening in the air. It almost had a colour and a visibility. It almost had a hum. It was as if the monk standing at the pulpit and reading had left an imprint. As if the words spoken over the blessing of food had magnified in power. A moment of true sincerity had done this. Maybe the young monk had been hungry, smelling food he could not eat, at least not yet. But he believed what he was doing was necessary, to bless the food, to give thanks. And now, long after the monks had gone and their lifestyle with them, this spirituality lingered and refreshed. A thickening, that's how she would describe it. Like normal air turning to smoke, like when you're making sauce, stirring the spoon easily through liquid waiting for a change and then it comes, almost imperceptible, that first hint of heaviness. This heaviness was here, in this room, she felt it.

When she went back to the cottage, she joined Moni in the garden. She sat on the grass and finished the bottle of water she had eventually managed to buy.

Moni started talking about the boy she had seen earlier but soon found herself running out of words. She couldn't describe why he had made such a big impression on her. Besides, Salma was asking her about Iman. 'She found coloured pencils on the shelf, next to the board games, and she's been drawing birds ever since.'

'That's good,' said Salma. There was always a tenderness in her voice when she spoke about Iman. Salma switched to talking about Lady Evelyn. She had noticed the book on the table next to Moni. 'Are you reading it from cover to cover?'

'Of course, how else?'

'I keep dipping into it, bits and pieces, but it stays with me. I liked how her granddaughter said she was frail but physically tough. When she went out hunting, her tweed riding suit would get soaked because she dragged herself over the wet heather, then she would come home, have a hot bath and the next morning put it on wet again!'

Moni made a face. 'I didn't get to that part yet.'

Salma launched into the benefits of physical exercise. 'You know, sitting is the new smoking,' she said. 'It's just as bad for you.'

Moni was unmoved. Salma looked fit and sweaty, emitting waves of heat. She put her bottle down and pitched herself forward, face down on the grass, and started to do push-ups. Moni was vaguely impressed but felt somewhat embarrassed for her friend. Salma was acting Western. Sometimes, Moni did sense a gulf between them and became actively conscious that Salma had crossed a line Moni would never cross. Salma had married a white Christian – of course, Moni knew that David had converted to Islam, that he had done so years before he met Salma, but still she could never think of him as 'one of us'. Besides, English was the language of Salma's household and she often spoke and thought as if she was British and nothing else. This was all alienating for Moni but still intriguing. Despite having worked in a bank and marrying late, she was conventional and compliant. By refusing to join Murtada in Saudi, she was not in principle asserting herself or flaunting convention. She was just unable to let go of what she believed was best for Adam.

A ringing command from Salma interrupted her thoughts. 'A walk,' Salma was saying, looking up at her. She had rolled on her back by then, ready for crunches. 'A brisk walk would do you good, Moni. Believe me. And not only physically. You will feel good about yourself too. Your energy would be boosted, your day-to-day chores would be that much easier. Remember, when we go up that hill to the grave, it will be four miles walking. We can go tomorrow now that we're having today to settle. Today you really need to practise.' When Salma wanted to persuade Iman to do something, she cajoled and flattered. But with Moni, her voice carried a patronising tone.

Not that it offended Moni. Her thoughts were of the little boy whose name she didn't know. She stood up. 'I will go for a walk right now.'

'Great,' Salma beamed.

Moni didn't want to walk. She wanted to see the boy again. She left the cottage and walked in the same direction he had taken earlier in the day.

In the afternoon it rained heavily and none of them went out. Moni baked cupcakes, making do with whatever ingredients she could find in the cottage. Salma wasn't pleased. 'Count me out. I need to watch my weight,' she said. The irritation in her voice was because she knew that she would be tempted by the smell of baking, knew that she would struggle to resist and there was a fifty-fifty chance she would give in.

Iman showed more enthusiasm over the cupcakes and even offered to decorate them. She sat at the kitchen table wearing a Cinderella costume, the brown bodice and an apron with false patches. The kerchief covering her hair and the long sleeves were similar to the clothes she usually wore. It made her look natural, almost as if she weren't dressing up. But she was more helpful than usual, more deferential to Moni.

Navigating the still unfamiliar kitchen, adjusting the recipe to suit what was available, were challenges Moni was happy to take on. Besides, she was baking for the boy. To thank him for the umbrella he had given her when he found her walking in the rain earlier. He had appeared out of nowhere carrying it and walked with her back to the cottage, still without saying a single word. If the rain cleared up later, she would go back to where his cottage must be and take with her a batch of cupcakes.

The rain continued, and tea and the cupcakes almost replaced dinner. Salma had a tuna salad and Moni ate the previous day's leftovers. Iman steadily ate one cupcake after the other and finished off with a glass of milk. When she complained of constipation, the other two were quick to blame her erratic eating habits.

While Iman struggled in the bathroom, Moni asked Salma the question she had always wanted to ask. How on earth had her parents ever allowed her to marry David?

Salma smiled and said, 'It was strange. Even now when I think of it, it just seems like fate. David was in Egypt working for BP. He had a good position with a nice flat and a car. That flat was a company let and the BP employee who dealt with the housing of the expatriate staff happened to be a long-time friend of my father's. Uncle Emad's wife was my mother's friend, so you could say that they were family friends. Uncle Emad was very impressed with David. Among the other BP employees, David stood out for him because, during his time in Egypt, David had converted to Islam. After he did that, people started telling him, you need a wife. And Uncle Emad went one step ahead and not only said "you need a wife" but "I have just the right wife for you."'

Here Salma paused because it was at this stage in the story where she could mention Amir. Usually she didn't. Even her children didn't know about him. But now she said to Moni, 'I was involved with someone else at the time. One of my fellow students in university: Amir. We had even started to talk about getting engaged. My mother had already met him. The three of us went out to a cafeteria together. I remember that day. She came to meet him behind my father's back. She was tense. Amir spoke well. He said he loved me and that he had spoken to his parents about coming over formally to ask for my hand in marriage. But, he said, it was a bad time for them. His mother had just had a mastectomy and his father was in debt and struggling over the difficult sale of a piece of farmland. My mother listened to all that Amir had to say but she seemed sceptical. She said he should go ahead anyway and speak to my father. He said he wouldn't do that behind his parents' back. She said how about sending an aunt or an uncle as a substitute for his parents. He said that he wouldn't feel comfortable doing that. She started to get annoyed. She felt he wasn't cooperating enough, wasn't flexible. She was being generous, she was giving him a chance. He was a student without a penny and after graduation he still had three years of military service to complete. She wanted him to make more of an effort. He, though, felt that she wasn't being sympathetic. I sat there between them barely getting a word in.'

Moni imagined a younger, hemmed-in version of her friend. It was not easy to do so.

Salma went on, 'There were rows afterwards between myself and my mother. There were rows between my mother and my father when he found out that she had gone to meet Amir behind his back. "Why should we believe him?" my father said. "All this talk of his mother's illness and father's court case could be a lie." In the middle of this poisonous atmosphere, Uncle Emad stepped in. "I have a fantastic suitor for Salma," he said.'

This was where Salma chose to pause in her story. It was an odd place to stop because it was a beginning. It was even before meeting David. A day in which she was at her desk trying to study, the atmosphere which she had described as poisonous wafting through the flat. For days, her mother hadn't spoken to her. It was as if she didn't exist. Without being told she was forbidden to go out, she had stopped going out. Classes were done for the year and it was study break. Usually she would have gone out to study at a friend's house (where Amir would also be) or she would have gone to the library. Now, she just stayed at home, staring at her notes. It was, she remembered, unexpectedly hot for that time of year. Her jogging bottoms, which she wore as home clothes, felt heavy. Her long-sleeved T-shirt was irritating. But it was her mother who always supervised the seasonal shift in clothes. A whole ritual in which the winter clothes were folded with naphthalene mothballs and packed away. Then the summer clothes would be brought out and aired before being used. Salma did not dare initiate a conversation with her mother about switching to summer clothes. She sat in her room with the window wide open and longed for a cold climate. Hearing Uncle Emad's jovial voice outside was an escape.

Moni interrupted Salma's thoughts. 'But didn't they mind that he was a foreigner? Didn't they think that one day you would leave the country and not be with them again? Wasn't the cultural difference a problem?'

Salma looked at her friend. She liked Moni's methodical mind. She had recognised it from early on, buried under the jam that was mother and carer. 'David's favourable circumstances drugged them. My parents discussed these things that you just said, they voiced these objections, but they came out muted, through a haze of wonder. He was so different from anyone they had known, so beyond their experience that they couldn't quiz him or doubt him or joke with him. They suddenly went flat; they put all their trust in Uncle Emad's endorsement and said that it was up to me. Instead of the poisonous atmosphere, they were suddenly tiptoeing around me, sort of in respect. Later, the cultural differences did become a problem for them. But by then, David's time in Egypt was coming to an end and we moved here. Funny enough, my parents were shocked. They never expected him to leave, they thought he would be in Egypt for ever. It's strange that they thought that way. And to answer your question, at first they didn't mind that he was a foreigner. But afterwards, when my younger sister got married, it was obvious that they were closer to her husband than they were to David. They got along better with him.'

Moni said, 'I'm surprised. The way you met is more conventional than I thought. I was guessing that you worked together in the same company and then fell in love. Did he accept this kind of courtship?'

'No, he didn't accept everything,' Salma said. 'For example, he didn't want to meet my parents until he had met me first. He was sure of that. He insisted that we meet up alone. We did. My father was adamant that at that stage David wouldn't pay for anything for me. Not even a coffee. So, we went to the Aquarium Grotto Garden and I bought my own ticket. It cost two Egyptian pounds. David had to pay fifteen pounds because he was a foreigner. I liked him straight away. There was nothing not to like. He didn't appraise me, I would have hated that. He never showed off. But once we got inside the park, I realised that I didn't want to be there. It was full of students for one thing and I was anxious that one of them would recognise me and tell Amir that they'd seen me. "Let's go somewhere else," I said to David. "Anywhere." He protested, "But your dad said . . ." and I said, "It doesn't matter, I live a double life. I don't always tell my parents where I go." It was easy to be honest with him. I was speaking to him in English and it didn't feel real. It felt that the normal rules didn't matter any more. Everything was different. But I didn't tell him about Amir. I could have easily, and I think he would have understood and gone away. But even then, I didn't want him to go away.'

'It's fate,' Moni said. 'You were meant for each other.'

Salma was conscious that she had been candid with Moni, but still there was something she was keeping back. A minor detail she had pushed to the back of her mind. 'I thought he would drop me when I told him that I lied to my parents. He just laughed about it and said I was sneaky. To me it sounded like an endearment: "Sneaky". When a language is new to you, the words can sound different than their meanings. They ring other chimes. I couldn't get over the fact that everywhere we went, he had to pay more for things because he was a foreigner. I had never known that. How would I have known? So, I started buying the tickets and speaking to the waiters. He wouldn't say a word. He'd let me haggle and bring the price down as I was used to doing. It made me feel important. With Amir it had been the complete opposite. He always had to take the lead, pay the bill and decide what we did. When his allowance from his dad ran out at the end of the month, I had to pretend that I was unwell and that I didn't want to go out, so as not to embarrass him. Amir was like that. If I opened a juice bottle he couldn't open or got a better grade than him in a test, he would sulk for hours. Suddenly, with David, I was free of all that. What I wanted mattered. What I wanted I got. He even stood up to my parents and took my side. That's when things went forward, and we started arranging the wedding and trousseau and all these details.'

She paused, trying to remember something in the background to this narrative. Something she was ashamed of, the degree of shame small enough that she could bury it. A little thing. It nagged her now, but she went on. 'When we first moved to Scotland, the tables turned. I suddenly didn't know anything. I couldn't even understand what people around me were saying. All the skills I had – haggling to bring the price down, crossing a busy street, finding an ingenious way to solve a problem – were useless. The prices were fixed, there were traffic lights and there was usually only one way to solve a problem. David would go to work and I would sit at home. I became dependent on him and I didn't like it. I finished my training and started to work. And here I am.'

'Successful, mashallah,' said Moni. 'We all look up to you.'

Salma smiled. She accepted the compliment. Hers was a story of accomplishments and it pleased others to hear it. She must put Amir out of her mind. There was no point in continuing to text him. What use would it do? And yes, it could be possibly harmful. But she would like to see him. For old times' sake. To apologise. She owed him an apology. She had treated him shabbily. Her parents had treated him shabbily. He was scarred by what she did. It took him ages to get over it. He had never lied or dragged his heels volun-tarily. It was true that, at the time, his mother was having a mastectomy and his father was indeed taking his cousin to court to sell their ancestral piece of land. It was true because of the evidence she had seen. That was it! The large envelope addressed to her. Inside it were some official papers. This was the detail she had not mentioned. The bit in the story she was ashamed about.

A large envelope had been delivered to her flat on the day she came back from her wedding-dress fitting. She had walked in still dreamy from seeing her bridal self in the dressmaker's mirror, the waves of white taffeta, the tulle sleeves and the floor-length silken veil. She had picked up the envelope and seen her name in Amir's handwriting. She scowled, irritated. What does he want? She was ablaze with the preparations, almost feverish as every one of her wishes for the wedding was granted. What right did he have to intrude? In the en-velope was a copy of the medical record of Amir's mother and a copy of the court case his father was pursuing. Bastard, she had thought, trying to bully me back to him, wanting to ruin my happiness, they're all probably forged. She had glared at the claims of weakness, before tearing them up. But the documents had been authentic. She and her parents had done him an injustice. How poignant that Amir desperately needed her to believe him. How young of him.

The following morning, they set out for the ferry. 'The weather is perfect for this,' said Salma, and the others were encouraged by the fresh sudden sunshine after the previous day's rain. They needed to find Mullin so that he could ferry them to the car. With the car, Salma would drive for an hour to Glencarron in Wester Ross. In Craig, they would come to a private crossing where she would need permission to cross the railway line. According to Salma's research, there would be a telephone at the level crossing, she would need to pick it up and hear when the next train was coming. Only then would it be safe to drive across. After that was a two-mile drive into the hills, then she would park the car near a hydroelectric turbine. Beyond the two miles, the road was impassable for an ordinary car; only a 4×4 could manage the rocky bumpy path. They would need to leave the car and walk the rest of the way to Lady Evelyn's grave.

Mullin was painting a fence that led down to the boathouse. He shook his head at their request. 'It's the stalkin' season. Ye canna drive into the estate,' he said. 'No permission.'

The three of them stared at him. Iman did not understand the word 'stalking'; Salma and Moni could not understand why it would present an obstacle.

Because it was Iman who needed the explanation, Mullin was happy to oblige. This time of year, he explained, gentlemen and ladies came from England and further to hunt the red deer of the Highlands. This was not only a fashionable sport but a necessity to prevent overpopulation and maintain stocks at a stable level that was healthy for farming and the environment. Only the defective deer were culled; those with uneven antlers, those who were old or weak.

'This has nothing to do with us,' said Salma, impatient to get going. Her natural inclination was to dismiss objections, belittle obstacles. 'We just want to visit the grave.'

'The car would faze the deer,' he said. 'They feel the slightest sounds, e'en a loose stone. They can see black and white too.' He stared at Moni. She was the one dressed in black.

Frustration made Salma's body rigid. The fear of failure. They would be right after all, the others in the Muslim Women's Group who had stayed behind. Visiting the grave was difficult, they had said, it was remote, inaccessible. But she must prove them wrong, she had come this far and would not give up. Her voice rose, 'We have the right to walk the hills, ramblers' rights.' This man might think her foreign and ignorant, but she knew about the Scottish Outdoor Access Code.

Mullin shrugged. 'If youse insist on going, it canna be with the car. You'd need to park in the Achnashellach Forest car park ower frae the level crossing, cross the train line by foot and then walk six miles intae Glenuaig.'

Iman put her hand on Salma's arm. 'We can walk the six miles, Salma. It's not a problem. Let's do it.'

'I'm not walking six miles,' said Moni. 'Six miles there and back. It's too much.'

Iman started arguing in Arabic and Mullin watched her with amusement. His presence was upsetting Moni even more than Iman's inconsiderate insistence. She caught him looking at her with contempt as if he knew she was slow and cumbersome. She belonged to cities and cars, not to nature and fresh air.

Salma was weighing the situation. She knew that Iman was deliberately supporting her, but at the same time Moni was saying the truth. Six miles were a lot longer than four. It would be twelve in total not eight. Challenging but doable for her and Iman; too much to ask of Moni.

'Is there a time of day when the stalking stops?' she asked Mullin. Perhaps there could be a window when she would be allowed to drive the two miles up into the estate.

'Sunday,' he said. 'Nae stalkin on Sundays.'

The three women looked at each other. Saturday was the day they were meant to leave the loch and go home. 'We can stay extra,' said Moni. 'I'm happy to pay for the extra night.'

'It would need to be two,' said Iman. 'Saturday night and Sunday night.'

'Fine,' said Moni. 'If Salma doesn't need to go back to work by Monday, I can phone the nursing home and tell them I'll pick up Adam a day later.'

'I can take Monday off,' said Salma. Hope was coursing through her again. And relief too.

Iman walked back to the cottage while Salma and Moni went to the monastery where the signal was stronger so they could make the necessary phone calls. Salma texted David to update him. Iman had no one to message, no one who cared whether she returned to town on Saturday or Monday. The gap that Ibrahim had left, who or what would fill it? Sometimes she fantasised about winning him back. But even if he did take her back, she would never feel safe with him again. He had showed her that she was easily disposable, her body and silly possessions.

When Moni and Salma returned to the cottage, they found Iman dressed in floating turquoise. She demanded that Salma take her out in a boat. She was a mermaid, she said, and mermaids need water.

Moni, still annoyed with Iman, took the opportunity to criticise her Ariel costume, the flimsy blouse revealing the purple seashell bikini top. 'You can't go out like this!'

'I can, and I will.' She was in a rebellious mood. 'You can't stop me.'

'No one will see her,' promised Salma. 'There really aren't that many people around and she can take her coat with her just in case. Let's go.'

They climbed into the boat. Salma was the one who rowed. It gave her pleasure to scoop the water with the oars, to push the combined weight of them forward. The loch at this end was narrow, almost like a river, but the water was still except when the wind caused the surface to ruffle. Tree branches bowed over the water. Mountains rose on either side, the close ones grassy, the ones further away brownish, the ones even further away grey and misty as if they were shadows.

To maintain balance, Moni had to sit alone on one side. She watched the green banks drift past. She was searching for him. The little boy who had played ball with her, the one she gave the cupcakes to. He was the real meaning of this place. Every minute with him counted. She smiled when she thought of him, when she remembered the things she said to him. He never spoke, only smiled and nodded, his face animated, his eyes understanding. It was all her monologue and she liked how she spoke to him, how she found things to say. She liked how she sounded, too, kind and entertaining, pointing out things, explaining, making connections. Next time she met him, she would tell him about this boat ride. She must make a conscious effort to remember what she was seeing, to enumerate the details, not everything – that would be boring – but only the things that would interest a little boy, like the ducks swimming alongside the boat. Maybe she could take him out on the boat. Maybe she could row like Salma. It was certainly something to aspire to.

Iman looked down at the water. There was so much in there. Pebbles and creatures that could sing. Fish that knew her. Plants that were stretching up to the light. She breathed in the smell of the water and saw the shadow of wings, the Hoopoe following her, his crown reflected in the water, his black and white feathers a shimmer. She pointed him out to Salma. Salma said that he was one of the animals of Paradise, one of the animals mentioned in the Qur'an. 'He was King Solomon's special messenger, carrying important royal letters in his beak.'

Iman started to say, 'My Hoopoe is modern and I'm not afraid to tease him,' but then she stopped. Moni was waving to someone on the bank. Iman turned to see a boy picking up a ball that had rolled away from him towards the water.

'He looks like Adam,' said Iman.

Moni's skin prickled. Typical of Iman: blunt and casual. But all the more reason to trust in her sincerity. Moni felt that she had been given a gift. The last of her negative feelings towards Iman evaporated. Iman would not make this up.

It must be true. He did look like Adam. Past the disability, there was a resemblance, and yet most people couldn't see past the disability. It was too big, too glaring. And here was Iman, in her usual deadpan voice, matter-of-fact, just like that. Delight and greed made Moni turn to Salma. Made her ask, 'What do you think, Salma? Does he look like Adam?' She wanted Salma's endorsement too, to seal the likeness, to make it official. But Salma had not seen the little boy and now it was too late, he had already stepped back from the shore, out of sight, and their boat trailed on.

Never mind, thought Moni. Another time, another day. One could not be disagreeable within this tranquillity. She brushed away at the wasps that circled Iman's head but didn't circle hers.

Iman dangled her arm outside the boat. Her fingers caressed the water. Such a busy world down there. She hummed a song for the dolphins, but if they came too close it would alarm Salma, so she sang softly instead.

Salma could row without getting tired. She was stronger today than yesterday. She turned her head and glimpsed the blur of red. There he was, jogging through the trees, along-side the bank, but she could row faster than he could jog.

Iman caught a glimpse of the man in the red T-shirt. Mindful of what she was and wasn't wearing, she hid herself behind Moni.

'We will soon lose him,' Salma said. 'He won't catch up with us.'

By the time Moni turned, the jogger was already far behind. She didn't even see the colour of his clothes.

Are you running after me because I ran after you the other

day? You will catch me only when I want to be caught, that is, if I want to be caught. I can run as fast as you can run. I am lighter than you, stronger each day, leaner and quicker.

Later, Salma posted a selfie of them at the boat on the group page, the serene water around them, the purple mountains behind. Not all the comments were the mix of envy and approval she was seeking. The queries, 'What happened? You couldn't get to the grave?' required explanation.

At night when the Hoopoe flew into Iman's room for the second time, she was not surprised. He told her a story about water. His stories made her not think about Ibrahim, not hurt and rage. Water, the Hoopoe said, is the essence of everything. We would not be here without it. He told her about the water djinn who could swim faster than a sailfish. Because they leapt out of the water, they covered more distance. The world of the oceans, the Hoopoe said, is a secret. People think they know, but what they know is only a little of the whole. It's incomplete. That's why the unexpected keeps on happening; that's why so much is out of control. People believe they have tamed the wilderness, mapped the stars, charted every inch of every continent. But there are still surprises out there. To leap up and slap them on the face. To humble them occasionally. Just because they think they know best.

But Iman didn't know best. Iman knew that she didn't know. And that was an endearing quality, she had been told. The Hoopoe was entertaining, but he was also a warning of what could go wrong, a warning of what was coming.

'Disappointment is around every corner,' he said. 'The way

forward is a circle. The other side is different only because it faces the opposite direction. If everyone could see the end of Time, their hair would turn white in fright.'

'Where do you live?' she asked him.

'In a garden.'

'Why can't Salma and Moni see you?'

'They did see me. But they would not gain anything now from hearing my voice. Not yet.'

'I didn't tell them about you. They will tell me I am dreaming. Besides, I want to have a secret all to myself. Something that I don't share or explain. Tell me a story.'

'Once upon a time in the snowy part of the earth there was a beautiful girl called Iman. She had blue eyes and blonde hair . . .'

'No, she didn't.'

'Yes, she did. This is not a story about you. It is about another girl, who just happens to share your name. Iman had a jewel, which she had inherited from her mother. The jewel was in a box and Iman kept that box under her bed.'

'I know what will happen next. Someone will steal the jewel. I just know it . . .'

'Iman was a light sleeper and she was confident that if anyone tried to steal the jewel from under her bed, she would wake up immediately. One day, Iman received a letter. The letter was full of medical advice. It said that recent scientific research has proved that prolonged proximity to jewellery could lead to a serious, debilitating disease. Women were warned to take off their rings and necklaces before they went to bed. And even then, they should store them away in a separate room. On the following day there was a news item about how the shop attendants in the top three jewellery shops in the city had all fallen ill. As a result, the shops were forced to close. Iman became alarmed. She was attached to her mother's jewel. It was a shimmering green diamond as large as an ostrich egg. It had belonged to her mother's family for generations. The lights flickered and danced on the diamond in such a way that one could sit and watch them for hours without getting bored.'

'I would get bored.'

'No, you would not. You think you would. But you too would be transfixed. You too wouldn't be bored. The following day, there were more reports of illnesses from people who owned jewels. Three of the shop attendants died. The authorities decided to call in all the jewels in the city. People were asked to deliver their jewels to the nearest police station and they were paid compensation for that. Iman didn't take her green diamond to the police. She kept quiet. She was not the only one. There were others too who were suspicious of the reports. Or they were not confident that they would be compensated fairly. One of them was a childminder who sentimentally held on to her engagement ring. When the youngest child she was minding fell ill and died, there was widespread alarm. Everyone was convinced that the new law must be more vigilantly enforced. That was when the police raids started. Police bursting into people's homes and taking their hidden jewellery.'

'Did they raid Iman's house?'

'Before they raided her house, she escaped. She wrapped the green diamond in rags and ran away from the city. She ran far away until she was safe.'

'But this doesn't make sense,' said Iman. 'How come she didn't fall ill like the others? Or even die?'

'Because it wasn't true,' said the Hoopoe. 'The scientific research was a hoax. The illness and death of the jewellery-shop attendants was a coincidence. The death of the child was caused by a gas leak and not the childminder's engagement ring.'

'But how did Iman know this? How was she sure that the diamond would not harm her?'

'She wasn't sure,' said the Hoopoe. 'She reasoned that the diamond had been in her family for generations, bringing good and not harm, so why should it be harmful now. She reasoned that a thing of beauty must not be destroyed. And she was right in the end. Tell me, do you have a diamond too, just like her, handed to you from birth? I think you do.'

'Oh no! My family are too poor for diamonds or jewels.'

'You value your faith too little, you take it for granted, the sacred words you were taught, the path you were born into.'

He was right. She did not think her faith was a diamond; she thought it was lines on her palms. She asked him, 'Did Iman have a happy life in the new place she ran to?'

'She felt safe and she felt happy. Especially at the beginning, when she first arrived. Like the camel in the story.'

'What camel?'

'A young camel who lost his way because he straggled behind. The trading caravan, a long line of heavily laden camels, including his mother and brothers, went off without him. You see, the day before, as they were resting and refreshing themselves in the oasis, he had gorged himself on wild berries. They will make you sick, his mother warned, and she was right. The following day he was too weak to carry the load he usually carried and so the owner of the caravan placed him at the very rear of the procession. On the road, the camel became violently sick. He vomited and collapsed and when he woke up, he discovered that he was all alone. The caravan and all that was familiar had moved on to the farthest horizon.

'Off the road he went, groggy and dehydrated. Unless he found vegetation, he would surely die. He stumbled here and there and eventually found himself in a valley where there was a running stream and lush vegetation. It felt like a miracle. Soon he was refreshed and started to gain back some of his old strength. Now, this valley belonged to a lion, who ruled it with skill and generosity. The lion believed himself to be a fair and magnanimous king. This perception of himself was important to him. Out hunting one day, he chanced upon the camel. The camel was terrified by the sight of the carnivore, fell to his knees and started to plead for his life. "Your Majesty, I beseech you to spare me. I seek refuge in your land, please grant me safety and your permission to live here." The lion was moved by the sight of the skinny mottled camel, by his fear and youth. "Camel," said the lion. "You are my guest for as long as both of us shall live. My valley is your home. Eat and drink as much as you need. I will protect your life."

'The word of the king is law and the other carnivores in the valley did not dare disobey him. The camel was given free rein and he was full of gratitude. With time he became plump and his coat glossy. Now, the lion's closest companions were three – an elderly jaguar, a gossipy black crow and an entertaining hyena. They circled the king and, for their livelihood, they depended on the meat the lion hunted. Their loyalty was unquestionable and when they spoke, the lion tended to listen.

'One day, whilst out hunting, the lion was badly injured by a bull. He withdrew to tend to his injury and, like other wounded animals, fasted from food. The onus fell on the jaguar to hunt for food for the others. But the jaguar was old and what it managed to bring in was barely enough for its own needs and that of the crow and hyena. The situation actually got worse when the king's health started to improve. No longer fasting, the biggest share of the meat went to him, while even less was left over for the other three. Taking the jaguar and hyena aside, the crow said to them, "This cannot go on. We will die without food. The only solution is to eat the camel. He is not one of us. He is a vegetarian and we are carnivores. He is a newcomer while we are citizens of this valley from birth. He is a lowly refugee while our ances-tors roamed these lands since time began. In these difficult circumstances that are beyond our control, it is the camel that must be sacrificed. I will petition His Majesty on that matter."

'The lion, however, did not even allow the crow to finish its speech. He was incensed. "Did I not promise the camel safety?" he roared. "Did I not give him my word of honour? How dare you make such a proposal?" He attempted to lunge at the crow, but the pain of his wound flared up and he lay down again.

'The crow was not deterred. It gathered the jaguar and the hyena and together they hatched a plot against the camel.

They went to him and it was the crow who spoke first. "Dear camel," said the crow. "The king is slowly starving. As his loyal citizens we cannot sit back and let this happen. Therefore, the jaguar, the hyena and I are going to formally offer him our lives."

'The camel was taken aback. The jaguar was old, the hyena a pack of bones and there was hardly any meat on the crow. "Will the king actually eat you?" the camel asked.

'"Of course not," said the crow. "It is merely a formality. A show of loyalty and gratitude."

'"Then I must join you," said the camel, and the four set off together.

'One by one, led by the crow, the animals laid their life down before the king. "The crow is a scrawny thing, there is more meat on me," said the jaguar. "The jaguar is old and tough," said the hyena. "Eat me instead."

'Roused by these noble sentiments of sacrifice and altruism, the camel cried out, "Your Majesty, I am young and healthy. Please eat me. Look at the lustre of my coat and the plump meat that covers my bones. I am the one most worthy of your palate."

'"He's right," said the crow and without further ado the jaguar leapt at the camel's throat.'

'Oh no,' Iman cried out. 'What did the lion do? Didn't he stop them?'

'No,' said the Hoopoe. 'The lion looked away.'

Chapter Seven

Salma was talking to Amir. She knew she shouldn't, but here she was in the cloister of the monastery where the phone signal was strongest, using up her data. He was miles away and she was safe from sin, the disloyalty symbolic not actual, too airy to be incriminating. This gave her courage, or arrogance; she could not be touched and so could not be blamed. This was a virtual game, which she could enter and exit, unscathed, incurring no losses. What was it like hearing his voice? Exactly as she remembered. Nothing had changed. All these years – eighteen, nineteen years – could have been weeks or months.

'What's your daughter's name?' she asked and immediately forgot his response. Her mind couldn't retain the new changes, though this was what they talked about at first. Bringing each other up to date, although they had already done that with messages and emails. There was a need to repeat the facts, though the facts continued to remain abstract. He now had a six-year-old daughter. So what? It had nothing to do with their shared memories, the future they had planned but never executed, the places they had sat in and talked about how much they meant to each other.

They spoke about mutual friends. Who was working where, who had married whom, and the ones who had died prematurely. They lingered a little over this last small group – the particulars of their illnesses or fatal accidents, where they last were, how old, but then they quickly moved on, leaving them behind. It was awkward talking about death when they now felt electrified with life. The deceased had exited too early, left the party in full swing, didn't see their children grow up. It was Amir doing most of the talking, filling in details. She listened to him, ignoring the chill gathering around her, the instinct to be inside. The door of the refectory was locked. She had tried opening it.

'Do you still play tennis?' she asked.

'Yes. I am on the board now.'

'Of the club?' She laughed out loud. 'That's such a grown-up thing to do. That's what people our parents' age did when we were young. And we used to be frightened of them. Remember. They would tell us off for messing up the net. "Whatever you do, don't touch that net, don't lower it, don't raise it. Leave it alone." Even though it was sagging, filthy and full of holes!'

'We have brand new nets now,' he said, a familiar bristle in his voice. 'In excellent condition.' So quickly defensive. She remembered the effort of circling him, humouring him, mindful of stepping on his toes. All this she had done with goodwill, without complaint. Full of energy she had been, optimistic and hopeful, flexible as only the young could be flexible. Photocopying past exam papers for him, queuing so he didn't need to, allowing him to win every card game and every tennis set, yet, at the end, she had completely floored him. But they would not talk about that today, not yet the reproach. That would be too intimate, too close and revealing. Safer the banter.

'You haven't changed at all, Salma.'

'That profile picture you're seeing is old.'

'How old?'

'Last summer.'

'See, I'm right. You haven't changed one bit.'

She liked hearing this. Of course she did. 'I don't play tennis any more, but I do keep fit. Then I'm on my feet all day, always busy.'

He understood straight away that 'on her feet' was a reference to work. He said, 'I was so sorry to hear about your PLAB exams.' There was warmth in his voice, a genuine understanding of that loss. No one else in the world had really cared. Not her parents far away, unable to comprehend that their daughter, the doctor, was not considered a doctor in Britain. Not David for whom her choices were her choices, who asked her questions and innocently believed her every answer. Do you want this badly? Are you sure? What could she be sure about with baby number two on the way by the time she had already failed the exam twice? He would cook so she could study, babysit so she could nap, but it hadn't been enough. To pass the exams needed too much of an overhaul, a surge to join an altogether higher league, and she was not able enough, not prepared enough. Sometimes she felt that David did not want to dirty his hands with her complications, specifically these complications that arose from that other continent, the guts and terrain she came from. But then he would be generous and considerate; so open and trusting that she would regret her complaints and find herself flooded with gratitude.

'Salma, you are a doctor and these exams were just an obstacle.'

'That's life,' she said on the phone, the bitterness surfacing through. 'People here complain about the health service being strained, doctors working long hours and yet they make it incredibly difficult for medical graduates from abroad to qualify.'

'You should have persisted,' he said. 'You should have cracked these exam requirements whatever it took. Made sacrifices. Got help. Come on, it's not like you to give up.'

She liked this reproach, his unshaking belief in her. But he hadn't known her as a mother, hadn't seen what pregnancy and sleepless nights did to her, time and again. It almost submerged her once and for all, but it didn't. She wouldn't be on the phone now with him if it had. Motherhood hadn't enslaved her, but it did dent her resolve, put her in her place.

'I tried, Amir. I tried my best. The circumstances were against me.'

'Nonsense. You needed help that's all, a bit of support. Your husband isn't a doctor, is he?'

His voice was neutral, but she knew it was a dig that did not require a reply. Amir was the surgeon now, his private clinic stuffed full of patients, his reputation high, the money coming in. No doubt his wife had a full-time maid, a beach house overlooking the Mediterranean, private schools for the kids.

'Do it now,' he was saying. 'It's never too late. Sit those exams again.'

For a second, the old ambition surged through her. It flared up like lust. She was conscious of her elbow touching her breast as she held up the phone, her hips brushing the column she was standing against. 'Or I could just pack it up and return home. Rewind the clock.' Her voice had an edge to it, an uneven attempt to sound flirty.

'I would be at the airport waiting for you.'

She could visualise it. To be whisked away, to be young again. 'Don't you have better things to do? I reckon you're busy.'

'Every day is the same as the one before it,' he said. 'My wife is Japanese.'

'Really? I didn't know.'

He laughed. 'Metaphorically.'

She didn't get the joke and imagined her children heckling in the background: 'Racist!'

Amir began to explain. 'She's super-efficient, methodical and organised . . .' He suddenly stopped as if caught out. He didn't want to talk about his wife any more.

Salma rescued the silence with chatter. The Wimbledon matches. It turned out he was following the coverage even more regularly than she was. They were the same people but heavier and slower, their responses taking more time, their words loaded with assumptions, presumptions and the solidity of the past. She told him about Lady Evelyn. Her wedding in 1891 was in the All Saints Church in Cairo. As a gift, the Khedive sent palms and flowers to decorate the church.

'What was she doing in Egypt?'

'Her parents owned a villa in Cairo and they spent the winter months there.'

'I know where that church is,' said Amir and she almost gasped with delight as he started to connect her with streets and landmarks she had forgotten. 'I badly need a holiday,' he said. 'There is no peace here. Continuous strife every which way I turn.'

She surveyed the scene around her. Fresh cool air, the almost empty lawns of the monastery, the blue-grey waters of the loch up ahead. 'Plenty of peace here.'

'I will join you,' he said.

She laughed. 'You will be most welcome. Bring a rain jacket.'

'Seriously. I need to get away. I feel stifled.'

'You said this years and years ago, the exact wording: I feel stifled.'

'Did I? What was the occasion?' He sounded more alert. They both had good memories. Brains that retained information to spill out on examination papers. But why start raking up the past?

She said, 'The first day of our clinical placement. We were put together.'

'Yes, I remember.'

Did he remember that he had hated it and she had encouraged him, neglected her own work to do his for him while he procrastinated? He never acknowledged her support or thanked her. But then she didn't need to be thanked. To be his love was enough. To bear his weight was enough. If she were to judge him now, she would say spoilt brat.

Mollycoddled at home as the only son, privileged everywhere else. But that was typical of their time and place. The hard knocks hit the men later in life, while vulnerable girls turned into venerable matrons who could do no wrong.

'Salma. Salma.' His repetition of her name pushed its way through her.

It was coming too soon, she wanted to press down the brakes, to keep the pace steady, to be in control. Instead she blurted out, 'I'm sorry. Sorry. Sorry.'

'Sorry is not enough. It's not enough.'

The whine in his voice made her laugh or sob or cough. A sound from the throat. She was far away. Cruel and far away.

'You can laugh all you want, but there are flights to London every single day,' he said. 'More than once a day.'

'I'm not in London.'

'Then how do I get to this forsaken place where you're at, another flight?'

'Maybe. Maybe not.'

'You're not taking me seriously.'

'I thought I was the one who was going to come back, and you were going to make a doctor of me.' Even while joking the hurt was still there, old but visceral.

'I will bring you back with me. That's a separate issue.'

'Ah, well. You would like it here. There's a tennis court. I've seen some people playing. I haven't played in years.' It was such a holiday thing to do. Search for equipment, play a sport you haven't played in years.

'I will book and let you know.'

She laughed, and he said, 'This isn't an empty threat.'

'I believe you.' She was playing along now. 'Bring some coriander with you.'

'What!'

'Freshly ground. It's not the same here.'

'What else?' His tone was bored. Even in this play-acting, he did not want to be the one to bring, the one to carry or go out of his way. Salma imagined his wife being totally in charge of the household, while he lived in an orbit of work, siesta and tennis club – actually not much different than when he had been a boy. His print on the household would be faint, his presence brooding rather than constructive. Or when he was in a good mood, his presence as sparkling as a holiday, the family hanging on every word of his clever banter.

She said, 'Long ago, when you used to tell me you felt stifled, I thought you wanted to emigrate. Do you still want to do that?'

'It's too late.' He sounded resigned. 'There are decisions that need to be taken at a certain time. You can't put them off for ever. I wasn't desperate about leaving, though. Not like you.'

So this was how he saw her. Desperate to get out. True, she had done the rounds of embassies – New Zealand, Canada, Australia, the US – come back with forms, which she read and summarised for him. The precious pages on the café table between them, the extra care lest a drop of tea fell on them. If she hadn't queued for the forms, he wouldn't have. That was their pattern, what came naturally to them both – she did the legwork and the research so that they could brainstorm and fumble towards a decision in which he would have the final word.

'I wasn't desperate to leave,' she said.

'Oh, you were,' he said. 'It's the only explanation.'

She felt pushed back, unable to come up with a defence. A defence that would not be a personal criticism of him. It was admirable, in a way, how he had justified her actions and protected his ego. She loves me but she's desperate to leave. She loves me, but a better opportunity came up. She loves me.

Salma said, 'Is this why you're back in contact? To prove that I made the wrong choice.'

'Didn't you?'

Her voice was stiff. 'There is something called fate and destiny, as you well know.'

'Sure. I don't disagree.'

'Let's not quarrel.'

'I'm sorry. I act disingenuous and it must be infuriating for you. You once let me beat you at tennis, didn't you?'

Once? She laughed, taken by surprise, the warmth back again, the edge gone. Such a concession from him! 'Of course not. It's not the sort of thing I would do.'

'But it is. It is. I badly needed the pretence, you were more mature, you held it all together.'

That was true when she was with him, when she was there, but not after she came here, not when she was repeatedly failing the PLAB – failure a new experience, an alien state – and the children were so small. It had taken all her strength to crawl her way out of that, to turn around and start from scratch, then make something of herself.

He went on praising her abilities. 'Remember the time when we went to Saint Catherine?' This was the college trip she had organised. Forty students, many of whom had never been away from home. She had been too distracted by her leadership role to appreciate the place, to be truly in awe. The burning bush seen by Prophet Moses, the place where he received the Ten Commandments. She remembered rocks the colour of sand, the way the monastery nestled in the gorge. Now she was standing in a monastery too, one that was converted and secularised, made frivolous and lucrative unlike that living, working monastery up in the rugged hills of Mount Sinai.

After she put the phone away, she felt as if she had time-travelled. A part of her had been with him in a firm and complete way. The years scrunched against each other, a folded fan, slim and easy to hold up, to control. To put away? To put away all these years: David and the children, the work and the friends, a whole life she'd built. Impossible. But for a short time she had been sucked into a connection with the past, electrified by every word said, by every word implied and not spoken. She had felt all the clichés – alive and rejuvenated. Even now her body hummed, the body that had never left the loch.

Moni held his hand. The little boy was balancing on the wooden climbing frame. 'Look at you! You are my height now,' she said. They were in the adventure playground and the rubber matting, covered in loose play bark, was soft underneath her feet. There was no fence encircling the playground and behind it was a pitch where a group of teenage boys were playing football. The empty, open-air tennis court could be seen further back, closer to the loch.

The boy smiled but never spoke. He was not deaf. She was sure of that. His expressive eyes responded to her words, his mouth rounding in surprise, his forehead creasing into frowns. Then there were all the delightful faces he made to accompany her monologues. She figured it must be only a matter of time before he spoke. More than anything else, she wanted to know his name. She wanted to talk about him to the others. She wanted to assign to him an identity that was special. Frustrating too was the fact that she never came into contact with his parents. They certainly allowed him plenty of freedom and were unconcerned about his safety. If Adam had been like this boy, able to walk and run and climb, she would have been possessive of him. She would have made sure that she knew his whereabouts all the time. She would not have been careless. Never mind. Here was this little boy; it was such pleasure to be in his company. For him, she willingly left the cottage. She followed him wherever he wanted to go.

When he let go of her hand and strode with new confidence across the wooden walkway, she sat on one of the big tyre swings and watched him make his way down the slide. The anxiety that she might be too heavy for the seat made her stand up again. She strolled around, enjoying the proximity of the other parents, flattered by the gift they were giving her – the unspoken assumption that she was the boy's mother. She wished that she knew his name so that she could say it out loud for all to hear. He was a good boy, respectful of the other children, giving them their space. The playground was all made of wood and the steps of the ladder, leading up to the walkway, looked like logs.

'Let's go look at the rabbits,' she suggested. In the lawns between the monastery and the loch, the rabbits were mounds
of brown fur, nibbling diligently. Occasionally, one of them
would dart across the grass and the boy would follow. She
did not allow him to follow the rabbit that scampered into
the monks' graveyard. There, the land was completely flat,
the grass marked only by short white crosses, with clubs on
the tips and a circle on which was written the name of the
deceased. No, he mustn't go in there; it was disrespectful.
The rabbits ate the grass of the graveyard because they didn't
know any better. Let's count them instead.

He loved the snack machine that was in one of the clois-
ters of the monastery, overlooking the garden. She gave him
coins and with great concentration, his body tense with excitement, he inserted each coin in the slot. A coin slipped
through his fingers, fell on the tiles and rolled away. 'Catch
it,' Moni cried out, 'quick before it gets away, before it es-
capes.' The drama in her voice as he scrambled to pick up the
coin, an exaggerated sigh of relief when he did, a clap of her
hands. He stood tall then, pushing the last coin into the slot.
Then he made his choice. The anticipation of the packet of
crisps sliding down, then dropping to where he could pick it
up, his small hand inserted through the rectangular compartment, not without a little hesitation, but still made brave by
the treat to come. And then, at last, the snack.

She taught him to share, showed him how to be generous.
He must offer her some of his crisps, he must give her a bite
of his chocolate. Then she would want a snack of her own
too. Back to the machine. Oh, do I have enough coins? I
hope I do. Have a look. Help me count. Alhamdulillah, I

have enough. Here, you get it for me. He would insert the coins and select the juice, her choice of flavour, the satisfying thud of the bottle down to the compartment. She must share it with him too. Would he prefer one sip each in turn or the last quarter of the bottle all to himself?

'I must call you something. You must have a name. My son's name is Adam.' They were on the croquet lawn, the water and mountains within sight. She showed him a photo of Adam on her phone. In the photo he was wearing a striped blue T-shirt and only a bit of the wheelchair was showing. She rarely showed Adam's photo to anyone. This one she had sent to her parents. The grandchild they weren't proud of.

Today was turning out to be the warmest day of the holiday. She lay on the grass and watched the boy drink the last of the juice. His lips changed colour. She checked her phone's signal and called the nursing home to see how Adam was getting on. The nurse said he was with the other children in the garden enjoying the fine weather. Moni watched as the boy stuck his tongue into the bottle and tilted his head back. A few drops of purple juice fell down his chin.

'This will stain your T-shirt,' she said, gently taking the bottle from him. 'Be careful. Get a tissue from my bag and clean your face.'

He wiped his face with the back of his hand, leaving streaks of grass and a bit of grit on his cheeks, then rummaged in her handbag, becoming distracted by her house keys and a leaflet about immunisation before he pulled the tissue out. 'That's right,' she said to encourage him. 'Wipe your face so that you can go home later nice and clean. Your clothes are always clean. Such a nice T-shirt you're wearing today. Smart.' He smiled as he looked down at the train design on his T-shirt and handed her the dirty tissue. A bee buzzed in front of her nose. She swatted it away and closed her eyes. When she opened them, the boy looked more substantial, as if he had moved to sit closer to her. She would miss him when the time came to leave the loch. The thought brought a prick of tears to her eyes. Silly to form such an attachment, exaggerated and sentimental.

'I don't even know your name. Next time I will bring a paper and pencil and maybe you could write me your name. Or –' she sat up, propelled by a sudden idea '– why wait for paper, write your name on my phone.'

She opened the Notes section. A new page. 'Here, type out your name for me. I am sure you know all your letters.'

When he handed her back the phone, she said, 'No, that's not your name.' Her voice was sharp. The boy's expression, open and full of goodwill, changed to disappointment, a slight frown in the attempt to understand why he'd been rebuked.

Moni started to explain, 'Adam is my son. Not you. It's not your name. You've heard me speak about him. That's all. But I wanted to know your name. I wanted you to write it down.' She made an effort to speak gently. She didn't want him to think that she was telling him off. 'I'll give you an-other chance. Here. Now write your own name, not my son's name.' She handed him her phone.

When he again wrote 'Adam', she felt the anger rise in her, the protectiveness. 'I don't know why you're doing this.' She took the phone away from him and lay back on the grass again. She closed her eyes and kept them closed until she heard him standing up. 'Where are you going?' She scrambled up on to her knees, but he was already walking away. 'There is no need for you to be upset,' she called out as he broke into a trot.

Later, at the kitchen table, she told Iman what had happened. They had drawn closer since coming here. Moni cooked, and Iman appreciated her efforts. Salma on the other hand acted as if Moni was deliberately sabotaging her diet attempts. She avoided the kitchen and all the rituals of cooking that interested the other two.

Iman said, 'Maybe his name *is* Adam. It could be. It's a name anyone could have whatever their nationality or religion.'

Moni was still sceptical. 'Perhaps.'

'There is no other explanation,' said Iman. She was dressed up in an outfit that was so ordinary and respectable that it didn't even look like an outfit. Moni had gotten used to her in one outrageous costume or another but now found her different somehow, reliable and smudged round the edges. What was she dressed up as now? Receptionist? Bank teller?

'You're right. I should have at least taken him for his word, pretended to believe him.' Now she may never see him again. She stood up and turned to the sink. Iman did not wash a single mug or dish. Salma and Moni did all the housework. Occasionally, Salma went up to Iman's room to make the bed, empty the bin and bring down dirty bowls and cutlery.

'Actually,' said Iman. 'Why don't you look for his parents? At the very least you would meet them and then find out what his real name is.'

The idea had already crossed Moni's mind. That day he had given her the umbrella, she had assumed he lived close by. However, on inspection she had found no cottages or lodges there. The cottages were scattered further in the grounds of the monastery. Approaching them, she would feel like an intruder. She could ask Mullin. He was often around doing one thing or the other. But she was convinced that Mullin didn't like her.

'Iman,' she said, her fingers in the warm water. 'Would you do a favour for me? Would you ask Mullin about the boy's family?'

It was always a mistake to ask Iman to do anything. 'Why me?' She tossed her hair back. 'Do it yourself. Or ask Salma.'

Salma was busy either with her phone or her fitness. She had found a gym in the monastery.

'Please, Iman.'

'No. Do it yourself.'

Moni was irked by Iman's response. She lifted the bowl she was just about to wash and slammed it on the kitchen table under Iman's nose. 'Wash your own dishes!'

Iman, taken aback, rose from the table. 'Don't get upset. It's not a big deal. It's nothing. I can ask him for you.'

Moni picked up the bowl and put it back in the sink. She wiped the spot of soapy water that was on the kitchen table because of her outburst and, without saying another word to Iman, finished doing the washing-up.

For this mission, Iman decided to wear something practical. There were even more outfits in the cupboard now than when she had arrived. Or at least there were ones that she had

not seen before. Whereas on her arrival, there was an abun-
dance of princess dresses, flouncy skirts and beautiful colours,
a more pragmatic mood was now on offer. There was a sailor
outfit, a nurse, even an astronaut! Now she chose to wear the
trousers and top that Jessie the Yodelling Cowgirl wore in
Toy Story. Iman hid her hair under the big hat and allowed
the belt to show off her waist. After leaving the cottage, she
took her time, not on purpose but because she was distracted
by one thing after the other. There was a squirrel, which
took up a good ten minutes, a rabbit she knelt to stroke and
flowers to sniff. The sounds that the frogs made held her
attention. She listened as if she could understand what they
were saying. Most of what they said were prayers. Prayers
for food and mates. At the edge of the loch, she found a tree
trunk that had been shaped into a seat. She must try it out.
Beneath her, the water was shallow and still. Further on, it
spread deeper, with the mountains on either side. This was
the southern end of the loch where it flowed into the river
or the river flowed into it – Iman wasn't sure. She noticed
the sound of the wind in the trees and how it ruffled the
water. A duck with a green head was swimming quickly to
the shore. Near Iman it waddled out of the water and she
could see under the simple white chain around its neck and
its smooth brown breasts, the pink webbed feet navigating
the pebbles on the ground. She could lose herself in all these
details, colours of placenta and milk. She could become of
these things and need nothing else.

Eventually she found herself at the monastery. It was too
imposing for her, too masculine. The gargoyles were the
colour of guns. The tall slim windows like ghostly sentinels

hovering above the ground. She stepped into the cloister. An atmosphere hung all over the building, she felt it on her skin. Salma had raved about the architecture of the monastery, but Iman felt a kind of heaviness. Like a responsibility. Knowledge is heavy. One can gain hold of the treasure and then lose it, or memorise sacred words and forget them.

She was about to turn away when she saw something through the window. A figure in costume. It must be a costume, a brown medieval cloak, warm woollen layers with a rope for a belt. The figure evoked a memory, not of an experience, but of something she had seen on television, an image in a painting or in a book. She pushed open the door of the refectory and when she entered, her knees felt weak. She leant against the door and looked up to see the figure climb up the steps to the pulpit. Before he reached the top, he turned and looked at her. Fierce eyes, dishevelled hair, body tilted forward. She was reminded of the Hoopoe's story about Nathan. That was how she had imagined him to be, intense and focused, someone who would be too busy for the likes of her. But here he was, stopping to give her a second glance; she had distracted him, delayed him from his prayers. She wished she was not wearing this ridiculous cowboy hat. In her own clothes, with her ordinary hijab, she would have better matched his medieval outfit. They would have understood each other, asked forgiveness from the same God, followed the Ten Commandments, experienced the trajectory of weakness, sin, regret, then redemption. But Nathan and his times were over, the monastery knew it, and the grounds; the silence because there were no more prayers, the blankness because no one knelt. The Nathan she was seeing now was a memory, his prayers did not count. Back out, she told herself. Already the air was thick with misplaced energy, the room closing in. This was a dead end.

Out in the fresh air, she caught her breath and walked towards the boathouse. A boat was moored on the lake. There she found Mullin.

'Hi lassie,' he said. He was crouching down in the boat, folding the canopy. 'How're ye getting on?'

It was clear that he liked her more than he did either Moni or Salma. Both had come across him in the past few days and complained afterwards that he was rude and gruff.

'Everything's fine,' she said. 'I'm looking for a little boy. He doesn't talk. We see him on his own, never with his family. Do you know where they're staying?'

'There's a fair number of young lads here. I don't mind which one you're talking about.' He stood up and walked towards her. 'Has he caused ye any trouble?'

'No, not at all.'

'There are families in the cottages at the other side of the monastery, near the start of the walking trails.'

She turned to go, following the direction he pointed to. Salma had mentioned the walking trails. They were graded in difficulty. Some more challenging and longer than others. They took you up through the woodlands and the scenery was meant to be breathtaking. Hiking was an activity Salma was determined the three of them would do before they left.

Iman walked slowly. This was partly from reluctance and partly a response to Mullin. At school they had studied an ancient poem in which the beloved was praised for, among other assets, swaying like a cow making its way through a muddy pasture. Iman must have imbibed these attributes, wore them like she now wore these costumes. Every man was to be won over for favours or expedience. A few must be snared and conquered. Not in sin but in lawful marriage. A rich husband was the easiest way to make a living. But this hadn't worked out, had it? And the failure bewildered her. Whenever she remembered Ibrahim, she felt stunned by loss. Her life was on hold, in shambles. What am I going to do with myself?

She should ask the Hoopoe for advice. But he just kept telling stories. One after the other, as if all the answers were inside the narrative, all the guidance embedded in the logic. Besides, she was fairly occupied here, engaged in her sur-roundings. She did not want to tackle the future. The loch staved off the problem of her homelessness and she was young enough to inhabit the present. The attic room was the best of homes; Salma and Moni her family.

It was a long walk to the other side of the monastery. Surely the boy didn't live that far, otherwise Moni wouldn't have found him playing near their cottage. It didn't make sense. But Iman did not abort her mission. She would look for the boy and his family today, as best as she could. She heard scratching and panting behind her, but before she could turn to look, a force pushed her to the ground. She started to yell and kicked at the large dog. This made it more aggressive and she gasped as the gravel cut into her palms, the weight of the dog crushing her chest and thighs. The grass rose up to claim her and, for the smallest increment in time, it felt as if she was being sucked into a warm smoky place. The ground, hard as ever but still capable of becoming concave, hollowed, as if it were a belly sucked in. She started to hyperventilate and, lifting her head, saw a bright red spot of blood on her palm. Even here. Even here, there could be fighters, snipers, violence. They surrounded her now, slipping the leash over the dog's head and pulling it back. The concerned owners talking and talking, to the barking, leaping dog and to her all at once. They apologised, was she seriously hurt? Their dog was new and friendly, his energy still unbalanced, and she was small. 'You shouldn't have fought him off,' the woman chided. 'You made him more excited.'

Iman pushed herself up and dusted her clothes. The Alsatian frisked around her. The sounds it made, its saliva, fur and smell – all were incomprehensible. Iman wanted to get away from these people who were too watchful, too talkative, too close. Her tongue betrayed her. She answered them in a language they didn't understand. She couldn't help it. The English words were out of reach, she knew them but could not retrieve them. They had slipped away, unreliable.

Her heart beat, ya Allah, ya Allah – forming proper words, while her tongue could only mumble.

'Let me see your hands,' the man said. Iman hid her hands behind her back. She did not want them to nurse her, to flutter over her.

'Go away, leave me alone,' she said, and it was a good thing that she could not be rude in English.

She hobbled back to the cottage, where Moni and Salma fussed over her. She lay on the sofa and cried out that her body hurt, all her bones were broken and, for sure, she must be dying. Alarmed, the other two surrounded her, examining and questioning. She had bruised her knees and cut her palms, but it was her mind that was more troubled. All the bad dreams that had belonged to dark nights flared up, brought to life by the sudden fright and physical pain. She saw, again, fresh blood spilt, whiteness that wasn't porridge but brain; she smelt charred flesh and heard children screaming. She hadn't escaped. In this idyllic location the war could come and not from the internet or the television screen. It could rise from inside her because she had not left it behind. She had brought it with her on the airplane.

And the earth had wanted her, had tried to hug her in, to cradle her. 'I was going to be buried alive!'

'You must have imagined it,' said Salma. She noticed that Iman was dressed as Jessie and, for all her bravery, she was terrified of dark enclosed places. 'We will go back to the very same spot where you fell, and you will see that the ground is flat and normal.'

Of course, it did not make sense. The earth was not like the wall of a stomach, capable of clenching. But the earth could contract, could it not? If Iman had been better educated she would have known. Or at least known how to find the information. Fear and muddled thoughts. 'Mummy, mummy,' she wailed. 'I want my mummy.'

Moni could no longer help it. She turned away from the scene on the sofa, struggling to hide her amusement. Salma, though, was visibly moved. 'My darling, you are fine, you are fine.' She fetched a pocket mirror and Iman examined her face with care. No scratch or blemish on the beautiful cheeks, that bluish black smudge on the chin certainly dirt and not a bruise.

Iman eventually settled down, her moans subsiding, her anguish blending into peevish requests. She became a queen reclining, with two ladies-in-waiting fetching and carrying for her. Moni was dispatched to the kitchen to make soup. Salma bustled with ice pack, hot-water bottle and paracetamol. Cups of tea. Iman sighed, and tears rolled down her cheeks. For a couple of hours, Salma and Moni sat on the floor next to her couch.

'No one is prettier than Iman,' said Salma. 'Even if she has bruised herself. Even if she is crying like a baby.'

'I don't like dogs,' said Moni. 'Even puppies. They are smelly and nasty. Why would anyone want them in their home, on their sofa, shedding hair everywhere? Then they take them out and let them run amok, leaping on people and frightening them.'

'It wasn't the dog that frightened her,' said Salma. She was speaking for Iman so that her friend could feel babied and cosseted, looked after and safe. 'Iman loves animals, don't you, sweetie?'

Iman didn't reply. But she looked straight at Salma as if she were hanging on every word.

Salma went on, 'My children have been nagging they want a dog.'

'Don't give in,' said Moni.

'They promise they would look after it. Take it for walks, give it baths, take it to the vet, but I don't believe them.'

'You'll be doing all that,' said Moni.

'That's what I thought. Why add to my chores?'

'And don't forget having to renew your wudu every time the dog touches you.'

'No, licks you. It's a misunderstanding. Its saliva is what is impure, not its fur.'

'I had no idea. Iman, did you know this?'

Iman turned to look at Moni. 'What?'

Moni repeated her question.

'Yes,' said Iman.

Moni and Salma exchanged looks. Salma said, 'You had a cat, didn't you, Iman?'

'Did you?' Moni smiled. 'Nothing wrong with cats. They're clean. What happened to it?'

'Got lost,' said Iman. 'Maybe stolen.'

'You think someone stole it?' Salma leant her back against the sofa. 'You didn't tell me at the time.'

'There was a group of teenagers in the building. Hanging around smoking joints in the backyard. I caught them frightening her once. Being mean. Maybe they stole her.'

'Whatever for?' said Moni, and the other two didn't reply. She shifted gear. 'I know a job Iman would be good at.'

'What job?' Salma sounded possessive.

'A receptionist.'

'A receptionist? Where?'

'At our clinic.'

'What clinic?'

'I'm thinking of this idea,' said Moni. 'The three of us could start a business together. A massage clinic for women. I have some savings that I can invest, and I can manage the business side. Iman would be the receptionist and you, Salma, could do exactly what you're doing now, but then you'd be working for yourself. What do you think?'

Every massage therapist contemplated becoming self-employed. Choosing her own clients and her own hours. But Salma was surprised by Moni's idea. The three of them working together, Iman as the receptionist. 'I'll think about it.' Her voice sounded a little stiff, her smile not genuine.

'I can be a receptionist,' said Iman. It would be a role, a costume she could put on.

'There you go!' Moni said to Salma. It was as if she had scored a massive point or won another board game.

Salma looked at Iman. 'You would be the best receptionist ever.' She sounded more patronising than sincere.

'But seriously, Salma,' said Moni. 'Aren't you uncomfortable massaging men? Are you even sure it's allowed, did you ask?'

'I asked two scholars,' said Salma. 'And they gave me different answers. One said yes, it's an extension of nursing, with the intention to heal, and one said no – only massage women and children.'

'You got the no answer first, I'll bet. Otherwise you wouldn't have tried again.'

Salma smiled. 'That's what happened. But I work in a hospital, so I rarely had the bad experiences other therapists had. There are weirdos and perverts out there.' She sometimes felt that her hijab protected her, made her hazy and distant, further out of reach. The signals she sent out were muffled by clothes, obscured by layers, buried out of the way. But Moni was right: to choose her clients would be a step in the right direction, to focus on women and children would make her life easier.

'You told me once,' said Iman, joining in the conversation, 'that most massage therapists are self-employed.'

'Yes,' said Salma. 'The pay is better if you're self-employed. But you end up working plenty of weekends and evenings. Then again, with better pay, you can train in other methods. I've always wanted to learn reiki.'

'What's that?'

They spoke about it for some time, how the word sounded like the Arabic ruqyah, the healing prayers accompanied by touching or blowing. Iman told them about a woman in her village who was believed to have been possessed by a djinn. Ruqyah was used to cure her.

With Iman now feeling better, the other two started to drift and to contemplate their exits. Moni longing to search for the boy, Salma to text again – *I'm not telling you where I am, stop asking.* Finally, when they left, and she found herself alone, Iman picked up Lady Evelyn's book, which Moni had abandoned on the coffee table. She looked at the pictures – the clothes and hairstyles. In 1895, the demure floor-length skirt and long jacket with puffed sleeves, hair held back and covered by a hat. In the mid-twenties, the soft bobbed hair and long pearl necklace. A pleated skirt, ankle length; a cloche hat, probably wool.

In a photograph taken at Glencarron, Lady Evelyn was aiming a gun, wearing jodhpurs that reached just over her knees, with long stockings underneath. Iman made the effort to read one of the captions. Her progress was slow, but she persevered. 'Evelyn in one of her famous tweed skirts.' Molyneux, the French fashion designer from whom she ordered her clothes, had his studio in the garden of her house in

Mayfair. If only the photographs had colour! 'Which outfit is my favourite?' Iman asked herself. She wasn't sure. In a photograph taken in Kenya, right outside a hut, Lady Evelyn was in a pair of high-waist, wide-leg trousers. This would definitely be Salma's favourite because she had a maroon pair that looked exactly the same.

Chapter Eight

Moni walked around looking for the boy. She scrutinised every child she came across. It occurred to her that perhaps his holiday had come to an end and he had left the loch. This dismayed her. Not only because she would miss him but because they had parted on unfriendly terms. She chided herself for not handling the situation better. Why had she over-reacted to him saying that his name was Adam? Why hadn't she, from the beginning, made attempts to contact his family? These thoughts beat her up as she walked around searching the playgrounds, the tennis courts, the public rooms inside the monastery. She even found herself at the indoor swimming pool, a congested, damp place where people looked indistinguishable in their swimming clothes and she looked odd, fully dressed.

She wandered into the refectory and recognised it as the room Salma had spoken about. It had been empty when Salma first saw it but now there were several people. Three teenagers were playing billiards. A mother sat on a tartan up-holstered armchair while her children played with a puzzle on the floor. The room had the effect of stillness on Moni, of arrival. She suddenly did not want to leave or keep searching for the boy. Here was peace and plenty, a connection to all that was good and right. Here was something of a replacement. She chose a high armchair in the furthest corner of the room, near the window. She sat and suddenly felt exhausted, her throat sore as if she had been frantically running around the whole of the estate, shouting out his name. But she hadn't done that. She had simply walked around without saying a word. Her calves felt heavy as if they were swollen. According to Salma, she ate too much salt and needed more exercise. What would it be like to care again about her body? To find the time and the willpower. Pull her stomach in as she pushed Adam's wheelchair, eat more fruit and vegetables. It sounded simple enough. Sometimes, she received emails about courses especially for carers, yoga or art classes, coffee mornings or even first-aid workshops.

Her phone, dormant in the cottage because of the poor signal, suddenly came to life. Every day, from the grounds, she phoned Adam's care home to check up on him, but she had not switched on her data. Now the wireless signal picked up messages from her mother and from Murtada. Missed calls too. The same reproach, the same disregard for her here and now. A new angle of attack from Murtada. *You are oblivious to my own needs and deprivations. If you're able to leave your son with strangers, then why didn't you come to me instead of going off on holiday with your friends? I've been patient but you have no compassion.* A direct command from her father demanding an immediate and urgent call. She called home without hesitation, alarmed because the message had been sent a day ago. Her parents' faces glowed from the screen.

Her mother in national dress, her father with a grizzly chin as if he had skipped shaving. The ceiling fan swirled above them and here she was, sitting in her coat. Murtada had reported her intransigence. She would not forgive him for this. Her mother led the recriminations – a wife's duty is to be with her husband. You cannot continue to live in Britain on your own. It's high time you gave him another child. They did not add that the next child must be free of fault, but it was implied. How odd that although her family and Murtada's all said that Adam's disability was Allah's will which must be accepted graciously, they all tended to imply that it was somehow her fault. She had fallen short. She needed to step up and make amends. She argued, as she had argued with Murtada. Adam, Adam, Adam, she kept saying because it was as if the whole world wished him out of the way, out of sight and out of hearing, a minor factor to be taken, only reluctantly, into the equation. Why couldn't they understand how fulfilled she was when the doctor examined Adam and said to her, 'Well done'? When the nurses treated her with tender respect. She would not find this care in any other country. Her father closed his eyes. He had heard all this before. Her mother cut her off. 'Listen here, you've been indulged enough,' she said. 'Murtada is not going to wait for you for ever. A man has his limits and he's been patient enough. How would you feel if he now goes ahead and takes another wife?'

This was meant to be the ultimate threat, the winning card. If you don't carry the bundle of your crippled son, drape yourself in a black abaya and hop on a plane to Saudi, your husband will take another wife. You will be replaced; your spot will be taken. Easily, because from the vantage point of his expat status, he would not struggle to find a successor to Moni. They are aplenty, and he could pick and choose from virgins to university professors, from those with salaries to those with influential brothers. How would you feel, Moni?

She was too stunned to reply. Where was this heading, divorce? She could almost hear the collective condemnation from parents and friends. They would almost certainly take Murtada's side. They would say that she had failed in her duty as a wife, she had put her child first and that was not proper, not natural. Will Adam ever thank you for this sacrifice? Will he ever give you anything in return? But instead of pondering these questions, reasonable in their own way, worthy of consideration, she revolted against the sarcasm between the words, the insinuation that Adam was incapable of gratitude, unable to give, not worthy of her sacrifice.

It is not sacrifice, it is me. Me and him belonging together. His discomfort mine, his inability my duty. She should find Salma and tell her that her marriage to Murtada was coming to an end. She would tell her that in her search for the boy she found the refectory and it was true, there was a quality in the room, something that lingered from long ago, magnetic and lulling; something that understood and welcomed. But before she could name this quality, the door opened, and he came in. She stood up, went forward and gave him a hug. 'I am sorry, Adam, I am sorry,' she repeated. He seemed more substantial than she remembered, taller. Perhaps because she was hugging him. She drew back. Adam.

He smiled and pushed past her. Not unkindly, but still

she felt chastened. She watched him climb up the stairs to the pulpit. When he reached the top, he stood and surveyed the room, his eyes scanning the whole area but dispassionately, as if he couldn't see her. She remembered what Salma had told her about the monks having their meals in this room while one of them would stand on the pulpit and recite the prayers. But he would not have been as young as that boy. Adam. She must think of him that way. That was his name.

She tried it out now. 'Adam,' she said out loud. 'Come down.' The mother who had been leaning forward over her children's puzzle sat back in her chair and gave Moni a quick look. The teenagers around the pool table, who had found the heated conversation in Arabic a curiosity, did not take any notice.

Because he ignored her, she raised her voice. 'Adam.' He smiled down at her and started to walk down the stairs. When he got to the bottom, he reached out for her hand. This was happiness. They were friends again. 'Do you want to play with a puzzle?' She would sit with him like that other mother. Moni was good at puzzles too, not just board games. She would teach Adam all the tricks and shortcuts, what to watch out for. He shook his head.

'You're still not talking?' She had almost forgotten that he didn't speak. It didn't matter. All that mattered was that she had found him and that he was not cross with her. It was true that his name was Adam. He had answered when she called him. So, she had been the one at fault, not believing him that other time. She must make amends. 'Are you thirsty? Would you like a drink of juice?' He nodded, and smiled when she swung his hand and said, 'Let's go.' It was a joy to treat him, to see him enjoying himself. Together they walked out of the refectory and headed towards the snack machine.

I am not a physiotherapist. Even that turned out to be unattainable. I'm a massage therapist. Anyone can become that. You just need O levels (the equivalent of the Thanawiya Aama) or a certificate in Anatomy, which all these university years amounted to. I do work in a hospital. That was not a lie. The pay is less than working in a private clinic – those alternative health ones that offer aromatherapy and reiki. And I would even do better if I was self-employed, but I've needed to say 'today at the hospital' or 'they need me at the hospital'. Over the years, my parents forgot that I wasn't a doctor.

'You *are* a doctor,' he said. 'To me you always will be. Here your degree is just as valid as mine. You're in the wrong country, that's all.'

'That's all?'

'Yes.'

'You make it sound as if I just stepped out of the picture for a few moments. As if I popped out for a break.' Twenty years of marriage, four children, a job, a house, the Arabic Speaking Muslim Women's Group . . .

'If we were together now, I would convince you. I would, which is why these calls aren't enough,' he said. 'We need to see each other, we need to be in the same place. Where are you?'

'I won't tell.' She felt powerful. Distance gave her power. A sense of invincibility. 'Besides, you don't have a visa.'

'Who says I don't have a visa! I have a five-year visa that I can use multiple times.'

'Bluffing.' She was safe. What was he going to do? Drop everything and hop on a plane. No one in their right mind would do that. She could relax.

'I remember your clothes.'

'Oh yes, I remember your clothes too.'

They list:

A red T-shirt, the sleeves just a little too short. They showed off his biceps. On purpose? Not on purpose?

The denim jacket she wore almost continuously in second year.

The headscarf with silver threads that shed all over the place. Cheap.

The sunglasses he forgot at the café and when they went back to get them, they were not on the table and the waiter who had served them denied that they had left anything behind. Do sunglasses count as clothes?

The striped top that hung well below her lab coat and looked dowdy.

His lab coat – the one that was incredibly white, so bluish white that it made her sing the lyrics of the Ariel ad.

His tennis top with the lopsided collar. It always curled, it could never fall flat.

Her green dress, the one she wore when he was ill and she came to his house to give him the notes he'd missed. Because she sat in the kitchen watching his mother cook, the dress afterwards smelt of garlic and coriander.

The jumper that ended up smudged with tears, mascara and snot.

He insisted that it was always harder for those who stayed behind. He was the one forced to move in the same physical space, circling the spot newly vacant, now abandoned, gnawing on the absence. While she had forged ahead into a better world, out of reach, learning, adjusting, improving – she had no time to think of him and he could think of nothing else but her.

She accused him of exaggerating. She only half believed these professions of misery. They had been young, after all, resilient and immature. Instead she took his reproach as an attempt to draw her close, perhaps even win her back. Or else it was part of the flirting game; it certainly was pleasurable.

I'm waiting for you, she texted. *It would be like you to surprise me by just appearing. No warnings given. No, Salma, I am arriving on such-and-such a flight. Or, Salma, pick me up from the airport.* She laughed at the thought of seeing him again. The comedy of it. Perhaps she would not fancy him at all and instead see him as another client. Someone she would caution not to sit too much, not to lift things too heavy. Why shatter the illusion and spoil the gentle flow of nostalgia?

On and on, the back and forth of it. Every time, it became less guarded; every time, she took more risks. A selfie. A photo of her new running shoes. He sent photos of his clinic – he was showing off. He sent a voice message she could listen to time and again. Speaking to him as she was lying down was different than sitting or standing up. When they were both lying down, when they knew they were both lying down . . . Now that it started, it went on, even when Moni noticed that she was sneaking off to send voice messages, even when Iman noticed her excitement every time her phone flashed with the arrival of a new text. The guilt, if there had been any at the beginning, was trampled by repetition. Any awkwardness was ironed out. She became bolder in what she said. What she said she wanted. In theory of course, always in theory.

They exchanged secrets. He could trust her because she was far removed from his social circle. She did not know the people he rubbed against each day, the movers and shakers in his life. He told her of an incident he was ashamed of, an incident in which he had broken the law. He had not spoken to anyone about this. A week after he first opened his clinic, late one night after all the patients and receptionist had gone, two men came in. You will accompany us, they said. We are state security, they said. He went with them in their car. They blindfolded and handcuffed him but were extremely polite. The drive went on for miles. When the car stopped, and they uncovered his eyes, he saw with the first light of dawn that they had arrived at a villa in the middle of the desert. It had a wide garden and a spacious drive. There was a sprinkler in the garden. Inside, the furniture was new and expensive. He was led up the stairs to a bedroom with the television on at full blast, a singing competition. A woman in a nightdress was on the bed, tied up, obviously bruised, obviously pregnant. But he had not been brought here to tend to her wounds. You will bring the contents of her womb down, the men said.

When he said no, they held a gun to his head. They said, a shame you would die in such squalid conditions, in a bedroom in the arms of a whore. That's the image your father and mother would carry for the rest of their lives.

He had trained as a surgeon, not a gynaecologist, he had never performed an abortion before. Not even on a willing mother. This one fought him with all her strength. And the baby, a girl, was big enough to breathe, at least for a few minutes.

He said that, for months and years, he lived in fear. In fear that the woman would surface and report him, in fear that the men would show up, in the fear that such a dirty secret would pop up out of nowhere and ruin his life. Even now, he said, after all this time passed, I still walk against the wall, with my head down. 'You're fortunate, Salma,' he said. 'You are more fortunate than you think.'

The confession drew her closer to him. The catch in his voice, the fear he invoked. She understood what he had gone through, at least understood the compulsion and the shame. He would never be the same again and no one would guess why. Later, when the men drove him back to his clinic, still polite as ever, he could not believe what had happened. A slice out of his life. A bad dream. Count yourself lucky. Among the disappeared and the imprisoned for years, his tragedy wasn't such a tragedy, his loss minute.

'They put a gun to your head,' Salma said. 'There was nothing you could do. You were forced into it.'

'I know,' he said. 'That's what I tell myself.'

'Were they really state security?'

'I don't know. How can I ever be sure? Gangsters, mafia. I don't want anything to do with them.'

'Why didn't they just get a corrupt doctor and pay him?'

'I thought of that too. I can't figure it out.'

The suppositions and making sense were part of the pleasure of their phone calls. She had not spoken like that in years. Every culture has its own way of reasoning. With him, she was untangling things the way she had done long ago. The same probes, the same logic. This is a function of that, this is correlated to this, correlation is not causation and, of course, there is the law of diminishing returns.

When it became her turn to confess, the mood lightened between them. She said that she had already told him about not being a physiotherapist. 'That can't be everything,' he said, which made her laugh. He was right, but it was Iman who was her confidante, Iman was the one with whom she shared her secrets. She could not bring herself to tell him about the shop assistant who sold her the gloves. He was handsome and young, most likely a student, and she had felt an attraction to him that was so strong that it was almost tangible; every second in his company loaded, the whole interaction heaving. It was all over the top and in telling the story to Iman, she had embellished the details, added more spice, to the extent that Iman insisted that she must see him for herself. The next day they went together to the department store and while Salma stayed away, Iman went over to the counter and pretended to be interested in gloves. Salma should have seen it coming. The attendant was warmer towards Iman than he had been to her yesterday. Even though Iman did not buy a pair of gloves, he gave her more attention and showed her more patience. Afterwards, Salma and Iman had coffee and cake and laughed about him. Iman said that he was too rough-looking for her taste. She said that the ladies' accessories section of this reputable department store could not camouflage the essential manual labourer in him. And they laughed even more.

The second crush/attraction/disloyalty to her husband – she could not decide on how to name it except that it was a secret – involved a client and was less light-hearted than the shop assistant. The dull, small, grey cubicle in which she worked lit up in crimson, warming her until she was flushing, the partitions narrowing until she felt the need to escape. It was a struggle not to drop the bottle of oil, an effort to keep her voice from rising a pitch. The second time he scheduled a session, he spoke to her in a way that made her realise that her hijab, which she had always depended on for protection, had become useless. It was flimsy and hypocritical. The fire was closer than ever. One word, one step, one stumble. The third time he scheduled an appointment, she called in sick. The fourth time he scheduled an appointment, she made sure she had the day off. The fifth time he scheduled an appointment, she assigned him instead to one of her colleagues who owed her a favour. He asked after you, he asked after you, she would hear and enjoy hearing. But she was sensible enough to keep away from the temptation. To save her soul, to save her marriage, to save her sanity. Keeping away was the right thing to do.

'Where are you, Salma?' Amir asked.

'Far away.'

'Tell me.'

'No.'

'Tell me.'

'No.'

He threatened he would find her, one way or the other.

This week or the next. After the holiday, she would return to find him in her city. He knew the name of the city where she lived.

'A big city,' she laughed. 'And you don't know my exact address.'

'There are two ways to get information,' he said. A bribe or a threat. He elaborated on how he would bribe her. She laughed and laughed. And the threats?

It was Moni who noticed the smell. Fastidious, squeaky-clean Moni having to share a room with Salma's running gear, the sweat-stained tops and soaking sports bra; the training trousers streaked with grass and whatever else. She wrinkled her nose and walked around the room, sniffing. 'Can you smell that, Salma? What is it?'

Salma was fiddling with her hair in front of the mirror. She reckoned it had grown thicker since they'd arrived. 'What kind of smell?'

'A nasty smell. Foul.'

'I can't smell anything.' Under a harsh light, the top front of her hair exposed glimpses of her scalp, but not as much. She had stopped parting it in the middle, an unflattering look. The past was where her luxuriant hair grew, in another country. 'Why do you care about your hair, when it's always covered?' one of her colleagues had asked when Salma moaned about the price of hair-thickening products. Moni or Iman would never ask such a question. They knew that their headscarves were as important and unimportant as a bra or a pair of sandals. Salma cared about her thinning hair. She just did. What she didn't care about was the smell in the room, if there was really a smell. It must be Moni's imagination.

Moni stalked the room, sniffing. She picked up objects and held them up for inspection. In the mirror, Salma watched her with amusement.

'It's your phone!' Moni pointed at it, lying on the side table near Salma's bed. 'The smell is coming from your phone,' she said with triumph.

Salma turned around in disbelief. Suddenly possessive, she sprang across the room and picked up her maligned phone. Now in her hand, it felt valuable and irreplaceable, barely a few days old. 'Phones don't smell,' she murmured, bringing it up to her nose. She barely sniffed it before wiping it on her sleeves.

Moni shrieked. 'Don't do that! Disinfect it or at least find out what's on it.'

'There is nothing on it,' said Salma. 'I had it on the grass earlier on. I remember chucking it in my shoes at some point.'

'I see. So, you then hold it up to your cheek and your ear.' Moni was astounded. 'I would be careful if I were you. All the germs you might pick up.'

Iman was lying on the floor of the forest. When she closed her eyes, she heard what she didn't want to hear – the distant sound of shelling. The sounds of nature should be louder than those of humans and their weapons. Early in the morning, she had sneaked off and gone on an adventure. She had taken the ferry and then the bus to the nearest town, walked into a hair salon and demanded a bob like that of Lady Evelyn. So much of her black hair had fallen on the ground. And how had she afforded all this? By stretching her hand into Moni's purse. Given Moni's carelessness with cash, she would never notice.

The crescendo of the forest suddenly in her ears. She turned and saw the trees blocking out the sun. A chill seized her body. She sat up and gathered her cape closer, over her hair and shoulders. Today's costume was that of Padmé Amidala. Iman had ached and almost begged the cupboard for a tweed skirt or jodhpurs, for a hunting suit fit for the Highlands, but that was not what she got. She stood up and dusted off the leaves that clung to her tunic. She shook the cape out.

A movement caught her eyes. A sniper in a tree. She leapt and struck him down with her lightsabre. It was imperative that she protected the forest and everyone in it. They needed her. And this sniper had been a scout. There would be others following him, the bulk of the enemy force. She must be alert. She was strong now and moving. She could jump up and leap forward, swing the heavy lightsabre this way and that. It thrilled her, this strength. Knowing too that it was temporary, that it went as easily as it came, and she had little control of it. Ever since the dog had knocked her down and the earth had hugged her, she had experienced this duality. It was almost as if she had to be weakened to gain strength, she had to simulate dying to throb full of life. The dark energy was there in the middle of the earth, under the surface, coming from molten rocks, carried in smoke. She who had always been helpless knew it was invaluable. Her life would never be the same again. Today she was Padmé, queen warrior, mother of twins. With the cape around her head and shoulders, the weapon in her hand, she was able to fight.

The forest witnessed a lightsabre dance. Here were her attendants, a female force, the fiercest in the galaxy. Together they practised their moves and she was the leader. They matched her steps and copied her manoeuvres. There was no need for words, her costume spoke for her. The Hoopoe watched and hovered as if he was the director of this scene. Enemies too were part of the drill. They loomed through the trees, monstrous shapes with grunts and clubs, with brutish strength but limited intelligence, masterminded by a force of supreme evil. Iman and her soldiers could defeat them all, one by one. She was not even frightened. In no time at all, she was done, alert and breathing heavily in case there were other challenges yet to come. When she was sure of her victory, she put her lightsabre away.

It was getting late. The sky was pretending to go dark. It would never completely darken, but still, a sunset was a sunset and it was time for Iman to head back to the cottage. Salma and Moni would wonder where she'd been. Ever since the episode with the dog, they had been extra solicitous, or at least Salma had been. All Moni did was stop asking favours or chores from Iman.

She heard them arguing as soon as she walked into the cottage. As soon as Salma saw Iman, she shouted, 'What happened to your hair?' As soon as Moni saw Iman she said, 'Doesn't Salma's phone stink?'

Coming in from the fresh air, Iman caught the sour, uric smell. 'That can't be coming from her phone!'

'There,' said Salma to Moni. 'This has nothing to do with my phone.' She turned away, 'Iman, who cut your hair for you? Is that why you've been gone so long?'

Moni did not allow herself to get distracted. 'If it's not your phone, then what is it?'

'I don't know,' said Salma. 'I can't smell anything. If you two can smell something, then look for it yourselves. Don't accuse my phone. Phones are phones. They don't stink. Besides, it's practically brand new.'

'Give it to me,' said Iman.

Salma handed her the phone. Instead of smelling it, Iman went over to the dressing table, picked up Moni's Obsession and sprayed it all over the phone's surface. Picking up a tissue, she wiped away the excess liquid. 'There you go,' she said. 'All sorted.'

Moni winced at the use of her perfume as camouflage. Now the bad smell was a mix. Whatever it was, urine or worse, drenched in an overdose of Obsession. From now on Moni would never feel the same again about her favourite scent. She would not be able to smell Obsession without smelling what it had tried valiantly to obscure. The audacity of Iman! She could have at least asked her permission.

Iman was pleased with herself. She had resolved the issue and stopped the other two from arguing. She congratulated herself on not being passive, on doing something for a change. There will be a new Iman when we leave the loch, she mused as she walked upstairs to her room. Someone who is stronger, who knows what she wants. She still had to attain that last bit. To know what she wanted. It used to be a baby, that was all she ever wanted, but she could want other things, even though she was not yet sure what exactly. Choosing had never been easy for her. A skill she had not practised because, in a world of little or no choices, it had not been necessary. No more. She was in Britain now and there were choices. More choices than watching daytime TV or children's movies. She could do this or that, be this or that. To know, to set herself on the right track, to strive, to achieve. One step at a time.

Salma grabbed her phone and stormed out of the cottage. She almost collided with Mullin who was riding a bicycle. He lost his balance and had to stop. 'Whore,' he muttered under his breath. Salma did not stop walking. She could not believe that he had just said that. Impossible. She must have heard wrong. He must have said, 'Whoa!' That's what he said, because she nearly knocked him off his bicycle. She wasn't looking where she was going. The next conversation with Amir would be laced with Moni's perfume and, by extension, Moni's disapproval. She did not need this reminder. She did not need pricks on her conscience. It was not that she didn't feel any guilt at all talking to him, it was that the other things she felt were far stronger.

Overlooking the loch, she took her phone out. It did smell. It did smell.

She bent down and dunked it in the water. Would it get damaged beyond repair? It was unlike her not to care. But she did not want Moni's perfume on her phone. And the other smell. It made her ashamed.

'Evil is often frozen,' the Hoopoe later said to Iman. 'Paralysed by weakness. Many a crime hasn't been committed not because of a lack of intention but because of a lack of means.' Iman thought of Salma, safe from sin because Amir was far away. That night, the Hoopoe's story was about the snake catcher who climbed the mountain. He climbed and climbed and the air around him grew colder. Near the summit, he found more than he had aspired to – a huge serpent frozen in the snow. It was a magnificent sight. The ice had trapped the movement of the snake's tongue as it lashed out, his fangs were in full display; the lustre of his coat was dazzling. The snake catcher could not believe his luck. This would be the most spectacular public display ever; the whole town would be agog. He carried the frozen serpent back down the mountain and, before he reached the town, he hid it under woollen blankets and tied it up with a rope. On reaching the town he started to call out, 'Come and gather to see the biggest serpent on earth, the longest and most amazing.' Soon an excited crowd gathered in the town square. It was a sunny afternoon and the mood of the gathering was festive. The snake catcher stood in the middle of the crowd with a large basket in which the frozen serpent lay covered under a blanket. With a flourish, the snake catcher whisked away the blanket and the crowd drew in its breath. The serpent was certainly huge, certainly stunning. The combined effect of the sun and the blanket had made the ice around it thaw. A twitch, a shudder. Had it really moved or was that the ice cracking? A blink. The serpent was alive. It had only been dormant, kept still by the ice. Suddenly, the serpent lashed out. It broke the ropes and immediately attacked the snake catcher. Crushed by its strength, he lay dying. The last thing he saw was the serpent wreaking havoc on the crowd.

'Did you understand the story?' the Hoopoe asked.

Iman, still thinking of Salma, said, 'It was the snake catcher's fault. He should have thought maybe, just maybe, the serpent was still alive. Or it could be that moving the frozen serpent from one place to another caused the problem. Up in the cold mountains, it was harmless and would have stayed harmless. Under the blanket, under the hot sun of the town square, it became the greatest danger. The snake catcher was disillusioned. There he was, full of eagerness and anticipation, carrying the very thing that would be his doom. We are our own worst enemies.' She was now thinking of civil wars, how they went on and on until there was little to win and more to fight over.

'But what is the serpent?' asked the Hoopoe.

It was lust and greed, all that lies frozen and dormant, that remains harmless until we warm it up and activate it, until we accidently bring it back to life.

The Hoopoe told her another story. 'Three fishes were swimming in a stream. They were content with their life, eating as much as they wanted, unthreatened by bigger fishes or other predators. One day, they sensed the approach of fishermen, men whose intention was to draw their nets. The first fish said, "To save my life I will escape from here. I will make the difficult journey to the sea. And I must do it alone and in secret. My friends will surely weaken my resolve. Their love of their home waters will persuade them to stay." Without saying goodbye, the first fish set out and was saved.

'The second fish said, "I am by nature crafty. I will play a trick on the fishermen. I will float belly up in the water and they will think I am long dead and discard me." This is exactly what happened. One fisherman caught it in his net but believing it dead, tossed it back in the water. The fish swam off and was saved.

'The third fish made no preparations. When the fishermen arrived, it panicked. Darting here and there in the water, it leapt high and fell with a splash. With greater agitation, it jumped again even higher and flopped down in the fisherman's net.'

Chapter Nine

On the morning that marked a week since their arrival, the rain kept them indoors, in each other's company. From the window, the sky was a low uniform grey. To Moni it felt like being in an airplane that was passing through dense clouds. She was the one least put out. To her, the outdoor life was still not entirely comfortable. If it wasn't for the boy, Adam, she would not have gone out at all. She spoke about him now to the others, how well behaved he was, how adorable and agile. If only he would talk to her.

Iman was wearing a warrior costume that none of them could recognise. It made her look bulky. 'Aren't you too warm?' asked Salma. She was the one most restless. With weather like this, she would not be able to run. The ground would be muddy. Besides, her phone had been confiscated from her, or at least that's how it felt. Moni insisted that it still stank and was not fit to have inside the cottage. The phone was now perched on the sill outside the kitchen window. Safe from the rain, but still exposed to dampness and out of earshot. Already since dunking it in the water, the screen was becoming blurred. In messages, certain letters needed to be guessed at. Salma wished she had her old one with her, but she had left it in the car.

Iman said she was not too warm. She did not know where the costumes she had worn earlier in their visit had gone and she was not interested in finding out. Cleopatra, the princesses, Cinderella – she had passed that stage. Now it was Padmé Amidala, the White Witch and other warrior figures. The choice was either to wear these new costumes or her own clothes. It seemed a long time since she had worn her own clothes. She wondered how Ibrahim would react if he saw her dressed like Padmé with a lightsabre in hand, her hair cut short in a bob. Conjuring him up in her mind, she found her sadness turning into anger.

Salma looked out of the window and suddenly asked, 'Shall we brave the rain and go for a walk? We need to practise for when we visit Lady Evelyn's grave on Sunday.'

'Better wait a bit,' said Iman. 'It might clear up.' She turned to look at Moni.

Moni hesitated. Perhaps if they now went out for a brief walk in the rain, it would substitute for a long and potentially exhausting one in good weather. Instead she said, 'Being in the cottage is part of the holiday, we paid for it. It would be a waste not to enjoy it.'

'All right,' said Salma. 'Iman wants to stay so we'll stay.' She smiled at her younger friend.

'I can't believe you just said that.' Moni's voice rose. 'I also said we should stay. Salma, why are you acting as if I hadn't spoken?'

Salma turned towards her. 'I'm sorry. I didn't mean to. I

agree with what you said. The cottage is part of the holiday. We'll stay.'

'That's not the point,' said Moni. 'Why do you treat Iman like a child? It's not helping her. She's a grown-up, perfectly capable of fending for herself. Yet you pamper and infantilise her. Like a pet. You don't even do that with your own kids!'

'I'm here, Moni,' said Iman.

'I know you are.'

'But you're talking about me as if I'm not here. I'm perfectly capable of talking for myself.'

'That's what I mean,' said Moni. 'Why this special treatment as if you're delicate china about to break. There is nothing physically wrong with you.'

'You don't know,' said Salma. 'You don't know everything that Iman went through during the war.'

'No, I don't know,' said Moni. 'But surely her dependence on you isn't solving the issue.'

Salma spoke in a calm voice. 'I think you're jealous, Moni. Because you don't have a special friend. Or any other special relationship. You're aloof with everyone. You keep your distance. Don't want to get too close, don't want to get involved, don't want to get your hands dirty . . .'

Moni gave a small tight laugh. 'So this is about your phone, then. Because I banished it, you're now saying all these mean things to me.'

'They're not mean. You look at Iman and instead of compassion, you're all self-righteous.'

'I'm not. I'm just pointing out that you're holding her back, Salma. If you want to be a true friend, then help her stand on her own two feet. That's what you need to be doing.'

To Salma's surprise, Iman blurted out, 'Salma, I do want to tell you something. I've changed. I do want to stand on my own two feet, like Moni says. I want to know where I'm heading. And you don't guide me, Salma. You're just happy for me to stay as I am, keeping you company, listening to your problems.'

For a minute Salma was lost for words. She turned from Moni to Iman.

'She treats you like a pet,' said Moni to Iman. 'I see it every day . . .'

'Stop,' said Salma. 'What's going on? I've known Iman longer than you have. Don't come between us, Moni. Stay out of it.'

'That's the problem, isn't it? You want to move people about. Maybe you mean to be helpful and you are sometimes, I won't deny it, but you sure are bossy.'

'You're interfering too,' murmured Iman.

Salma, her body rigid with surprise, wondered where all this, this *insubordination* was coming from. 'How dare you speak to me like that! The both of you. I will leave you. I will take the ferry, get in MY car, MINE, as you seem to have forgotten, and drive back without you. Then you can be stuck here if you're so keen on independence.'

She knew she sounded ridiculous even as she spoke. Moni laughed out loud. Iman giggled. Trying to remain in control, Salma forced herself to smile as if she had been joking all along and the outburst had been in mock anger. But some of it she meant. The reminder that the car was hers, that she had driven them here and they were dependent on her to get them back. It was lame, she knew. This need to assert her authority, to remind them and put them in their place. She was squirming now and wanting the comfort of her phone, the messages from Amir. Through him, and with him, time had different proportions so that her life back home – yes, home in Egypt – became long and eventful, her life in this country short and flat. All the married years, the children growing up, condensed into a single episode, one that was busy but minor, full of details and events that all had the same colour.

She started to walk to the kitchen, to retrieve the phone from its banishment. Enough was enough.

'Don't you dare bring that stinky phone in here,' said Moni.

'You're hallucinating, my dear. I'm sorry to tell you this. The smell is all in your imagination.'

'Iman smelt it too.'

'By suggestion. From you.'

Moni turned to Iman for a defence. Iman said nothing. Emboldened, Salma said, 'I will take my phone all the way to the monastery where the signal is strongest. A bit of rain won't hurt me.'

'I know why you're so attached to your phone these days,' said Moni. 'Iman told me everything.'

Salma stopped and turned to glare at Iman. Her friend refused to meet her eye. Iman had told Moni about Amir when she had specifically told her not to. And here it was now, the predictable telling-off from Moni.

'It's wrong,' said Moni. 'You need to stop this, Salma. It's beneath your dignity. It's playing with fire. You'll ruin your life and all that you've worked hard to build.'

'Oh, the drama,' said Salma, sitting down again. 'It's only texts and a few phone calls. Hardly enough to get me stoned to death.'

Iman said, 'In your heart and thoughts you're cheating on David. That's just as bad.'

'I thought you understood me, Iman,' said Salma. She could take all this from Moni, but not Iman.

'Stop contacting him,' said Moni. 'Stop it now before it gets out of hand. Can't you see what's going to happen? You will get so caught up with him, you won't be able to be with your husband any more. Your relationship with him will become strained. He has rights on you and so do your children.'

'Ah, the expert on marital bliss is talking. What do you know about successful marriages? You've put your son's needs above your own husband's. Above your own needs. How is that fair?'

'She's right,' Iman said. 'You're not a good wife, Moni.'

Moni's face flushed. She opened her mouth to speak, but Salma interrupted her. 'Don't give me lectures on a wife's duty, Moni, when you lock your husband out of your bedroom at night.'

Iman raised her eyebrows.

Moni wished she had never told Salma that particular detail. She had been so keen to demonstrate what a devoted mother she was, sharing her bed with Adam, keeping her husband out. One night, when Murtada had come whispering her name so as not to wake his sleeping son, she had raised her head from the pillow and hissed, 'What do you want?' in a way designed to make him shrivel. The next time he travelled away and came back, he found that she had installed a lock. Moni drew in a breath. 'I might not be a good wife, but I have my virtue, thank you very much. I'm not two steps away from adultery.'

'Up to your neck in disobedience instead.'

'I neglect my prayers for the sake of Adam. You don't think I would neglect Murtada?'

'Oh, the martyr,' said Salma. 'It's all about motherhood for you.'

'I can't help it if my son is disabled.' There it was, the pride in her position. 'You're the one who should be ashamed, Salma. Not me. Is it any wonder that your phone stinks, with all that disloyalty passing through it day and night? Have some self-respect.'

Iman spoke up, 'We want what's best for you, Salma. David is such a good husband. You say that yourself. How can you do this to him? He's done you no wrong.'

'I'm not doing anything to him. This is separate from him.'

'How can it be nothing to do with him?' said Moni. 'How would you feel if he was having some virtual relationship with someone else?'

She would be hurt, of course, her self-esteem dropping to zero. It would matter who this other woman was, what kind of rival. It would make a difference if she was a younger version of herself. It would make a difference if she was white, or prettier, or with a better job. She would never forgive him.

'Think of the children,' Iman said. 'Is that how you want them to know you? You're their role model.'

'No, I'm not,' snapped Salma. 'They're ashamed of me.

Ashamed of my accent, my background, my opinions. I'm losing them. Day by day, they get older and more British and sometimes I hardly know them any more.'

'That's nonsense,' said Iman. 'They love you. I know that.'

'You're the foundation of their life,' said Moni. 'They take you for granted. They probably take their father for granted too. But both of you, and the strong relationship between you, that's what's holding the family together. Don't break that.'

Salma wished for tears of remorse, welling from a sense of shame. Instead she felt anger grow inside her. Moni couldn't understand. Iman, who had more sympathy and imagination, was being obtuse. She had told her explicitly not to tell Moni about Amir. She turned to her now.

'What happened to you, Iman? I trusted you. What got into you?'

Iman shrugged. When the other two stared at her, wanting her to explain, she started choosing each word with care. 'I've been thinking about myself and my future, wondering what I really want. For a long time, all I wanted was a baby of my own, all I could imagine for myself was to be a mother. But that didn't happen and it's not likely to happen soon. It might not happen at all. No, don't start to interrupt and insist that I must hope. It's not about optimism or despair. And it's not all about you, Salma, or how you treat me.'

She took a breath in and continued. 'Every day since we've been here I wear a different outfit and I become someone else. Every costume has a story and comes with a way of behaving attached to it. If it's pretty and feminine or if it's practical. Some of the clothes in the cupboard here are heavy and some of them restrictive. They made me think about my own clothes. Why do I dress the way I do? Because that's how my mother dressed and the women in my village. Or that's how my husband of the time wanted me to dress. Each one had an opinion. The first wanted me to wear these long, loose abayas or plain coats. The second thought I should lighten up and wear trousers and colours, not attract attention to myself. Then Ibrahim encouraged me to copy you, Salma, and we started to go shopping together. There was never time to think, what do I want to wear and why? Well, I've made a decision. I'm not clearing it with you or asking your opinion. I'm just telling you so that you know and don't act all surprised. From now on I will stop wearing hijab. That's it. I will take my headscarf off.'

The announcement stunned Moni and Salma. They had not seen it coming. It made no sense. Yet Iman continued to talk, and they followed her peculiar logic, an argument connected to uniforms and costumes, roles and camouflage.

'If I'm not dressed for a role, then who am I?' she said. 'If I don't know who I am, then how can I know what I want? The hijab wasn't forced on me against my will, but I wasn't given a choice to wear it or not, either. It was what the other older girls in my family were wearing. It felt natural that at a certain age I would wear it too. But if I were free to choose, I might not have chosen it. I might have chosen something else. Maybe I would have dressed like Mulan or like a cowgirl. We think we are the ones wearing an outfit, but it's imprinting itself on us.' Iman could not believe her own fluency, how she was talking and the other two were listening. It had never happened before. Not one stutter, not one fumble for words. She went on. 'Maybe no one in the world really has a choice. Even men. If you're born in a certain place or a certain century, you just fall in line and dress like everyone is dressing. The kind of clothes you would find in the shops. It's artificial. And I want what is natural, what is true to myself, the self I was born to be . . .'

'Go naked,' said Moni, half sarcastic, half challenging. 'Nudity is the natural state. That's how we're born. That is who we really are without the dignity of clothes.'

'I tried it.'

Moni and Salma gasped. 'No, you did not,' said Salma. 'Lunatic.'

'I did it once in the forest.'

'Do it again and if Mullin rapes you, don't come to me crying,' said Moni.

'Oh Moni,' said Iman. 'I got cold and had to crawl in the ground. I covered myself with leaves and branches. It was like being buried. And I thought to myself, like you just said, that's what I was wearing when I was born, nothing. And that's what I will be wearing when I'm buried – a shroud over nothing. I learnt from that. Clothes are about living, not hiding away. Clothes are protection from the cold and wind. I felt vulnerable without them. The pebbles on the ground cut my feet, there were thorns, dirt and insects and little animals. Let alone the cold.'

Moni rolled her eyes. Salma was aghast. She was losing Iman; little by little, her special friend, the younger sister, was slipping away. This was not the Iman she had always known. Not with this fluency, this waywardness. Salma could not reply. It was left to Moni to talk and argue. She went over the basics, tried different tactics, but Iman would not budge. She was not going to wear her hijab any more.

'Lady Evelyn didn't wear the hijab.'

'She did when she went on pilgrimage,' said Moni.

'But not here,' insisted Iman.

'We went over this,' said Salma. 'She was restricted by her social position. And the times she was living in. She couldn't go around dressing up as a foreigner!'

'She could if she wanted to,' said Iman. 'She was brave enough.'

'It's not about courage,' said Moni.

'Besides, you of all women, shouldn't do this,' said Salma. 'You're so attractive. Already men are all over you. What will it be like when there is more of you to admire, have you thought of this?'

Iman shrugged. 'I never cared for all that.'

'Liar,' said Salma.

'Look who's calling who a liar,' said Moni.

Salma turned on her, 'You think you're better than us both.'

Moni made a face. 'I'm not the one cheating on my husband or taking off my hijab.'

'You're an oppressor,' said Iman.

Moni was shocked. 'Me?'

'Yes, acting as if no one in the world has more troubles than you do. You're full of it.'

'That's completely unfair,' said Moni. 'You two are free to do what you like, but my duty as a friend is to caution you.'

'So why don't you accept caution from me?' said Iman.

'Because I'm not doing anything wrong.'

'Pushing your husband away is wrong.'

'I am fighting for my son's well-being. I should be applauded, not told off!'

'You need to do both. Care for your son as well as your husband. Teach your husband to care for his son.'

'You need to stop phoning Amir.'

'You need to dress like you've always dressed.'

Outside, the rain continued to lash down, the wind rattled the windows. It was difficult to believe that this was summer.

'Punishment,' the Hoopoe later said to Iman, 'can sneak up on you. Justice can take many forms and the one who administers it might not necessarily be aware of his role. This is the oddest story I will tell you, the one that is the most difficult to understand, its message the hardest to accept. Remember it, though, when things become too difficult and your instinct is to scream out, that's not fair, that's not fair. Because more likely it is fair, even though by all accounts and appearances, it looks like nothing of the sort.

'A travelling knight came across a waterfall. He got off his horse and decided to have a wash and a drink. He took off his clothes, bathed and refreshed himself. When he got dressed, he forgot to put on his belt and galloped off. That belt was a money belt full of gold coins. It was later found by a young boy who went to the waterfall for a swim. The young boy could not believe his luck. He grabbed the money belt and ran off. Meanwhile, the knight continued on his journey. When he eventually realised his mistake, he turned back. When he reached the waterfall, he found an elderly man making wudu in preparation to pray. "Where is my money belt?" asked the knight.

"'I haven't seen any money belt," said the elderly man.

'The knight drew out his sword and killed him.

'You would think that the elderly man was innocent and unfairly killed. You would think that the young boy stole what did not rightfully belong to him. But there is a back-story to this tale. One that even the protagonists didn't fully know and would never have been able to put together. For many years, the knight had employed the services of a loyal hard-working couple. The labourer looked after the knight's stables and his wife worked in the scullery of the castle. The couple worked faithfully for twenty years, but the knight never ever paid them their wages. They did not have the means to challenge him and get their rights. The young boy who ran off with the knight's money belt was their son.

'As for the elderly man. A long time ago, in the arrogance and strength of youth, he had cruelly killed the knight's father.'

Chapter Ten

When Iman took off her hijab, Salma took it personally, as if Iman was rejecting her, turning away towards another ideal, ditching all that they had shared. Alone, she found herself in tears, shocked and speechless as if betrayed. She did not fight back or try to argue with Iman. Instead she caved in and, quite unlike herself, experienced for the first time what she would have identified in others as low-grade depression. The reluctance to get out of bed, the disinterest in jogging and the constant dragging down of anxiety and guilt. Glimpsing Iman in the grounds of the monastery among other people caused a surge of envy. Iman's hair was shining and luxuriant; with the new haircut, the ends bounced round her ears. Instead of approaching her friend with a greeting, Salma ducked out of the way to avoid coming face-to-face with her.

Careful to avoid Iman even in the cottage, she found herself turning more towards Amir, towards their shared past, a time of certainties and hopes. The regret that she had married David and moved to Britain began to gather into an emotion, almost a fact. She had made a mistake. Amir was her ideal mate, her home city the true beloved, medicine her rightful vocation. She was forty-five and her life was a mistake. A mistake that could be rectified, or perhaps it was too late and it could not be rectified. That was what she considered as she lay down staring at the ceiling. Pull out now or go on knowing that you are living out a sentence. Which option was doable, which option was the right one? Then the sound of Iman up in the attic would bring her back to the loch and she would register how Iman now came and went without telling her, without urging her to join her, without checking up first on what she wanted to do.

Moni clashed with Iman. Right was right and wrong was wrong, and Moni was confident of her position. She lectured Iman on the need to be mindful of Salma. In this country, who else did she have to look after her, except Salma and David? Whatever she did, Iman must not jeopardise her relationship with them, and taking off her hijab wasn't helpful. Moni surprised herself by caring. It had been a long time since anything had penetrated her bond with Adam or was even able to distract her from him. Briefly, she was released and found herself sounding like her old self: the Moni who worked in the bank, who followed and gave orders, who understood the legal structures, the stock options and the fluctuations in interest rates. This was the same Moni who now faced Iman. It mattered little to her that Iman was not responding, not budging from her position; she was not even following Moni's arguments. Moni was flexing a muscle she had thought long atrophied. It made her feel better.

When she did come across Iman in public, riding Mullin's bicycle on the path leading to the forest, Moni's reaction was completely different from Salma's. She found Iman without her headscarf indistinguishable from other women, one and the same. The special aura of vulnerability and preciousness that had surrounded her was gone. She was another glossy, wind-tousled head of hair, bland and common. And because Iman was small, there was even less reason for her to stand out. When she whizzed past and waved at Moni, who was on the phone to the nursing home, it took Moni a beat to recognise her.

Iman avoided her friends. She no longer cosied up to Salma or hovered around Moni while she cooked. Instead, she stayed out most of the time or up in her attic room. The cupboard continued to yield costumes. One was a US army marine. Iman put it on and rummaged in the cupboard for a gun. It was not there. She sat on the floor of her room and waited. The idea of a loaded heavy gun excited her. She did not want to harm any person or animal but walking about with a gun would indeed grant a sense of power and protection. No one would dare hurt her. They would be afraid. No one had ever been afraid of Iman. She attracted others and did not repel. But she was tired of all that. The emphasis on her beauty. It had not given her security or allowed her to understand herself. Beauty itself was a mask, a barrier, all that other people could see of her. They did not want to listen to her, they did not want her skills or her opinions. They were content with her presence, like a flower in a vase, pleasing and uplifting, a lovely scent to refresh and intoxicate, a brilliant colour against a drab, unappealing world.

Moni cooked and ate by herself. She looked out of the window at the rain that again kept her away from the boy. It did not keep him away though and on hearing a knock at the door, she found him, to her delight, wearing a bright blue anorak with a hood and wellington boots. She fussed over him. 'Adam, are you hungry? What shall I make you?' He opened the fridge and took out the carton of eggs. She made him an omelette with feta cheese. 'You must have been hungry,' she said, as he wolfed down the food. 'You need to eat to grow. I can almost see you growing right before my eyes!' It was an expression, an exaggeration, but it did seem to her that he was bigger since the first day she had seen him. Not older, but bigger in size. It was a strange observation. As children grew older, they became leaner to some extent, losing their baby roundness. He, though, just seemed to be getting bigger, his cheeks chubbier than ever, his chin soft. She must be imagining things.

'Have you never had a feta cheese omelette before? Do you like it?' He shook his head and then nodded. She was used to the fact that he didn't talk or couldn't talk. He did make sounds, though, a high ah of surprise and pleasure, a frustrated growl when he stood on the kitchen chair and couldn't reach the top shelf of the cupboard. There was a kite stored there; it had caught his attention and he wanted it.

'Not on such a gloomy day,' she said. 'You need good weather for a kite. You also need your father to take you out. I would not be of any use to you flying a kite. I'm sorry but I know nothing about kites.'

When he climbed down from the chair, he gave her a hug. 'You are a lovely boy,' she told him. 'The cleverest, nicest boy.'

His eyes, brown and full of expression, kept her captivated. They baked together. After getting him to wash his hands, which he did while making the most comical of faces, he shaped cookies and afterwards decorated them. He was clumsy with these tasks and she enjoyed instructing him on how to keep his hands steady, how to move without spilling. When he concentrated, he opened his mouth. It made her laugh.

In Lady Evelyn's book, she showed him photos of Toby Sladen, Lady Evelyn's grandson. 'Look, here he's the same age as you are now. His shoes are funny! But that's how little boys dressed in 1922. Every school holiday he would spend with his grandmother on her estate. He must have loved it – all the fishing and exploring – he even went hunting with her too.'

She read out a letter written from Lady Evelyn to Toby. 'I was so pleased to get your letter, my first post since I left London which seems years ago . . . I have now got permission from the King to do my Pilgrimage – I will be the first European woman to enter the sacred Cities – but it means that I won't be home again till towards the end of April – so you must arrange for your holidays . . . I'll write Grant to put the two housemaids back in case you want to go there for a bit.'

For reasons she could not understand, the letter moved Moni, even though she had read it before. She felt tears welling up as she steadied her voice to explain. 'Grant was the gamekeeper at Glencarron. At the time of this letter, Toby was seventeen years old. He was still at boarding school.' She sensed a restlessness in Adam and put the book away. It was time for him to leave.

She gave him most of the baked cookies to take home

with him. She covered them in cling film and put them in a plastic bag. He would have to walk in the rain and that made her feel ever so sorry for him, grateful that he had come to see her.

After he left, she went to check up on Salma. Having given up on counselling Iman, she had turned, since yesterday, to Salma. They shared a room after all and it was natural to lie on the second bed and converse or come in and out asking after her.

'Shall I bring you something to eat? There is rice and aubergine stew.' Moni knew by now that there was no point in offering the freshly baked cookies to Salma.

Salma shook her head. She lay on her back with her arm across her face. This was a way to hide the tears.

'But you haven't eaten all day,' said Moni. She remembered the raw food diet that Salma had been following on and off. 'Shall I get you the nuts you like? Or some grapes.'

'I had some earlier.' Her voice was thicker, slow. 'Thanks for getting me the water.'

Moni felt sorry for her. 'Salma, you're not yourself. What's wrong with you?'

The tears rolled down Salma's face. She could not hide them any more. 'I know this sounds stupid. It sounds stupid to me, but when I think of all the time that's passed and how I can't get it back . . . I want to undo things and I can't. How do I pull my children back so that they're little again? It can never happen. I just have to keep on, keep on, but for how long? Everyone is thinking this, I am sure. If people spoke the truth they would admit how sad it is to get old.'

'You're not old,' said Moni. 'You are fit and healthy. And yes, you are young.'

'These are platitudes, Moni. Forty is the new thirty. Fifty is the new forty. These things that are said so that people can be cheerful. When people are cheerful they get on with their lives better. They go to work, they shop. That's what it's all about. Then, at a certain point, sooner or later, they drop dead. And it goes on and on. One generation replacing the other, making a mess of things one way or another.' She was talking about this, but she would have preferred to talk about Iman. To untangle her mixed feelings. But Moni was so sure of everything, so black and white, she would never understand.

Moni said, 'Maybe you're tired, Salma. You do too much. You're always pushing yourself. Maybe you're just exhausted and need a break. There is nothing wrong with that. A lie-in. You certainly deserve it.'

Salma nodded, 'Thank you, Moni. Maybe I could have a cup of tea.'

'Sure,' said Moni and she went to the kitchen to make it for her.

When she came back, Salma was sitting up in bed. She had smoothed down her hair and tied it up in a scrunchy. 'Have you seen her in public, Moni?' She was talking about Iman without her hijab.

Moni sighed. 'Yes, briefly. I almost didn't recognise her. I don't know why she wasn't content with our garden here which is secluded.'

'I saw her,' said Salma. 'I was walking back from the monastery and I came across her talking to Mullin. It was a shock, seeing her standing there with her hair showing. If she had the hood of her rain jacket up, it would have looked natural given the weather. But there she was, as if she was being defiant. I didn't know what to do. I dodged away from them. I just couldn't face her.'

'I wonder what Mullin said to her,' said Moni. 'Or if he even noticed.'

'Of course he noticed.'

'But people here never comment on appearance. They're very polite.'

'It doesn't mean they don't notice,' said Salma. 'My mother-in-law loves a good gossip. She doesn't interfere though. She wouldn't say why are you wearing this or that, not even to her own son, there is a distance. But she does notice things.'

Moni shrugged. 'It's pointless talking to Iman. She's made up her mind. We have to accept it.'

Salma felt, again, the wash of sadness. Iman mattered to her and she had thought, and all the evidence pointed to the fact, that Iman was dependent on her. Now this was an illusion. And if their old relationship was untenable, was there anything left that could replace it? 'She is not good at articulating her thoughts,' said Salma. 'I've learnt not only to listen to the words that she's saying. With her, actions speak louder than words.'

'She's praying again,' said Moni. Yesterday Iman had a bath and washed her hair. Her period had lasted six days.

'Yes, I noticed,' said Salma. 'And that reassured me.'

'It happens,' said Moni. 'Friends on social media. Suddenly there's an updated photo and they're not wearing it any more. The pressure, I guess, especially in the US or France.'

'Iman doesn't have that excuse.' Salma was surprised at herself. Why could she not be more forgiving? It was not as if she was blameless herself, immune to temptation. When it came to Amir, she could find a thousand excuses for herself. Another thousand for not giving him up.

'I have something to tell you,' Moni said. 'It's a deadlock now between me and Murtada. I won't go join him in Saudi and he's not accepting any other arrangement. I have to do what's best for Adam's health.'

This sudden announcement, though not surprising in itself, caused Salma to snap back to herself. 'Don't rush this, Moni. It's hard enough caring for a disabled child without being a single mother as well. Try and see things from Murtada's point of view.'

'I'm already a single mother,' she said. 'Considering his input and interest.'

'I don't think divorce is a good option for you of all people.'

'Why not?'

'Don't take this wrong, but how many men are going to marry a woman with a disabled child? If you give up Murtada, there will be no substitute for him. You'll be a divorcee for the rest of your life.'

'So what?'

'You mean this? You'll be fine with celibacy? Fine with not having any more children?'

'Isn't this exactly what my life is like now?' Moni gave a bitter laugh.

'But you can reverse it. It's in your hands. What Murtada wants from you is not unreasonable.'

Moni picked up Salma's empty teacup and took it to the kitchen. Was she rattled by what Salma had said? Maybe, maybe not.

Salma took out her phone from the sealed plastic bag. This was Moni's idea, a compromise to keep the phone in the room while at the same time hemming in its smell. The smell which Moni was imagining, as mobile phones do not smell. And yet somehow Moni had convinced her of this and she had dunked it in the water. Now, drawing the slim, smooth object out of the bag, Salma too caught a whiff of something. She pushed the phone back into the plastic bag, sealed it and lay down on the bed again.

When she closed her eyes, she saw the envelope. It was meant to be white but had gone beige with handling. There were smudges on it and it was crumpled at the edges. It was addressed to her, her full name including Miss, written in Amir's handwriting. She saw with less clarity the documents that were in the envelope. They were both official. Originals, not copies, stamped and authenticated. There was a doctor's report on Amir's mother's mastectomy. There was the registration of the court case involving the convoluted sale of the piece of land which belonged to Amir's father and his cousins. The envelope contained proof to Salma and her mother that Amir had not lied to them. Yet Salma had torn this proof up. In fact, had not even bothered to tear it up properly but scrunched it and shoved it into the kitchen bin. Pushed it among onion peel and chicken bones, the smear of tomato paste left over in a tin, the slither of courgette peel. Then she had forgotten it. How dare he intrude on the day she had just come back from the dressmaker, the day of the final fitting for her wedding dress. The gorgeous swirl of white taffeta, the silky veil, the embroidery on the bodice. How dare he grubby such a day, paw at it with his muddied circumstances, with his need to prove himself!

And after the wedding, another memory, even more pathetic. Amir had wanted the envelope back. Bureaucracy demanded the original copies. He had called and called her mobile phone – her first – until she changed her number, and then he had shown up at her parents' door. All this, and she didn't tell him that she had thrown the envelope away, that he needn't bother.

In the bin.

I'm sorry, I'm sorry. She ran out of the cottage. She held the phone in her hand and the rain did not matter. She had remembered what she had excelled at forgetting. I'm sorry.

He said, 'I was angry with you at the time to the point that I fantasised about strangling you, hurting you as much as you'd hurt me.'

She listened to the venom in his voice and did not reply.

'All those so-called friends sneering at me, saying hard luck buddy, with a twinkle in their eyes.'

'Did you just say strangling me?'

'Yes, strangling you.'

She laughed as if he had absolved her. 'But I'm not as puny as you think. I would fight you off. Did you not know that I pretended I couldn't lift things, that I let you beat me at tennis, win when we raced? You have no idea how muscular I've become; how heavy I lift in the gym. I'm not afraid of you.'

She wanted him to laugh with her, but he didn't. 'You should be, Salma. You should.'

There was a silence after this. Hours when he did not contact her again. And it was revealing of how often they were texting and talking that six hours without him felt long and strange. The world became quiet again without the buzzing and flashing lights of her phone.

When it finally did ring, it was not him but Norma. 'I'm still away, Mum. Is your shoulder not a bit better?'

'Still away?'

'Yes, I'm sorry. It's only been a few days since we spoke.'

'I'm aching all over, Salma, and the heating pad hasn't been much help.' There was an impatience in Norma's voice. 'I suppose you must have your holiday.'

'I'll be with you as soon I get back. I'll pop round and give you a nice massage. I promise.'

'What if I come to you now instead?'

She had to stop herself from laughing. 'I'm nowhere near you, Mum. It's best if you take some codeine.'

Norma grunted and ended the call.

Still no message from Amir, no calls, no wishing her goodnight or good morning. Instead of waking up to sobriety, feeling relieved or at least chastened, she felt deprived. Norma's call hadn't jolted her back to reality, back to weighing all that she could potentially lose. Neither had the messages from David and the children. Instead, she was sickening for Amir. When she could no longer bear the withdrawal of his attention, she texted him with her exact location, the address of the loch. She added the nearest airport, the nearest train station, the bus that could take him to the nearest village. 'I'm waiting for you,' she wrote.

She justified it to herself by saying that the least she could

do to make amends was to give him the opportunity for re-
venge. He would not come, and she would be the one who
had begged him to, the one who had lowered her pride and
sullied her values for his sake. This time he would be the one
to reject her. Then it could end. Fair and square between
them. An even score.

The forest in the rain was dark and cold. Iman shivered. Her
hair was wet. She was waiting for the Hoopoe. He no longer
came to her room. Ever since she had taken off her hijab,
he no longer told stories especially for her. She sensed his
aloofness, his silent rebuke. She was meant to learn from his
stories, to become spiritually nourished, to tame her ego and
strengthen her resolve. Instead, the pull of the other current
was visceral and strong. The costumes more intimate than his
stories; her anger louder than his voice. But still she wanted
to listen to him, the wisdom of his words mesmerising if
difficult to apply, comforting despite being cautionary. To
listen to the Hoopoe now, she must join all the others in the
forest, sitting as if she were one of its inhabitants, no longer
a princess with a crown, no longer high up in the attic. And
she must wait and interpret. She must interpret because the
language in which the Hoopoe spoke to other creatures
was not her language, not her mother tongue. Here, with
the wind blowing, with the sounds of the frogs, birds, deer
and foxes, gulls, rabbits and squirrels, she must listen more
intently. The story that the Hoopoe told sounded like an
echo of another tale, a classic of two sides, someone turning from friend to foe, from companion to devil, someone
becoming something else. And, by doing so, stepping far

away, detaching, springing out of reach. The animals did not listen quietly, it was not their custom to do so. They heckled the storyteller, they threw in snippets of their own stories, insisting on adding their trials to the pot. There were wails and chuckles, grunts and screams that substituted words. The Hoopoe was revered but taken for granted. He was given time and freedom to speak, but his listeners knew better. Usually Iman did not cry when listening to a story, but this time she sensed the loss and the confusion, how change was the nature of life, whether violent or subtle.

Chapter Eleven

It was Saturday, the day before they were due to drive to Glen-carron and visit Lady Evelyn's grave. Salma proposed that they go on a forest walk. A shared activity, she believed, would bring them together and help mend the ruptures that had taken place between them these past few days. The weather was slightly better, and it was something she had always planned they would do, a positive way to end their holiday at the loch. To voice this suggestion, Salma had to rehearse and build up her strength. It no longer felt natural to take on a leadership role. She did not even sound confident as she spoke, but it was her duty to try. The future of their friendship was unclear. Iman neither spoke nor acted as if she was going to move in with Salma when they got back. All the declarations about being independent, all the accusations about Salma being domineering, were hardly pointing to a future under one roof. Besides, without her hijab, did Salma really want Iman in close proximity to David? In the past, it would have been easy to joke, 'Gorgeous, keep away from my husband,' now it wasn't. And yet she would insist that Iman moved in with them. It was the right thing to do. The poor girl had nowhere else.

At breakfast, Salma explained to them again that the forest trails were graded by difficulty and time. Left to her own devices, she would have opted for the longest, most challenging route that involved a high climb. Iman too was quite willing to make the attempt. But it was tricky enough persuading Moni to go on any walk, let alone one that was anything but short and basic. 'We can compromise,' Moni said. 'I could go with you half the way and then come back. You two can then do the rest of the walk.'

'That's fine.' Iman gave her usual indifferent shrug. In the past she would have then looked at Salma to confirm the final verdict. Now she just turned and walked up the stairs to get dressed.

Salma, disappointed in her, turned to Moni. 'That's a good idea. Maybe you will change your mind and keep going with us. You might surprise yourself.'

Moni made a face as she stood up. 'I'll get some snacks ready and make a few sandwiches.' She no longer spoke of her plan for the three of them to set up a massage clinic when they got back. It had appealed to Salma more than she had let on. Iman as the receptionist, Moni the business manager, and she free to concentrate on the clients. It could work. She could visualise it being successful. Or, more precisely, it could have worked. A deep sense of loyalty to Iman stopped her from initiating the kind of conversation in which Moni might cruelly say, 'I don't want her working for me without her hijab.' So, Salma did not mention the clinic, though she continued to think about it as the brake to prevent her from sliding further towards Amir, an alternative that would make her present life more appealing and, by extension, save her marriage.

When they opened the door of the cottage, it was as if they were setting out into a new season. The rain of the previous days had given way to washed sunshine, clean air, satiated earth and plants. They walked in silence, with Iman a little ahead, as if she was leading the way, claiming the forest as familiar territory. Salma matched her pace to that of Moni's. Moni was walking as fast as she could, but for Salma it felt like a warm-up.

'You will tire out,' she warned Moni. 'We can go more slowly.'

When they did, the distance between them and Iman grew. 'What's the hurry?' Moni panted.

The question did not require an answer. That first day at the castle, Iman had hurried to the spot where Ibrahim would later repudiate her. She had rushed towards an appointment with pain. It must be a human instinct, pondered Salma, this running towards what would ultimately destroy, this head-long trajectory towards death. 'Iman,' she called out. 'Slow down!'

Iman stopped and turned towards them. She was wearing camouflage, the grey-green of a soldier, not as tight as Tomb Raider but the same colours. Her hair, darker and wavier, was tied back in a Lara Croft style but with a shorter ponytail. Was that who she was trying to emulate? Her body language said impatience, indifference, independence. In other words, I don't need you any more. Where was this strength coming from? Salma wondered. From taking off her hijab? Or was it the other way round? Salma wasn't sure whether to laugh at the triviality of it all or to feel sad.

To walk as a group, their pace must match the slowest. To

walk as a group, Salma needed to curb her enthusiasm, Iman to become more patient, Moni to exert a bit more effort. It occurred to Salma that the best tactic would be to engage Iman in conversation. In that way, Moni could concentrate her efforts on the walk itself while Iman could be distracted from the need to hurry.

'You haven't sung to us for a long time,' she said to Iman.

Previously whenever Salma made this observation or some variation of it, Iman would break into song. Now she was silent.

'What's wrong?' Salma could not hide the nervousness from her voice. She reminded herself that Iman was the same person, with or without her hijab; nothing had changed, nothing could change. She needed these reassurances.

Iman shrugged. 'You didn't stand up for me. You didn't take my side.'

Salma was taken aback. 'When?'

'In every situation I can think of.' Iman lowered her voice. 'When Moni was mean to me in the car, you were silent.'

Salma could not remember Moni being mean to Iman in the car. The whole car journey seemed a long time ago.

'See, you don't even remember,' said Iman. 'It's nothing to you.'

Salma was lost for words.

Iman went on, 'I'm not going to move in with you. I can't live in your house.'

'Don't be silly. You have nowhere else to go.'

'See. That's your response. Is that all you can think of saying to me? Is that the best you can do?'

'Half of your things are in our garage. Remember. I told Ibrahim to give them to David.'

'I will get my things, Salma. Don't worry. I won't burden you with my rubbish.'

'It's not a burden. Why are you talking like this? We're sisters. We've always been. I want you to move in with us. Is that what you want me to say? Of course I do. Why should you even doubt it?'

'I am over doubting it. To you, I would always be young—'

Salma interrupted her. 'But you are younger than me. It's a fact. I didn't invent it.'

Iman sighed. 'You always think you know better. And I'm tired of this. Of being told what to do. Constantly.'

'Because you don't know what you want. You've told me yourself, time and again, you're not sure what you want.'

'I want to be independent.'

'But how practical is that, when you can't support yourself, when you don't have a job? Be reasonable. And it's not as if I ever stopped you from being independent. I was furious when you quit your job at the supermarket.'

'I don't want you furious and I don't want you pleased with me, Salma. I want to answer to myself, to make my own decisions.'

'What decisions? You're not making sense.'

'I don't have anything more to say, Salma.'

Salma, of course, did. But she did not want to say, I did this for you and I did that for you, be grateful. It was on the tip of her tongue. She did not want to say that for someone who doesn't have anywhere to go after this holiday except my house, you sure are acting uppity. She did not want to dish up threatening stories of homelessness and being vulnerable to abuse. These thoughts must have slowed her down for she found herself level with Moni, while Iman was now ahead of them on the path.

Moni said, 'Salma, I shouldn't have come with you. I will do my best tomorrow, I promise you, but I don't know why you insisted on this walk. It's not for me.' She was out of breath, but not too much.

'It's doing you good, Moni. You need to practise for tomorrow.' Salma did not sound enthusiastic. Why had she insisted that they go out together when togetherness was not important to either Moni or Iman?

'Maybe it is doing me good,' said Moni. 'But I can't last much longer.'

'You're younger than me, you shouldn't be so unfit.' Irritability crept into her voice. Salma's hopes of improving Moni were dwindling. Perhaps these aspirations had been presumptuous in the first place. Salma wished she were with Amir. But she was not. Here was her life as she had made it, as she had chosen it. From the very first time she had met David in Cairo and he had been happy to let her order for the two of them at restaurants, haggle on his behalf in shops, drive his car, save him from the city's beggars and swindlers, she had fallen in love with action and autonomy. Freed from Amir's need for her to be passive and secondary to him, she had surged ahead, enjoying the flex of her muscles, the importance of her voice, the power to achieve a difference. Now, years later, she was wondering if her achievements truly amounted to anything. And why had all these freedoms built up to no more than little pleasures?

You choose, David would say. The choice is yours. No one had ever spoken to her like that before, no one had ever asked her to choose. She had been thrilled at what he was offering. He listened to her opinion, which did not need to be the right opinion and the right opinion did not need to be his opinion. She had valued this so much. It had pumped her up and made her radiant, made her voice louder and her chin higher. Looking back now, it seemed such a frivolous victory, such a flimsy version of autonomy and self-importance.

Over the years, David and British society had given the children the same freedoms – they would not be subservient to her as she had been to her parents, they were independent and well rounded. Her daughter could throw away the chance to be a doctor, the doctor Salma wanted her to be because she couldn't. At home, Salma was no longer a queen who reigned; when she barked orders, she was either ignored or humoured. The pressure was on her all the time to be a supportive, comforting mum. Unconditional love was what was expected. 'There for them all the time' and certainly not the boss.

Someone should have warned me, thought Salma, explained to me. But the explanation had always been there. Everything had a price. She had paid with her home country and medical degree. Her position in the world. And now to lose Iman too, who spoke her language, who looked up to her as no one in her household did. Salma moved away from Moni. She fought back the urge to break into a run. She was too young for resignation. A long, heavy midlife looped down ahead of her, complete with health scares and children leaving home, David losing his mother, a smaller car, holidays without the children. I can still get out, there is still time for a fresh start. Admit that I made a mistake, that it was all a mistake, that I am a ghost here, neither necessary nor effective.

Iman sloshed through wet leaves and little puddles. Every day and every minute, her impatience with Salma and Moni was growing. Tomorrow's visit to Lady Evelyn's grave she was looking forward to, but the thought of leaving the loch the day after was unbearable. To get in the car again, with Salma bouncing in the best of moods, smug that they had achieved their objective, with Moni self-righteous that she was a good mother returning to care for her son. Iman did not think she could bear it. She must find a way out. Her instincts led her towards male assistance. Perhaps Mullin could help her. But he would want something in return, they always did. If her alternative to Salma's house was the women's refuge in the city, perhaps there was one closer to here? Then at least she would be near the loch and far away from Salma. She did not think she could live in a city any more.

When Moni had mentioned her idea about the three of them opening a clinic, Iman had been able to visualise herself as the receptionist. The one welcoming the patients, taking down appointments, being the first point of contact. But there were bad feelings now between the three of them. And Iman could not stand this atmosphere, it made her feel suffocated.

To be a tree or a squirrel, to be a pond or a fish, to be moving and living. Iman wished for another kind of existence, beauty that wasn't a responsibility, needs that could be easily fulfilled. Why was I born human? I don't want it!

She walked faster, certain now that she did not want Salma to catch up with her, did not want the sort of conversations aimed at pulling her back to the cosy past. They were on the blue trail, but when Iman came across the next wooden sign dabbed with blue, she hesitated. She could follow it or head in a completely different direction. To stay on the blue trail meant that Salma and Moni would catch up with her. They would find a picnic area, sit down and eat their sandwiches. Moni would fuss over the sandwiches because she had made them. She would expect some show of appreciation or at least acknowledgement for her efforts. How tired Iman was of all this.

Moni was struggling to keep up a decent pace. With every step, she lagged further behind the other two. At least I don't feel cold, she thought. When they had first stepped out of the cottage, she had felt the fresh breeze on her face like a smack. Now she needed it on her flushed cheeks, swallowed it in gulps. At least the floating jellyfish and sharp black spots that usually beset her when she exerted herself hadn't yet made an appearance. If they blocked her vision, she would stop walking. She would give up and just sit on the floor of the forest, leaning her back against a tree. Now she must keep walking. Around her, the trees rose high and the sunlight needed to work hard to filter through them. The forest would always be damp and fungal, sour-smelling. Moni knew she did not belong here, but this was the last full day in the loch. They would be at the Glencarron estate tomorrow. That was bound to be memorable, especially now that she had read Lady Evelyn's book and been touched by her special friendship with her grandson, Toby. They had been so close that he had asked to be buried next to her. Moni trudged along after the others. Knowing herself, she guessed that she would forget this forest. It would slide from her memory. She would, though, always remember Adam. He was the loch and the loch was him, and all these past days were about him. He would stay in her memory while the physical features of the loch would blur and mix up with photos she had seen or with scenes from television. She might remember the interior of the cottage, the kitchen where she had spent most of her time. Most likely she would also remember the refectory in the monastery, the dense feeling in the place. She had been looking for Adam that day and he had suddenly walked through the door.

The memory made her smile. The boy was the best that the loch had offered, the highlight, the pulse. She must see him later today to hug him goodbye. That's right, think of pleasant things to take your mind off the ordeal of walking. It would be good to become old and infirm, she thought, free to indulge her natural laziness. No one would expect much of her then. She could spend the whole day in bed or in an armchair watching television. But resting was not for Adam's mother. Her days were a variation of this walk, pointless effort, on and on. She missed him, missed his skin and presence, all the rituals she had built around his care. Most likely, no matter how fast Salma drove, they would arrive back in the city in the evening, well past teatime and it might be too late to bring Adam home. She would spend the night alone in the flat and then first thing the following morning take the bus to the nursing home. But if they set out from the loch first thing in the morning, there would be time to pick up Adam. Did they need to stay until twelve noon, the time they had agreed with Mullin, to hand over the keys and have him help with their suitcases? Perhaps he would walk around checking that everything in the cottage was in order before taking them across in the ferry. Had he not said that everything in the cottage must be as they had found it? Moni sighed. The kitchen needed attention.

It was the perfect excuse to stop walking. Salma, who was a little ahead of her, turned. 'Are you all right?'

Moni, panting, explained why she needed to return to the cottage. Salma tried to dissuade her. 'The kitchen can wait. I will help you.' Moni shook her head. She handed the sandwiches to Salma. She turned her back and was surprised at how easy it was to exit this outing. Salma hadn't protested as much as she thought she would. What a relief! Returning was much easier than starting out. Going down faster than climbing. She laughed a little, happy that Salma couldn't hear her now.

It occurred to Moni that they should have left the loch a day ago, two days ago. They had stayed too long. Every holiday had a perfect length and then it turned into an indulgence, time sitting heavy on idle hands, the mind free to find fault with life left behind, too much friction between people, familiarity turning to contempt. Every holiday was a threat.

Chapter Twelve

When Moni returned to the cottage, she found Adam sitting on the doorstep, waiting for her. The sight of him from afar made the last bit of the walk easier. She enjoyed moving closer to him, seeing him with greater clarity bit by bit. First, he had been a speck to be guessed at and then she could see what he was wearing, that he had his yellow ball in his hands; she could even see the expression on his face and meet his eyes with a smile of greeting. It was a good thing she had turned back and not continued with the others. She paused to catch her breath before walking the last few feet towards him. This would be their last time together. A goodbye gift would have been nice, but there were no shops in this place. Even if there were shops, she would have been lost and not sure what to get him. She would have just taken him with her and bought the first thing he pointed out. How sad that he didn't speak and that his parents were negligent. She must remember to take a selfie with him. It would be her holiday souvenir.

'Are you hungry, Adam?' She unlocked the door of the cottage and led him into the kitchen. 'Salma, Iman and I have to eat everything in the fridge before we leave the day after tomorrow otherwise it's a bother packing it all again.' There wasn't too much food left, but there was a mismatch. Too much milk, for example. Rice with nothing to eat it with. Cheese but no bread. The eggs needed to be finished. She warmed up some soup and they each put a spoonful of rice in their bowl, but still there was a lot left over.

Moni suddenly felt warm and sleepy. She did not want to say goodbye to Adam, but she wished she could have a nap. Just a short nap before the others returned.

Adam was pointing to the oven. He pulled open one of the drawers and took out the cookie cutter. She must bake for him if this was what he wanted. They had baked before and he had enjoyed it. He could take the cookies away with him and that would be her goodbye gift. Moni made herself a cup of coffee to recharge her energy.

She spoke to him as she gathered the ingredients together. 'I made sandwiches this morning, nice ones, but I didn't get to eat any. I put pickles and mustard in them and made them special. I even added fresh mint from the garden.' The sandwiches were all up on the trail with Salma and Iman. Maybe they would come back with one for her. Knowing Iman, she would crumble Moni's share and feed it to the birds. 'That's how she is. There's war in her country but the people are well fed. That's why she has no qualms about wasting food. In my country it's the other way round. That's why I'm never wasteful. I never throw food away. I always eat it. Maybe that's why I'm overweight.'

They baked the cookies together and the smell filled the cottage. 'I'm going to miss you, Adam,' she said. He didn't understand what she was saying. Abstract words. With her phone, she took photos of him wearing the oven gloves, biting into the first cookie and finding it too hot.

She left him to go to the bathroom and after that she prayed in the bedroom. When she finished praying, the bed looked so tempting that she could not resist the need to stretch out for a few minutes and listen to the hum of her aching muscles. It had been silly to join Salma and Iman on that walk, out of character. She had done it to be nice to Salma; that was all. Now she was relieved that it was over. Tomorrow they would visit Lady Evelyn and the day after they would go back to their normal lives. Her son was waiting for her. She had been away long enough, and he could not be left to stay with strangers for ever. This holiday had been a break from caring for him. At first, she hadn't appreciated the need for it or been grateful to Salma for taking upon herself all the organisation. She must remember to thank her, even if she did not look up to her as she had done before. That business with Amir had certainly made her reconsider.

When Moni opened her eyes, she wondered if Adam had got bored and left. She didn't want him leaving without the cookies. This thought propelled her out of bed and into the kitchen. No, there he was, still sitting at the kitchen table eating the cookies. There was even more of him, he was taking up more space, growing before her very eyes. She gasped at what she was seeing. Adam was ballooning, becoming wider, taller, fatter. He seemed unperturbed by this and continued chewing, half a cookie in his hand, and it was as if every crumb were making him grow. He was now her own size and yet still the child features: smooth chin, chubby cheeks, the missing tooth in his mouth. He was bigger than her, too big. Moni felt she must do something to help him. She must call the emergency services, she must contain this terrible growth one way or the other. Poor boy, poor boy. Yet he smiled when he saw her as if everything were normal, as if this was just another visit and she had just popped into the bedroom and returned to the kitchen again.

This isn't right, this isn't right. The kitchen chair collapsed under his weight. She screamed. He looked more startled by her screams than by landing on the floor. She ran towards him to stem the tide of flesh rising and overflowing, to hold back what would harm and hurt him. This was too much for his own good, too fast, unnatural. He was now too big for the kitchen so that she had to back out. The kitchen was full of his springy, healthy flesh, his smooth skin and softness; and there was no space for her, she was squeezed out to the corridor. The bigger he grew, the smaller she was becoming, crushed and forced. He was now too big for the cottage. Out, Adam, out. You have to leave. You have to go. He stood up and banged his head on the ceiling. He moved forward and got stuck at the door, his head jammed at the top, his arms cutting the frame. He whimpered in pain. He sat down and his head, still growing, reached the top of the door. He was now taking up the whole width of the kitchen, his elbow wedged underneath the kitchen tap, his hair touching the ceiling. In the vestibule, there was less and less room for Moni. She was hemmed in by his expansion, squashed by his need for more space. She was squeezed by what he had become, and she knew that she hadn't acted fast enough. If only she had got him out of the cottage in time, or if only she had run to save her own skin. Instead they were both trapped. And if he went on growing, the cottage would explode.

Her screams and his cries of distress. I'm sorry. I'm sorry, Adam. She was the responsible adult and he was a child in her care. She had miscalculated, she had overindulged, and this was the result. So much less of her, so much more of him. He's suffocating me, she realised. He doesn't want to, but he is. He can't help it. It's not in his control. She pushed back at him. To save them both. But there was too much of him pressing against her. The constriction in her chest increased. She blacked out.

What is worse than a nightmare is waking up to find that it is not a nightmare. When Moni opened her eyes, she found herself rolling like a ball from side to side. She found herself tumbling and somersaulting in a concave enclosure criss-crossed by fine grooves. Her body had become round. Her arms hugged her legs, her forehead rested on her knees, her feet were drawn in. She had become bunched up. Constriction was her new consciousness, plus the lack of gravity, this loss of substance and weight. Where was she? Certainly not in the cottage. There was sunlight and air. She was outdoors and moving, carried along. It was Adam who was carrying her in the palm of his hand. The springy enclosure was his hand, the fine grooves that stretched out beneath her like patterns in a carpet were the life lines on his palms.

She screamed when his face loomed in close to her. The sheer magnitude of it. Nothing menacing in his smile or eyes. The same rounded cheeks and boyish chin. He could not help any of this. He had been eating the cookies she had baked and suddenly he had grown. 'Put me down, put me down.' He could not hear her. Hers was a small voice under the sky and she was no longer standing tall. Moni could not untangle herself. She could not stretch out. Her hands were clasped round her knees, neck arched forward, feet drawn in. She twisted and bounced in his palm. He was holding her loosely, but he could crush her if he wanted to. All it would take from him would be a gentle squeeze.

Rolling like a ball, rolling like a ball. Moni would be on her back looking up. Then she would be on her knees, looking down. On her left side and right side. There was no constancy, no stability. Put me down, put me down. She felt him moving in the forest, swiping at tall trees with his arms, terrifying and jolting her in the process. This is a temporary aberration, she comforted herself. He will return to normal, I will return to normal. This cannot go on. Surely. Surely. All the kindness I have given him, all the sacrifice.

He dropped her. Inadvertently or because he had heard her, she would never know. The free fall made her scream like she had never screamed before. With all the power in her lungs, with every ounce of energy in her body. It felt as if her insides reached the floor of the forest before she did. As if all the organs in her body were squeezing down her birth canal and she must give birth to them. The landing was not as painful as she expected, if she could think straight enough to expect. Her new body shape saved her from injury. She rolled on the damp floor of the forest. She was the same size, but all perspectives had shifted.

The silence was the absence of her screams. She was bruised, and she could not stand up. She was still contorted, forehead to knees, feet drawn in, but her body was more relaxed. Her hands were no longer gripping each other. She could unclasp them and move them around. But she could not stretch out her legs or arch her back. She lay down on her side and looked around her. Something blue caught her eye. It was a dab of paint on a wooden post. Comparing her size to that of the post, it would seem that she had not shrunk: it was Adam who had expanded. And this was where she was, back on the blue trail in the forest. Iman and Salma would not be far. They would find her, and they would help. She could depend on them.

'Iman. Salma,' she called out.

When hours passed and there was no response, she began to despair. The trail continued for several miles and her friends could long have passed this spot. Finally, something moved towards her. Because it did not speak out in response to her cry for help, she assumed it was an animal. A deer or, worse, a fox. Normally these forest animals were harmless, but nothing for Moni was normal any more. Her body was poised for a fight, the instinct to defend herself. But what shambled over to her was as harmless as a cow, as elegant as a cat, as lustrous as a peacock. It was an unidentified creature, a mix of mammal and reptile, horrific and yet beautiful, repulsive and yet compelling because of the sad dignity with which it carried itself.

When it moved closer to Moni, she caught a sweet scent from it, more herb than animal. A perfume that soothed Moni's nerves, stopped her from fidgeting and trying to unlock her body from the distorted ball position it was now in. When the creature leant over to look at Moni and their eyes met, they recognised each other. It was Iman.

Chapter Thirteen

After Moni had left them, Salma and Iman walked in silence, enjoying the challenge of the climb. Without Moni to hold them back, they built up speed. Salma had the longer strides, but Iman could keep up. For considerable stretches of time, they forgot the bad feelings between them. It was almost how things had been in the past, with Salma leading the way and Iman finding it natural to follow. They crossed a running stream, the water transparent over the dark rocks, the clatter of their feet on the rope suspension bridge. They passed other climbers, couples and families, three men who talked among themselves in a European language. Salma was the one who exchanged greetings, slowed down for a few friendly comments. Iman ducked her head and said nothing. She had the ability to stop thinking, to simply feel and exist in the moment. At times she almost forgot that Salma was there, just a little ahead. But Salma was not making the decisions. She was not choosing right over left, it was all about following the blue trail. This put them on equal footing. It made Iman relax and even seemed to point at a new kind of relationship. One in which they could be equals.

They came across a picnic clearing, an array of wooden tables and a large rubbish bin. Without discussing it, they stopped to eat the sandwiches Moni had made. They did not speak while they ate, passing the water bottle in silence, flicking away crumbs from the table. In addition to her own sandwich, Iman ate half of Moni's and kept the other half to crumble for the fishes and the birds. There were enough bits of leftover food in this picnic area without her needing to add more. She would make sure to carry the half sandwich deeper into the forest, to a place that was less trodden, that was rarely brushed by the debris of humans.

If only Salma hadn't spoken, but she did. To reproach her yet again, to remind her of their shared past, their sisterhood; the times they prayed together and broke fast together. The times Salma vetted suitors for Iman. The times Iman refereed arguments between Salma and her eldest daughter. And the times I was your sidekick and dogsbody. The times you laughed at my views and treated me like a doll.

If only Salma wasn't speaking. She was spoiling the day with her voice, all this analysis. She was egging Iman on to talk, to say again what she had said before. How she disliked direct confrontations! And yet to Salma they were the solution. 'We must talk this through,' she kept saying. 'We can discuss this and resolve our differences, Iman.'

'You are oblivious to my feelings,' said Iman. 'You don't know me. If you knew me, you wouldn't talk to me here like this.' What she wanted to say was the forest should not be sullied with their pettiness. They should walk in silence, be in awe. They should be one with nature. But that was what Iman knew and Salma didn't. That was the difference between them and it was greater here than it could ever be in the city.

'I was happy walking,' said Iman. 'This outing today was your idea and I was going along with it and then you have to spoil it by talking.'

'I'm talking because I'm disturbed. And I'm disturbed because you've changed, Iman. Why have you changed to-wards me?'

'Because, because, because. Enough.' She did not want to explain. She was forever struggling to explain, to put words to feelings. Salma would outsmart her with words. Salma would win every argument. She said, 'Salma, there is no point. Get it through your head. I'm not going to move in with you. It's final.'

She saw tears spring to Salma's eyes, watched her jump up, scrunch the kitchen towel that her sandwich had been wrapped in and throw it in the bin.

They followed the trail in silence, Iman averting her eyes from Salma's face. Never had one of them cried without the other comforting her. But there was nothing more to be said. It had come to this. After all these years and hours of laughter. Friendship was not much of an investment after all, instead it was sand pouring down the hourglass, water meandering downhill; an act of defiance against the natural state of loneliness. A sound caused them to stop and turn around. Was it a deer thrashing through the forest, pursued or believing it was pursued, heading towards them or past them? Or was it a man running? A reddish-brown streak ap-peared through the dappled green of the forest, veering away in another direction.

In an instant, Salma was off the track, following the sound, that red moving through the green. Iman caught a glimpse of her tear-stained cheeks, the excitement in her eyes, and then she was on her own.

Iman continued walking. Without Salma, she found herself slowing down, more in tune with her surroundings, listening and watching. Looking up at a lapwing flicking from side to side, listening to its soft waa-waa sound, she tripped on the protruding root of a tree, stumbled forward and fell. On her knees, the smell of damp earth and vegetation went to her head; the darkness of the forest was womb-like and welcoming. Rest after motion, stillness and laxity. She could give in to this. No more resistance or arguments, no one asking questions, circling her, lassoing her in. She could be what she wanted to be, in a state of existence that was un-threatened, that did not need to be accounted for or earnt. It would be easier that way. No ability to attract or need to repel advances. She would be left alone, to sing if she wanted to sing, a song for the joy of it and not in order to entertain.

The Hoopoe was hovering above her. 'Stand up, stand up, stand up.'

She started to get up, but then decided not to. He had wasted his time. All that special tuition in her attic room, as if she were a princess. When she took off her hijab, he stopped visiting and she could only find him outside. She could only hear him when others heard him, she could only see him as they did. These were the rules now; she had chosen to become one of the crowd.

So if he was here now especially for her sake, then she

must be in great need, maybe even in danger. He too was possessive about her, not losing sight of where she had gone. He too believed she needed protecting and saving. No. No more preciousness. No more responsibility either. The solemnness in which she had been told that her beauty was to be cherished and guarded; hidden and kept from harm. She wanted away from all that. Far away where she could be left alone. Like a sunset was left alone or a flower bed or a butterfly. She would not take any more orders. Stand. Sit. Fetch. Don't come back. Send us money. Leave that bit of chicken for your brother. Marry him and not him. Make sure you remove every thread of your hair that's tangled in the shower plug.

'Stand up, Iman.'

No, she would not.

All she had ever wanted, truly wanted, known she had wanted, was a baby. Was that too much to ask? Her mother had more children than she wanted, and Salma had all the children she wanted. But she was like a doll, never pregnant, always slight and slim. Husband after husband, month after month. All she had ever asked for was a child. And, at first, she had thought it would be easy, just like that, marriage then baby, one following the other, the consequence of the other. Every cycle, she hoped it would be the last time she bled for a long while, but month after month, every month, a disappointment. Iman had always been in tune with her body. Unlike other girls, who could be fussy, who disliked the smell of what leaked out of them, who were terrified of their husbands on that first wedding night. Iman was a natural. She took it all in her stride. Surely hers should be the body to grow ripe with child, the body that was brimming with fertility, the potential for life. Go to school, ensnare a husband, become a receptionist – all to bide time for her true calling, her understanding of the meaning of life.

Yet neither the Hoopoe nor Salma spoke to her about this. They did not face her disappointment head-on. They did not explain to her why Moni was a mother and she was not. Why Salma had four and she had none. They would say it was Allah's will and she knew that already, but why was it His will? What was the logic behind it, the purpose, the intention? As long as she did not know, she would be bewildered, killing time, waiting to find out the purpose of her humanity.

She had asked Salma once, 'Is my constipation stopping me from getting pregnant?' And Salma laughed and said, 'Don't be silly. There's no connection.' But how was she expected to know what connected to what and what caused what. She had been bored at school, lessons that were too abstract, patriotic songs which meant nothing, all the silly fuss about clean copybooks.

Hands and knees on the ground. Under her palms, the soil seemed to give way, to cave in ever so slightly. Oh, so this would be like the other time when the dog knocked her over. The earth sucking her in and this time she would not be afraid. She would not resist. She did not want to continue walking without Salma, it was not worth it to complete the challenge of the trail on her own. She rolled on her back and saw the disapproval in the Hoopoe's eyes. 'Stand up, Iman.'

She smiled at him. 'I don't want to, and you can't force me.'

'Didn't I teach you? Didn't I warn you?'

She did remember the stories, but did he want her to apply them to her life? She had never been good at school, she had told him that, yet he still went on teaching. 'What was I meant to learn?' The ground was welcoming, cradling her back.

The bird made sounds that irritated her ears.

She laughed. 'Is that all? I know I'm human.'

Again, being told what to do. Be responsible. Be mature. Total uninhibited freedom is not for you.

'Go away,' she shouted.

'Stand up.'

'No.'

'Stand up.' He was flying all around her now, zooming in close as if he would swipe her cheeks with his wings, peck out her eyes.

'I'm not scared of you.'

'Listen.'

'No.' Enough with the patronising. Enough with the holding back.

He said, 'There are consequences to everything you do. A price to pay. Go against what is right and here of all places you will find the tangible consequences. They will not be postponed. Get up.'

'No, and you can't make me.'

His sadness was palpable, it descended upon her like a shroud. She would live the consequence of her disobedience, be punished.

A hollowing was taking place underneath her. Gentle, nothing to be frightened of. This was her fate, even if misgivings shrouded it. This was the inevitable consequence of who she was, the sum of her actions, the manifestation of her intentions. She submitted to it.

It was not a grave. One is placed in a grave, wedged in with care by the living, those who are still in the queue waiting their turn. She was not dead, and it was the earth that wanted her, a place of incubation, temporary and necessary. Her metamorphosis was painful. Limbs stretched and contorted, skin scorched and punctured, her hair not her hair, her fingers not her fingers. Her mouth felt tight, her tongue started to swell. It pushed between her lips and the fatness of it was new and uncomfortable. And it was not only her mouth, every part of her was in pain. The combined physical sufferings of womanhood: the cramps and torn hymens, the invasion and press of pregnancy, bruised pelvic floor and cracked nipples, even the aches of beautification, the sting of waxing, the pierce of earlobes. She could not trace how it all had started. The day she acknowledged that beauty was a burden, her femininity overpowering her soul, the day she admitted that she did not want to be human any more. Because a tree always had a home. A fox did not need to be told how to find food. A bird did not need clothes.

She was submerged now. Above her and around her, soft granulated soil. Her feet touched hair, her skin grazed cold bones, her ears caught the sounds of the creatures made of smoke. They did not want her presence. She sensed them fretting. There was a silliness about them despite the ability to move seamlessly between air, water and earth. The djinn knew no barriers. An enviable position, but still their lack of weight counted against them. Iman felt the pain subside into rawness, all the sensitivity of new skin. There was no rush. She could sleep and dream of the Hoopoe. In a dream, he would tell her another story.

There was a story that he had not completed. It was about two tribes in a forest. One tribe was made up of small gentle people, highly skilled and peaceful. The other tribe were monsters, greedy and violent. The small people lived in fear of the monsters. All their efforts and intelligence went into protecting themselves from attack. They devised methods of predicting the movement of the monsters, they laid traps for them and studied their weaknesses. The monsters were foolish. They survived on their brute strength. In the style of the Hoopoe's storytelling, there were epic wars and myriad adventures, heroes and heroines, tales of escape and subterfuge. Yet what had moved Iman the most in that story, what made her blood run cold, was the origin of the monsters. They were not another species. They were not foreign or alien. In fact, they were the children of the small people – some, not all of their children. At the toddler age, if they were destined to become future monsters, they would start to eat more and more. They would guzzle and become aggressive. Not finding enough food in the village, they would move to the woods and forage as much as they wanted. A small mother could come across her daughter or son, call them by name, beg them to come home, but they would ignore her. The next time, as their monster form developed, the mother would barely recognise her own flesh and blood. And they, well into becoming fully fledged monsters, would no longer have any memory that she was their mother.

Iman, though, was not losing her memory. When the earth finally gave her up and she stretched up as tall as a small tree, when she shook off her torn clothes, she remembered the human she had been. In the cartoons she often watched with Salma's children, transformed characters could see their new reflection in water. They gazed down into a pool of blue and their face swayed up at them. Iman searched for water, her movements ungainly, her sight blurred. She found a running stream, gurgling and frothing. But it did not reflect her face.

She guzzled and snorted the water. She farted and rolled in dirt. Her new body was not under her control. There she was, leaping to tear apart a squirrel. The sort of squirrel she would have cooed over a day ago. Now it was food, a mess of muscle and bloody fur. She felt the pleasure of it, the wanton recklessness of it, and wanted more.

She no longer knew the names of what she could see, hear and smell. The names of the other animals and plants. She knew that a rabbit had long ears, a twitching nose, but she could not remember the word 'rabbit', whether in Arabic or English. She no longer knew how to count; two plus two had an answer but it was elusive. She could not remember the verses of the Qur'an she had memorised and daily recited. Whenever she tried to speak, her tongue got in the way. She could only make sounds, grunts and moans. Parallel to this, a part of her was still self-conscious, still curious. What do I look like now? In my new life, this life of freedom? A tree did not need a home. A cow did not need a mirror. A chick did not need clothes.

She lumbered through the forest without any fear of cold

or getting lost. She felt a fullness in her belly and, absent-mindedly, emptied her bowels, just like that, no need to hide or squat or wash. All that fuss. Other animals sniffed her and were satisfied that she was genuine. Insects buried themselves in her coat. As time passed, she drifted seamlessly from waking into sleeping; there was no need to plan or make a strategy. A scent and a sound caught her attention. It was a human body squashed into a ball, rolling and unable to straighten up. The face was familiar and seemed to recognise her too. Iman felt as if she hadn't seen this person for a very long time. Was it someone from back home, a relative, a friend? No, it was Moni, reduced and distorted. Iman came close to her and their eyes met. 'Where is Salma?' Moni said. Iman heard her voice as if it were gushing through water, the words garbled and echoed. Salma. Yes, Iman remembered Salma. Salma with a child hitched up on her hips, one hand supporting him, the other hand stirring soup in a saucepan. Salma stepping out of her car and looking up as Iman gazed down from her window.

Moni was speaking about Salma. She would help us as she had always helped us before. She would know what to do.

What would Salma think if she saw Iman now? A snake might not remember the year before, the month before. That desire to know, to check, to measure against, was human. Iman had moved from one container into the other. Her soul was in an animal's body after years of being in a human. The outside form could change but not the inner. Her human shape itself had been a costume, like the princess ball gown she had found in the cupboard, like the warrior trousers. It

233

had not been about the hijab covering her femininity after all, but it was about her femininity covering her human soul. There would always be Iman, the soul, heading out and returning. Her soul was the origin from which there was no escape.

Chapter Fourteen

Salma had seen his red T-shirt through tears. Tears she was hiding from Iman. It stunned her that Iman would insist that she was not going to move in with her once they left the loch. She had known that Iman was gestating a rebellion, weaving daydreams of independence that could never materialise. And this had given Salma comfort. Soon enough Iman would come to her senses. She would move into Salma's house, sharing a bedroom with Salma's eldest daughter. Salma would take her to a lawyer to claim as many rights as she could possibly get from Ibrahim. They would spend hours discussing Iman's future, the kind of job she could do, whether Moni's idea of the three of them running their own clinic was feasible, whether Iman was eligible for benefits or an educational grant or an apprenticeship scheme. All the sensible proper things that needed to be done. And, by extension, Salma too would practise what she preached and become sensible and proper. She would stop the messaging and phoning, the dreams of packing up and leaving. She would shrug off the holiday fantasies and get on with being a good wife and mother. She would stifle all Egypt, the Beloved nostalgia and buckle down.

But instead, Iman was abandoning her, and Amir had come all the way for her. All that he said on the phone had not been empty promises and threats.

So, she ran after his red T-shirt through the forest. His was not a well-beaten trail, clear of trees and rocks. Instead there were branches sticking out to jab at her side, there were stones that threatened to twist her ankle and trip her. But she must not lose sight of him. It was him, for sure. After coming all this way for her sake, he was playing hard to get. He wanted her to be the one chasing him. He wanted her to say sorry. She was sorry, and she was happy too that he had come. No, not happy, but so excited that she couldn't think straight, couldn't figure out where she was heading. She called out his name, but he didn't slow down. She could not see him clearly, not as clearly as she wanted to. The distance between them should narrow, but it didn't. The forest was larger than she would have thought. Here were the first leaves of autumn, leaves as bright as tangerines. She crossed other trails, red, green and purple. Those she had earlier disregarded as too easy or too difficult for the three of them to attempt. The blue trail was far behind her. So was the cottage and the monastery. She was getting out of breath, which meant she must have run for a long time, covered a good distance. She jogged every day; she was fit and had told him so. And he played tennis, he didn't jog. So surely this chase could not go on for ever.

The trees were thinning around her. This would be the edge of the forest, now, closer to the village. She found herself facing a house or at least a building. A period house that looked like it was no longer a home, one of those places too expensive to maintain, part of an estate which perhaps had also, in the past, included the forest or at least some of it. All of this was conjecture. There was no sign or information. A wooden gate had been left open. It was evidence that Amir had passed through here, that he had entered the building ahead of her.

She closed the gate behind her and ran the last few steps to the entrance. Up close, the building was imposing and unwelcoming. It was the grey exterior and official look that made it like that. But if he was inside, she would find him. It was already too late to turn back, to retrace her steps. Iman didn't want her. And if Amir did, enough to travel all the way, enough to put his life on pause, enough to take such a risk, then he had earned her. She owed him. Why else had she given him her address? And here she was doing the chasing, running and running, calling out and pushing open doors to ruffle up the past and dig her way deep into it.

It was how she had imagined Lady Evelyn's hunting lodge. Victorian, with eleven bedrooms on an estate of 15,000 acres. The kind of home a lady came back to after a day of brown-trout fishing on the River Carron. Walls on which hung one stag head after the other. But no, this place could be a museum, unlived in, with the carpets and paintings of long ago. With the faces of the Scottish aristocracy gazing down at Salma, viscounts and earls, their clans and tartan. All around her was silence. No attendants or guides. The lights were off, and the curtains were drawn. Perhaps they had all gone but forgotten to lock up. It was not right that the valuable past be left without protection. A thief could come in and take these antiques. She, for sure, would not take anything, neither would Amir. Stealing? It reminded her of the time in the car when she asked Moni and Iman what sin they would choose to commit if it would never count against them, a sin that would not have repercussions either in this life or the next, a sin that would go unpunished. Iman said something confusing about freedom from accountability. Moni said she would kill someone. Murtada probably. Then Salma had sent a message to Amir asking him what he would do, and he had said exactly what she was thinking of saying. He wrote that he would steal what didn't belong to him – such as another man's wife. She wrote back that she would steal what didn't belong to her too – perhaps another woman's husband. It had made her laugh that Amir and she were thinking along the same lines, that their thoughts were in harmony. It was all tongue-in-cheek and disingenuous, reducing adultery to theft, twisting a major sin into one that carried a lesser punishment. They were flirting. And now the time for flirting was over. Here they were in this stately home at the edge of the forest, both foreign and free to roam. If she called out his name now, he might answer her. She took out her phone, but the screen was a complete fog. Even if there was a recent message from him, she would not be able to read it.

In another room, there were floor-length tapestries, scenes of hunting and ceilidhs, picnics and battles. One, of a Scottish queen with her only child, reminded Salma of Norma and David. The reddish tinge in their hair, the pale, heavy-lidded face of the woman. The way she was holding her son, his feet balanced on a table – in a black and white photo at home, there was a photo of Norma, her hair in a beehive, balancing David in the same way but on top of an armchair.

It surprised Salma that she could make such a connection, and it struck her now that through her children she was part of the history of this country. No matter what happened, even if she did leave, and now she had every intention of leaving, this connection would always be there, stretching back generations through glens and cottages, through woodlands and coastlines. No matter what happened, her lineage would remain, bits of her DNA. She might be forgotten but her mark would have been made. In the far future, a greatgranddaughter would wonder about her black hair or how easily she tanned or where her full lips came from.

Salma walked from one room to the next. Her heartbeat was settling, her sweat cooling, but she was still on high alert, waiting to turn a corner and find him. Any minute now, they would be together at last. In a further room, there were the stuffed animals that presumably the family had hunted. There were guns on display. A trophy and then suddenly a tribal mask from another continent. Here were the acquisitions, what had been bought from far away or won, what had been looted or stolen. To her surprise, she found herself standing over an Ancient Egyptian coffin. A man whose skin was gold, with a large, heavy black wig, a white shroud. But of course, it was not a shroud, it was a casket with four gold bands drawn around the lid and the base. The collar around his neck was green, black and red. The combination and tone of the colours were perfect for Salma to wear. It would not look out of place if she had a dress in these beautiful hues. She lifted the lid of the coffin. It was empty, of course. Did she really expect a mummy? Here was where death had served time, year after year. Now all that was left was a light layer of dust, a musty smell. She put the lid down and stared at the black eyes heavily lined with kohl, the magnificent eyebrows.

She was conscious that she was getting distracted, that she had come to find Amir and was instead roaming around. Perhaps fate was giving her the chance to reconsider, to back out before it was too late. But already it was too late. When she sent him the address, when he decided to come, when she saw him in the forest, when she left Iman and ran after him.

Why was he leading her through this house which held remnants of the past? She crossed an atrium with a glass ceiling, the sun shining through, and it was as if she were in another continent. A place that was hot and bright. She quickened her steps. To go back in time is like diving into water. The body is out of its natural habitat, an intruder in the home of fish. Salma gasped as she walked into one of her favourite memories, the one in which she was wearing her green dress. She was in the corridor of Amir's flat now, heading towards his room, her back to the kitchen where she had just been sitting with his mother. He was ill, and she was carrying the notes to the lectures he had missed. Because of his mother's cooking, Salma's dress smelt of coriander and garlic. Her heart was beating because she was in his flat and she had never been in his flat before. She was seeing what he saw every day, what he touched and smelt. Behind her in the kitchen, the lids of pots wobbled over a high flame and Umm Kulthum was singing on the radio. There was nothing particularly unusual about Amir's flat or his mother, not much different from her own flat and mother, but she felt an added closeness to him. Now she knew about him what the outside world didn't need to know, because she was special to him, she was his love and worthy of his privacy.

In the real past, the past that had taken place, she had not entered his room. She had stood at the door, clutching the notes. She had stood at the door because it was the proper thing to do, because she had promised her mother, because his mother was there in the background and even though she had said to her, 'Go in, my dear. Amir is still running a fever, he's not eating, do go in,' she would judge her if she did so. She could hold it against her in the future and Salma wasn't stupid enough to fall into such a trap. So, she had stood at the door and when he saw her, he jumped out of bed, completely taken by surprise, dishevelled and sweaty in his pyjamas. Handsome, she had thought, and she was flooded with dread, thinking, oh no, oh no, what if he did not have influenza as his mother said but one of those deadly diseases they had been studying.

In the real past, she had giggled and not returned his hug. She had averted her face and said, as primly as she could, 'Do you want to pass on your flu?' In the past she had behaved as one behaves when there is everything to be gained. But now this was not the true past, the past that had happened, it was only an echo of it, a mirage to dip in and out of, her chest constricted, her body knowing full well that it did not belong in this fantasy, that it could not last long and soon she would pop back into the present. When the dead are brought back to life, they are not brought back to live. When the dead are brought back to life, they do not linger. The miracle is in the resurrection; it is not a reversal of destiny.

Now, Salma the woman entered Amir's room. She did not

hesitate, she did not giggle. Like the diver and the mountain climber, she knew that her time in these depths and these heights was limited. She must make her mark and leave, there was no time for preamble, no time for shyness or playing hard to get. She would not avert her face, she would not be prim. But the bed was empty and that came as a shock. He was not here. He had led her that far, all the way to his bedroom, and then he was not here. The anger made it even more difficult to breathe, the gasp of disappointment an unyielding attempt to suck air in. She must back out, to search for him elsewhere, in another version of the past.

His room led to another room, a heavy door to push and suddenly she was outdoors on a university campus where she was surrounded by students coming and going, their loud clamour, their youth brushing past her with its uncertainty and deceptive promise. She squeezed her way through the throng. There was hardly any room for her here; she was not welcome. A voice from a loudspeaker announced the start of an event or a rally, the latest graduation photos up for sale. Salma could not make out the words. If he was here, embedded in this crowd, how could she ever find him?

She was shoved and pushed out the way. It was congested to the extent that the students would trample on her if she fell. And yet she had to keep going. She had ventured further than intended, covered more ground than she should; already it was too late. The portals behind her had shut, she could not retrace her steps even if she wanted to. Perhaps that portrait of the Scottish noblewoman and her son should have been sufficient for her, that tapestry which recalled her husband and his mother. Gratitude should have held her in check, made her reconsider. Perhaps that Ancient Egyptian coffin should have reminded her of the temporariness of life. Staring death in the face, she should have felt awe and remorse, or at the very least caution.

On she went, fighting to reach him, crossing a busy road where there was no provision for pedestrians. She zigzagged her way through jammed cars and buses, impatient motorcyclists and children selling boxes of tissue paper. Car horns and vendors shouting. Although she could not see Amir in front of her, she did not feel lost. She followed her instinct and it told her not to turn right but to go up ahead. She knew which building she should walk into.

It was a clinic, his clinic. She recognised it from the photos he had sent her. He was showing off, that's what it was, bringing her to where he could be in an advantageous position, where he could remind her that he was the successful doctor and she was not. Who was the smarter one now, the one with the higher grades, the neater notes, the one the teachers praised? In his clinic, she must be humble. She must know her place. After all, she was a mere massage therapist and he was a surgeon with a scalpel.

There was much to admire in the clinic. It was big, clean and well equipped. Minor surgery was performed here, as well as medical consultations. There were no patients now, but that was because the clinic closed in the middle of the afternoon. In the evening, after Amir had his siesta, it re-opened, and he worked late into the night. He would happily schedule a patient in for midnight and not get back home until two a.m. All this he had told her on the phone. She had coaxed the mundane details of his life out of him. What he considered dull, she considered nourishment. What he saw as matter-of-fact, she saw enhanced and plumped up with nostalgia. She let herself slow down, allowed herself to linger and indulge her curiosity. She looked at the rows of chairs, she noticed the calendar on the wall. She smiled at the stack of magazines in the corner, the water cooler next to them. A receptionist or even two worked here, nurses who were young and pliable. Did he flirt with them or lead them on? Envy made her skin damp, her cheeks flushed. And there he was when she turned, at last, wearing his red T-shirt, just as she had imagined him, just as she had thought he would be. All there, skin, height, smell and smile. The bulk of him. Not only the voice but flesh and blood.

She walked into his arms and that was the end of it. The end of the chase and the waiting, the speculation and the games. She would never be the same again.

Afterwards, when he left, she lay flat on her back on the operating table. She looked up and counted the circular lights beaming down at her. One, two, three, four, five, six. She closed her eyes and she could still see a blurred equivalent of them, also six. She tried to move her arms, but she couldn't. She tried to move her legs. She turned her head to see where all her strength had gone. There was a pail and it was full of muscle tissue.

She screamed until her voice was larger than the pain, bigger than her anger. It flooded her, and she passed out. Even then she could see the surgical scars and the stiches all along her arms and thighs.

'Salma, Salma.' She thought it was one of her friends come to rescue her. They owed her this at least.

But the face looking down at her was neither Iman's nor Moni's. 'Mum,' said Salma. It was Norma as Salma had never seen her. The loose sixties dress, the beehive hairstyle, the warm red in her hair.

Norma looked down at her. 'You poor thing,' she said. She dressed Salma and then she pushed the bed. She pushed it through the clinic and down the street, she pushed it across a whole city. Salma dozed and cried, she rambled about how she had come to him with desire and he had greeted her with a surgical scalpel. When she remembered who was helping her now, she said, thank you, thank you.

'You help me too,' said Norma. 'You've always been kind.'

Salma couldn't remember what she had ever done for Norma. Nothing special, nothing to be proud of. A free massage once in a while, taking an interest in her aches and pains. Nothing more. Perhaps that's what counted at the end, the actions one considered small and casual, not the big ones carried on the peg of self-righteousness.

Back through the university campus, back through the corridor of Amir's flat, back inside the museum, past the Ancient Egyptian coffin and the stuffed animals. Out again to the fresh air. When they reached the edge of the forest, Norma lifted Salma and laid her gently on the ground. 'That's as far as I can go,' she said. 'You have to find your own way now.'

It took Salma time to figure out how she could move. She could not crawl. There was only one way. Using her elbows, she could drag her body after her. Slowly, slowly. She made her way into the forest, trying to get back to where she had come from, back to the blue trail. She started to call out, 'Iman, Moni.'

They heard her and came to where she was. The three of them recognisable to each other: Iman, Salma, Moni. They exclaimed and swapped stories – at least Moni and Salma did, Iman grunted and yowled. They wept with sorrow, not sure whether it was for themselves or each other, for it appalled Iman to see her bold friend flat as a doormat, it pained Salma to see Moni, once tall and regal, reduced to a Swiss ball. And Moni could not get over the shock of what Iman had become – without dignity, inhuman and unable to speak.

'He took my strength instead of my virtue,' Salma said. 'That's what happened. He dug inside and took my muscles.'

For a long time, the three of them purred and comforted each other. They murmured laments and whined in rhythm. They were freed from pride and convention, freed from the need to put on a brave face or pretend that things were not as bad as they appeared to be. They were friends again and eventually, after they cried themselves to sleep and woke up with the sun, they asked, what now? Iman and Moni looked at Salma. She was their leader and always would be. No matter what, they would always look to her for guidance. They trusted her. 'What now, Salma?'

Chapter Fifteen

'We must return,' she said. That was all she could offer. The others understood her in their own way. A physical return. Their bodies back to how they had been before, able to stand tall, to bend when they wanted to bend, to move with ease. This was the most pressing kind of return. A return to dignity, to humanity and strength. How else to imagine a future, a way of picking up where they had left off. A literal return to the grounds of the monastery and from it to their cottage? The cottage was only theirs until Monday morning. If they did not get there in time, what would happen to their things? Mullin would gather them all together, haphazardly no doubt, but with enough finality to prepare the cottage for the next set of holiday tenants. A spiritual return? Not yet. Their insides were too dark to contemplate a revival, their burdens too crushing.

We have to move, said Salma. The three of us together, we must find a way to make progress. She was the least mobile of them, the most helpless.

Moni said, 'You must be in the middle, Salma. Iman and I

will be at either side of you. You will tell us where to go, but we will be the ones pulling you.'

They pulled her like a rug, dragged her across the floor of the forest. Moni clutched one arm under her elbow, Iman slung the other around her shoulder. There were no blue trails any more in the forest, no red trails or orange. They were on their own. Salma stared up at the bits of sky that showed through the treetops. She saw the sun and she said, 'We need to head east, we need to move back this way instead of straight ahead.'

They moved as a group. Salma had Moni to her right, Iman to her left. Their pace was slow but matched, their progress even. Salma's back began to ache. Dragged over roots and uneven paths, her skin became raw and bruised. They stopped for frequent breaks, to tend each other's wounds, to catch their breath. For it was not only Salma who was struggling, Moni too had her fair share of bruises and Iman, although more suited to the outdoors, was often distracted and fretful, her protruding tongue a source of irritation, her whines more frequent.

'Iman wants to sing for us,' said Moni. And Iman did sing. Or at least tried to sing. She had forgotten all the words to her Euphrates laments. The tunes were still there, embedded in her altered mind. And though she was yowling, it made her feel better, achieving a certain kind of release. Tears came to Salma's eyes when she remembered Iman's beautiful voice. When she remembered Iman's hair and her smoky eyes. We must return, she said to herself.

The trees became shorter and thinner, their leaves turning brown and falling. The three made their way out of the forest. There were soft white flakes on the ground, the air at first cool and then much colder. On they went until the ground was covered in snow. Salma slid faster, Moni rolled more easily, and Iman enjoyed digging her weight into the softness, leaving prints behind her. The sun shone bright. They were cold, but the quicker movement soothed them. They were making progress and soon found themselves up against a cluster of figures standing still; all of them statues made of ice. Famous people and their belongings. Tennis stars with their rackets, actors with their Oscars and smiles. There were ice sculptures of Mother Teresa and Gandhi, of Princess Diana and Martin Luther King. Moni was the one most entertained by these sculptures, identifying each one quicker than Salma could. Iman was oblivious. She could not remember these iconic figures, their household names beyond her reach.

The snow stretched out for miles and they were part of its whiteness; they were cold and numb, but being out of the forest lifted their spirits, made them feel that they had advanced. Sliding, rolling, falling off snow ridges, they clung to each other. It was Moni who was the first to laugh, followed by Salma, then Iman. Was there room for happiness? Only the kind that rose from a shared purpose, a unified effort. 'We are together,' said Moni. 'We are together,' said Salma. 'Speak, Iman, say the word "we". The word "we".' But Iman shrugged off Salma's arm and this caused Moni to stop. Iman moved in a circle. With her prints she drew a large round circumference and then she joined the other two inside it. That was her understanding of 'we', the three of them together.

'I missed you both,' said Moni, and she told them about

what happened to her at the cottage. 'I missed you both,' said Salma and told them what happened to her with Amir. I missed you both, Iman wanted to say but could not put into words her transformation, her free romping in the forest where it was eat or be eaten, where no one knew her name.

Moni was not sure where they were. The snow did not make sense. It was meant to be late summer, wasn't it? When they stopped and Iman made the circle around them, Moni was surprised at her own stillness. It was as if she had been rolling for hours, it was as if rolling was now her natural state and stillness an aberration. She was not as cold as she expected to be, as she usually was in the thick of winter, struggling to keep warm. Snow was not as hostile as she had always thought it to be. She was not in fear of it. Nor was she out of breath any more; she had kept pace with the others. Granted, Salma and Iman were not in peak form but, then, neither was she. She gazed at the glitter around her, it was not different from a desert, but with snow instead of sand, with white instead of yellowish brown. Ripples and curves, ridges and uneven surfaces that the wind had shaped and furrowed. How unlike Moni to take such note of her surroundings, to see and experience!

Iman was learning language all over again. Opposites intrigued her. Black fur, white ice. Warm breath, freezing snow. She swallowed huge gulps of it, felt it turn to water in her mouth and body. She must listen in order to learn. She must listen to Salma's voice, trying to reach her, to filter through what she had become. Iman. Iman. Salma was saying her name, repeating it, so that Iman could never forget it. Never forget its meaning and how it was a simple word that was as light as a spark, as pretty as a glow, as necessary as air, always special.

Salma felt warm and safe between her two friends. They would not harm her, they were here for her. Out of the three of them, she was the one who had full faith in friendship. The one to whom sisterhood was the most valuable and worthy of investments. Moni and Iman might see her as their leader, but she was the one who needed them. She could not now move an inch without them. When would her strength come back, would it ever? When we return. That was the answer. They must keep on moving. They had stopped long enough. It was now time to soldier on. Moni on her right, Iman on her left, dragging her through the snow.

They plunged, the three of them, holding on to each other, cascading through snow as the ground fractured and gave way beneath them. An avalanche. They screamed and fell through a cloud of white, a flurry that gathered momentum, lifted them high and swiped them down the mountain slope. Down they tumbled until they could not hold on to each other any longer, could not see at all, each one in her own white darkness, each electrified by her own shock. Eventually there was a stop, a deposit, a pile-up and they were beneath it, buried.

It was Iman who was able to scramble out first. Iman, who pulled out Salma and then, with Salma directing her, was able to find Moni and pull her out too.

'I thought I'd died,' said Moni. 'I really did.' She was like a snowball herself, almost invisible in this landscape. It had taken Salma and Iman a long time to find her.

At the bottom of the mountain, they found a gathering

of people. But these people could offer neither hospitality nor directions. These were eating themselves, chewing on a hand or pulling up their knees and gnawing on a foot. Each of them was alone, absorbed in themselves, they would not eat each other. Nor were they interested in the three women who were passing through. They could barely look up at them, so intense was their concentration on their own pieces of flesh.

Salma insisted on drawing them in conversation. 'Why are you doing this to yourselves? There are plants that could be eaten, fish and other good things. You are harming yourselves.'

Her pleas were unanswered. What she said fell on deaf ears. Iman and Moni, sensing danger, dragged their friend away. She protested, saying that they had a duty to help others, to save them from themselves, to guide them to what was right and safe.

'Are we in a position to preach?' Moni scolded her. 'Look at us.'

'Better than them,' said Salma.

'I don't know any more,' said Moni, 'who is better than whom.' And when she said that, her body relaxed. Her neck, perpetually bent forward, became less stiff. She could move it a little from side to side, even though she could not look straight up.

They kept on moving.

'I must eat,' said Salma. 'If I am to grow my strength again, I must have protein.'

A chill ran through Iman. She remembered a story the Hoopoe had told her. A story about a young camel, a jaguar, a hyena, a crow and their king, the lion. Iman began to cry. She began to whimper and scratch the ground.

'Oh dear, Iman. I would never eat you,' said Salma. 'How can you even think it? Don't you know me? Don't you know who I am? If I had the use of my arms, I would be hugging you now. Please don't cry.'

'Hunt for her,' said Moni. 'Catch her something to eat.'

So Iman was sent to hunt and she came back with a mouse and a toad. To Salma, the taste and texture did not matter. All she wanted was to build her muscles again. But it would take more than food. They had to keep going, keep moving; they must return.

The land turned rocky, its colours lighter than before, the vegetation thinner. They passed a group of people whose mouths were sealed across with stiches and whose eyes blazed with shame. 'What have you done to deserve this?' Salma asked. They must have spread lies, she thought, or bore false witness; they must have killed with their tongues. They must have said yes when it should have been no. They must have ruined lives with a word or more than one word. 'What have you done?' But no one could answer her, they could not move their lips. At the end, one of them pointed to an inscription on the rocks. 'They kept silent when they should have spoken out.'

Iman, Salma and Moni kept on moving. To protect Salma from the path that was now rocky, Iman carried her on her back while Moni rolled along. This slowed them down, so they went back to dragging Salma on the ground, bumping her along, while she kept her eyes shut and tried not to cry out from the pain.

The landscape turned mountainous around them. There were no longer any trees or any shade, just the sun pressing down on them, scorching their heads and stabbing their eyes. A path led them up to a hill and the cool interior of a cave. As soon as they stepped in, they heard the drip-drop sound of water, touched the wet walls and their eyes were soothed by the shadows that flickered around the cave. Further in was a hot spring, its water releasing vapours that were irresistible. Thirsty and dirty, they did not even confer but plunged in: Moni with a splash, Iman diving head first, pulling Salma with her. The water was everything they needed. It was comfort and welcome.

Iman felt the water penetrate the fur of her coat, reach deep to her skin. Her human skin was buried under the fur, a distant mark of her identity. She dived down and found that she could hold her breath for longer. She was like a seal, gliding away from her friends and back again. She felt the strength of her body and when she opened her eyes under the water, her tongue was safe in her mouth, her legs were her legs, her lower body that of a woman, her feet human. She struck through the surface of the water, pulled herself up but found that she was exactly how she had been when she first dived in.

In the warm water, Moni relaxed. Bobbing on the surface, she gazed at the walls of the cave, paintings in blues and reds. They were children's paintings, flowers as big as faces, bodies as thin as sticks, mops of hair and everyone smiling. Moni smiled too. She did not know how to swim but she was not afraid of this water, not worried that she would sink. The water was washing her, and she had always appreciated cleanliness, enjoyed the smells of soap and detergent, the scent of lemons and pine. In the water, the stiffness of her body eased. She could spread her legs out, she could raise up her arms and stretch. How good that felt, to be tall and straight again! But it was only in the water. As soon as she stepped out of the pool, she sprang back into a ball, her knees up to her chest, her arms tight around her knees, neck craned forward.

Salma too, in the water, became her former self. The strength flowed back into her arms and legs. She could stand up, her feet touching the slippery bottom of the pool, her weight held up by the warm water. It was just like normal, how it had always been. She was not doomed to life flat on her back. The three of them were heading in the right direction; they were surely returning. This optimism lingered even when she pulled herself out of the water and found that, again, she had no strength. Again, she was unable to stand up tall or even to crawl. The water had not altered any of them. The water only showed them what they could be. But 'only' was not the right word, for the water gave them what was just as important as change. The water gave them hope. The water made them stronger in faith.

So, on they went. Through the valley of fear, where shadows played with their minds and sudden noises made their skin crawl. They saw visions of their own future deaths, the ultimate agony and ugliness, the loneliness of the grave. And that was not all. In the valley were spectres of known fears so that Salma submitted again to Amir's scalpel and Moni was made smaller and smaller by the boy's growing body. Iman was in a war zone again, dodging gunfire, stumbling over a corpse, touching softness that was mangled flesh, limbs torn off and flung. In the valley of fear, the three of them clung to each other as the shadows pounded them with nightmares and squeezed their hearts with fright.

Daybreak saved them. The first rays of the sun drove out the malevolent shadows. 'We used to pray,' said Salma when she saw the faint layer of light over the night. 'What happened to that?' None of them could remember when they had last prayed. When they had last prayed properly and it was not like brushing their teeth, going through the motions with their minds elsewhere. Noon jumbled into night, sunset mixed with dawn. They had come to the loch with their prayer mats and copies of the Qur'an, but they had not looked after them, they had not kept them safe. They had come to a country where people had stopped praying and not realised that they were the ones brought here to pray. They did not consciously take up the worship which others had left. They did not realise that they were a continuation, needed to fill a vacuum, awaited by the ancient forests and masses of rocks. They misunderstood their role. They underestimated their own importance and exaggerated their shortcomings. They inflated their problems and followed their egos, counselled each other but rejected what was right. Their quarrels taking up space, their connections weakening. And now they were far away, deep in the realm of consequence. Iman could not remember the words, neither Moni nor Salma could stand up straight. But they could pray with their hearts, couldn't they? With their eyelids, with the breath they pulled in and out. They could, weakened as they were. Imperfect prayers, like those of the unclean and those who had not yet fully repented. Feeble prayers, but sincere because they were in genuine need.

The sun shrugged off the clouds and they saw ahead of them green and water, woodlands and glens. Beautiful and familiar, but suddenly Salma could no longer lead. 'I don't know the way,' she said. 'I'm not sure any more.'

They lingered and counted seven directions that they could take. North, south-east, over that hill, back towards the river. They could go straight, or they could go west, or they could head down to the beach.

Iman looked at Salma for guidance. Moni said, 'Salma, you decide.'

But Salma could not guide them any more. She had brought them this far and now she was stumped. There was nothing she could add, no insight, no ideas. After saying, 'We used to pray,' she had run out of knowledge, she had reached the end of her usefulness. They were stuck. Time passed. A whole day passed. Perhaps Iman would sniff out a new trail. Perhaps it was Moni's turn to take the lead. They waited for guidance, their urgency gone, the impetus disrupted.

Iman was the first to see the Hoopoe. He hovered over them and he was not the cute bird who had perched on her windowsill telling stories. Not any more. His wings were powerful, his crown iridescent, his plumage lustrous. He was now the mightiest of the birds, and if they accepted, he would be their guide. If they said yes, he would show them the way.

Chapter Sixteen

'In every journey,' said the Hoopoe, 'there comes a point, around three quarters of the way through, when the traveller, without a guide, can go no further. But not everyone finds a guide. Not everyone accepts a guide. Not everyone is convinced. Many would rather keep fumbling on their own, trying and trying again. They would rather risk not completing the journey, they would rather risk getting lost or content themselves with the advance already made, than follow in trust.'

So, it was up to Iman, Moni and Salma to decide. Would they follow the Hoopoe, or would they continue on their own? Would they make this spot their new home and go no further or would they try to return?

The Hoopoe circled them, and they watched the black and white stripes of his wings, the way the sun touched his crown. Then he flew a little bit further away and perched on the branch of an aspen. The three friends were left to confer. Iman did not hesitate. She had known him the longest and now it made sense that he was the one who could lead the way to salvation. Moni weighed the pros and cons

and decided she had less to lose and more to gain. Salma was
the one who struggled. She had left her country and followed
David, she had run after Amir's red T-shirt, she was tired and
bitter. But she would not remain alone without her sisters. If
they were going with the Hoopoe, she would go with them
too. After all, she could not go far on her own.

Iman moved closer to the Hoopoe.

'I accept you as my guide,' Moni said.

'I will go with you,' Salma said. 'Show us the way.'

He flew, and they followed. They moved as before, with
Moni and Iman on either side of Salma, dragging her on
the ground. A few feet. They had barely made progress
when there was a change. Unexpected, because it came
early, because it happened unannounced, without ritual or
preparation. But it was the transformation they had all longed
for, their burdens slipping away. Iman became human again.
Moni unfurled and straightened. Strength coursed through
Salma's body.

They laughed and hugged each other. It seemed like an
eternity since they had last heard Iman speak, seen Moni
standing up, felt Salma's firm embrace. For a long time they
celebrated, touching their own faces and bodies in wonder.
Moni raised both arms up in the air, Salma lifted Iman –
she could do that – and Iman started to sing the loudest she
had ever sung. Salma did jumping jacks, Moni clapped her
hands, Iman combed her fingers through her beautiful hair.
All three knelt and touched their foreheads to the ground, in
gratitude.

They forgot about the Hoopoe and they forgot how ur-
gently they had wanted to return.

When Iman noticed he had gone, she reassured the other two that he would come back. 'We must wait,' she said.

'Can't you call him?' said Moni.

'No,' said Iman. 'He will come on his own.' She told them all the stories the Hoopoe had told her. She told them the one about the bear who killed its master by mistake, the sad tale of the selkie, the story of the young camel and that of the frozen snake. She told them the story about Nathan, who long ago lived at the loch, of the sin he committed and how he tied himself up with chains and threw the key in the river. How he travelled to Jerusalem and how one day he cut open a fish and found the key to his freedom.

Moni and Salma listened to her for hours, captivated by her voice and the tales she was spinning. 'Iman, you are no longer shy,' said Salma. The petulance was gone and the studied boredom. The revulsion against being cast as feminine, or even human, all melted away. Iman had grown up. She wore maturity like a cape and it was the best piece of clothing she had ever put on.

'I love life,' said Moni. And the other two laughed. This did not sound like the Moni they knew. But here she was, cross-legged on the grass, a flower in her hand. She was beginning to look around her, to see all that was beautiful and fascinating. To step away from herself and her problems. To be more than a mother of a disabled child, more than a full-time carer. It should not be a burden looking after Adam, a sacrifice to be self-righteous about, it should be carried with firmness and ease. With gratitude too, because he was special in his own way, unique. If she let her guard down, she could be more generous, more willing to mother another child, a sister for Adam or a brother. That would be moving on – members of a family, each with their weaknesses and strengths. My children, she would say to others. Show photos of Adam being loved and accepted by another child, someone who would never judge him, someone who would know him in a new way.

And Salma. How had she changed? She would not tell them. 'Speak to us,' said Moni. 'Why are you quiet?' asked Iman.

Salma could not yet translate her hurt into words, it was not only her body he had carved into, taken out her strength, tossed it away in a surgical pail. It was not only that. She moved away from her two friends. She lay back on the grass even though she could now sit and stand up. She could braid Iman's hair and do push-ups. She rolled to her side and cried because she had not had a good cry for a long time. And they came to her, they did not leave her to cry alone. Iman to comfort her and Moni to say kind words. Salma had always been the strong one, the one whose life was sorted, the one who was envied, who knew what to do and what she wanted – but all that had been fragile.

'I want to tell you about my mother-in-law,' she finally said. 'And don't expect a mother-in-law joke.'

Moni laughed out loud. Iman smiled. She had met Norma many times. There was nothing remarkable about her, nothing of note. She was, to Iman, another chore that Salma slotted into her busy life.

'She saved me,' said Salma, and told them how Norma had carried her out of that clinic, back through time and countries, to the forest, where they were waiting for her.

Iman said. 'It wasn't her that saved you but what you did for her over the years.'

'Nothing special,' said Salma. 'Nothing that anyone else wouldn't have done. If David had married any other woman, she would have treated his mother the same way.'

Moni raised her eyebrows, 'Given her free massages?'

'Not necessarily,' said Salma. 'Not if she wasn't a therapist.' And when she said that, she felt a whole sense of satisfaction that she had eased someone's pain. That she had helped. Why all these years putting herself down, ashamed that she had failed her PLABs, that she was not a doctor as she had always dreamt of being? Hiding her low self-esteem beneath the efficiency, aggressively pushing her children to achieve what she couldn't, the years she lied to her parents, the low salary she continued to accept just to be able to say, 'I work at the hospital.' And when Amir surfaced on social media, all she had been willing to give up because he had addressed her as Doctor. She had been unfair to herself.

They waited for the Hoopoe. They chatted and waited. They sat in silence and waited. Salma grew restless. Perhaps they should set out on their own. They could complete the journey without the Hoopoe, figure out a way, instead of this endless waiting. Moni was thinking ahead to all that needed to be done to get back to the city; this wait was a waste of time. Perhaps, she thought, the role of the Hoopoe was over. To re-store their bodies was no mean feat, a miracle in itself. Did they still need him now? Iman listened out for the sound of wings; she scanned the sky. She was sure that it was not yet over. If they set out, they would get lost, they would not return. 'Wait a little longer,' she urged her friends. 'Be patient.'

The sun began to set. Even if the Hoopoe were to show up now, it would be too late. They would not be able to make progress in the dark, they would have to wait for day. They were almost asleep, huddled together under the tree, when the Hoopoe came back. He came to them not as guide but as storyteller. The story he told was for the three of them, not only Iman. It was Attar's fable, *The Conference of the Birds*. They had known it – read it, heard it, saw the bird illustrations in a book – but then, over time, forgot.

'The birds of the world,' the Hoopoe said, 'gathered to discuss a prospective journey to find their king. Many found excuses not to set out. The journey was too arduous, they said. We would get lost, they said and stayed behind. The group that flew out did face many perils. They flew over deserts and mountains, for years they travelled and at times it felt as if their whole life would be spent on the route. Some got distracted by the charming scenery, some were eaten by wild animals. Some went mad from hunger and dashed themselves against the rocks. Some were burnt and drowned and molested. Only thirty birds survived to the very end. They reached the majestic court battered and bruised without feathers or strength. Why on earth would His Majesty receive you? the court's herald said. You are nothing to him. When they begged and cried, they were granted an audience. At long last they were in the presence of their Beloved. What did they see? They saw the whole world and other worlds, myriad suns and stars, lights upon lights. Within this dazzling reflection they saw their greatest shock – they saw themselves. Thirty birds. How could that be? they wondered. It was as if they were looking into a mirror. It took them some time to solve the puzzle. Their existence was within him because nothing existed outside of him. The birds merged with the one they had flown towards, the one who was themselves and everything else. From the lowliness, they rose again so that seeker, destination and the way became one.'

In the morning, the women followed the Hoopoe down the mountain and across the valley. They climbed up a small hill and looked down at a clearing near a lake. They saw men busy constructing a building. They were dressed in clothes only seen in paintings and films set centuries ago. The men were not using any modern building technology and they were singing as they worked.

'It's the monastery,' said Salma. 'We are watching it being built.' Her relief that she was near a familiar landmark overcame the oddity that they had been swept back in time. The monastery meant that they were close after all to where they had started. They had indeed returned part of the way.

Caution made them hold back, made them hide themselves under a tree. The scene before them was all freshness and hope. A house of worship rising. They felt the sincerity that fuelled the manual work, men toiling to build what they might not live to see, working for a necessary grandeur and elevation. Moni, Iman and Salma saw the monks come in and takes their vows, some of which they would keep and many of which they would not be able to uphold. Vows of celibacy that were not imposed on them by the Almighty, which they took on voluntarily and then fell into sin. Iman, Salma and Moni saw the years sweep over the monastery, the waning of faith bringing with it corruption and corruption further eroding faith. They saw the abuse of little boys and the unlawful accumulation of wealth. They saw worldliness encroach upon the sacred, the secular triumphing over the religious, how this life became more important than the next. They saw enthusiasm dwindling and distractions growing until the place was empty, devoid of prayers. Then the renovations began. Architects hired to restore the original features, designers to make the apartments fit the theme. The chapel becoming a swimming pool.

But not everything was swept away. There was something of the prayers left behind, a concentration of what had been the most sincere, a density. The three of them had come upon it in the refectory, Salma first, then Iman and Moni. They felt the print left by the priest who had read the prayers up at the pulpit while the monks ate their meals. Men deprived of women experienced the deepest thankfulness for the food on their plates.

'You can see him now,' said the Hoopoe. 'If you go down and look through the window, you will be able to see the whole scene.'

The three held hands and ran down the hill. The sun shone down on them and afterwards, for the rest of their lives, they would remember this as one of their happiest moments. They would recall the anticipation and how young they felt, like little girls, with all their strength and flexibility, with easy joints and laughter in their throats. Iman held Salma's hand and Salma held Moni's hand. It started to rain, a light drizzle that sprinkled them as they moved. The water touched their heads and made them special. The hill sloped down, and they gave in to the pull of gravity, the acceleration of their steps and heartbeats. Each of them was self-conscious, aware of her restored body, how good it felt to be whole, to be upright. How good it was to have a clear mind and balance, to have a tongue that could talk and feet that could hold up her weight with ease.

'It's Nathan,' said Iman, when they looked through the window. 'I thought at first he was Mullin, but it's Nathan. He is the one reading the prayer. He is the one grateful that he had lost his chains. He came back home and had been forgiven. It is he who built the monastery.' She recognised him from the Hoopoe's description, from spending story time on him and his journey to Jerusalem. She recognised him from that time she had glimpsed his image through the window and thought he was, like her, dressed up in costume.

There he was now, through this window, no longer in chains, understanding what he was reading: every word. They recognised him as one of them, a believer, though he had not lived long enough to know the Last Prophet, nor to hear the final revelation. They had in common with him the knowledge of their Creator, the desire to seek forgiveness, the trajectory of slip and rise, the journeying to come close. They understood him, and he would have understood them too, if he had lived in their own time. The similarity between them was more than the difference. Through the window, the medieval scene was as exotic as a European painting, the rituals alien but acceptable. They had an affinity to it, an understanding that existed despite the barriers of time and race.

The scene could not last long. Just long enough for Iman to make her guess and for the three of them to bear witness. Then it flickered and was gone. The refectory was empty, the monastery in a further period of time. It could even be the future, as the furniture was different from how they had seen it, the tartan chair no longer tartan, the billiards table replaced, the design more minimal. But the pulpit was still as it was, the wooden panelling, the door and the large window. 'The room is waiting for you,' said the Hoopoe. 'It is your turn now.' That was the last thing he ever said to them, the last they saw of the shimmer of his crown and the black stripes of his feathers. 'It is your turn now.' For the final steps of the journey, the guide does not need to be there. It is the traveller's private time, the traveller's specific destiny and not that of the guide.

The three stepped into the room and they knew what they had to do. It was obvious. One after the other, they climbed the pulpit. They sat, they did not stand up. They did not need paper or book. The words were in them, memorised and often practised. Each one recited as much as she could recite. If she made a mistake, the others corrected her; if she stumbled, they nudged her memory. Each one of them had her own way of remembering. Moni kept her eyes shut. Salma looked down as if she could see the pages in her hands. Iman recited in a melodious way, unhurried and rhythmic, less of a reading than a chant. Between them, they managed whole suras and hundreds of verses. They did what they could, and they did better than they ever thought they would be able to. The walls heard them, the building heard them, the grounds too had been waiting to hear them. They were adding to what was already there, supplementing what had already been granted. There was nothing radical in what they were doing, nothing contrary. It was a continuation. A flow meandering but not changing direction, because the direction had always been the same. The paths might be infinite, but the destination one.

When they finished, it was time to go home, but the door of the refectory would not open for Salma. Iman tried the window and it would not budge. They were stuck without the Hoopoe to ask for advice. They had come this far and now here was another obstacle. They were locked in.

They conferred and even shouted for help. Moni rattled the door, Salma banged on the window. It was no use. But suddenly when Iman turned the handle of the door, it opened. They rushed to get out, but it closed again. Only Iman could open it, only Iman was allowed to pass through.

'I will not leave you,' she said to the other two. 'We came together, we leave together.'

'No,' said Salma. 'Go and our turn will come.'

Moni hugged Iman goodbye. She could do that now, the tenderness in her, the spontaneous gestures of affection coming out.

The door closed behind Iman and the others paced the room in silence. When Moni tried the window, it opened for her. She understood straight away that she would have to leave alone. She would not be able to take Salma through with her. It was futile to protest. All she could do was hug her friend and then climb out with a joke, 'I would never have imagined being able to do this.'

Salma was alone. She tried the door, she tried the window, but neither were to be her exits. Was she the one destined to stay here on her own?

Unless there was another way out. A way that was not a

window or a door. She paced the room and found it – a hatch at the bottom of the wall panel. Small but not too small. She squeezed her body through it and found herself in a tunnel with damp soil around her. The air was dank and all lay in darkness, but she crawled along the earth, crawled slowly and crawled more. It took a long time, dragging herself through the damp soil, inching forward, waiting for a glimpse of light. Trusting that it would be there, the darkness could not go on for ever. A chink, and the sun was there ahead, at last, there it was ahead. Salma increased her speed, no longer feeling the effort now she was nearly there. When she finally emerged and stood up, she found herself staring straight at her car.

Moni and Iman were waiting for her. They had packed up all their things, including hers, and left the cottage.

'It's Monday,' explained Iman, handing Salma the car key.

Salma kicked the car wheel in frustration. 'We were meant to go visit Lady Evelyn's grave yesterday. Sunday is the only day. Now I can't drive the car into the estate!'

'We can still go,' said Moni. 'I don't mind walking. I can walk now. We'll leave the car at the forest and cross the railway line by foot.'

'It will be twelve miles, Moni. Can you do this?' Iman's voice was gentle.

'I'll try my best.'

'We can't not go,' said Salma. 'It's why we came in the first place. We have to.'

Chapter Seventeen

They heard the clap of gunshot and the stags bellowing in the distance. Around them, the hills and crags were in shades of rust and copper, stretching out for miles, and the more the three of them climbed, the more they felt that there was nothing else except them and the glen they were walking through. The path was muddy and often there were rocks that were sharp to step on. The gradient was not steep but gradual. Often, they forgot they were climbing, until a dip downwards afforded them a larger view of clouds touching the brown mountains, the vast moorland spread out with hills dotted in white rocks and yellow heather. Slopes of hills with ancient, unpronounceable names, rocky valleys and rough grass. A waterfall just like that, appearing out of nowhere, the gushing sound of it, then a smaller one and another. A river ran parallel to the path, sometimes twisting narrow and becoming shallow as a stream with islands of pebbles and greenery. Sometimes, as they were walking, the water was just there, within reach, and sometimes instead there was a steep precipice leading to the river. The gurgle came from every side and above them. It filled their ears and they sensed the flow underneath them, clean and cool, running under the grass, coming down from the heights of the deer forests and peaks.

Salma was following the map in Lady Evelyn's book. They were walking the dotted line that paralleled the river and curved around the mountain. Moni felt a pressure in her bladder and the continuous sounds of flowing water didn't help. She tried her best to ignore her body and keep walking. The path was wide enough for one large car, more than ample for the three of them, and they walked at the same pace, not speaking much, except to say that the weather was good, no rain, no fog, neither too cold nor too hot. And where were the hunters? they wondered. Up there, out of sight, stalking the deer in the forests and further glens? From time to time, the roar of a stag could be heard, sounding very much like the bellow of cattle. Or was that a horn to call the deer? Mile after mile, they walked. Whenever Iman glimpsed a large rock projecting up high on the hill, she thought it was Lady Evelyn's grave. But it was too early, there was still a long way to go. Whenever there was a bend in the path, Salma would think that it was the last bend, the turn after which they would see the hunting lodge ahead of them and there on the left, up on the northern hillside, would be the headstone they were looking for. Iman illusionary, Salma too optimistic, Moni more and more anxious about her need for a toilet.

There's the headstone. There it is. Wishful thinking. Seeing what one wants to see. They must keep on.

Salma had parked the car in the Achnashellach Forest car park so they were able to walk across the level crossing.

Because they were on foot, they did not need to telephone for permission to cross the railway line. A sign explained that they should just look and listen to make sure that a train wasn't coming. Once inside the estate, they followed the road upon which, if it wasn't the stalking season, Salma would have been allowed to drive her car. After two miles there was a turbine and a deer fence with a locked gate they had to climb over – Iman nimbly, Salma with care, Moni with effort. On the other side of the fence, the path was rugged, suitable only for a 4×4. They continued on.

In January 1963, when Lady Evelyn died in a nursing home in Inverness, a telephone call was made to the mosque in Woking. The story the imam heard was strange. An aristocratic Scottish woman, over ninety years old, had laid down the terms of her funeral in a will. She wished to be interned according to the rules of her faith, a faith that was not that of her family or the people around her. She wanted an imam to read the prayers in Arabic. She wanted bagpipes to be played and no Christian minister must be present. She wanted to lie facing Mecca in a place where the red stags could run over her grave. The imam took the overnight train to Inverness, far away, he later said, like the distance between Lahore and Karachi. He was met at the station and driven sixty miles by car through the mountains to the hunting lodge in Glencarron. There the family were gathered, people from the estate, those who had known Lady Evelyn and spent time with her. Apart from the imam and the deceased, there were no other Muslims in the funeral procession. Severe frost covered the ground, an icy wind carried the tunes of 'MacCrimmon's Lament'. The ground was difficult to dig but it was dug.

With no one to understand his words except the deceased, the wind, the rocks, angels and djinn, the imam asked Allah Almighty to forgive Lady Evelyn her sins and to grant her paradise. To fill her grave with comfort and light, to accept all the good she had done and overlook all that she should have done but couldn't. As was her request, the verse of light was later inscribed on an inset bronze plaque over her grave.

It was the verse which, whenever she had opened her copy of the Qur'an, she found before her. She loved it because she understood it. And she understood it because it spoke to her of something that she had known, had always known, had glimpsed in these hills that were empty but not empty, that were more rough than pretty. Even their colours were un-polished. Her spirit was here where she wanted to be buried. The people who walked at her funeral knew it and now the three women sensed it too in the gentle wind and the tough climb, in the mists that lowered over the dark peaks and lifted.

They had moved, as she had moved symbolically, from the built monastery near the loch to the emptiness of the moun-tains. Left behind the hushed, thick, sombre atmosphere of organised religion and travelled up to where there was sim-plicity and balance. Not the indulgence of the secluded life, neither the gratification of service, nor the voluptuousness of identity. No, here was aloneness. The nothing of it. Just to be small, a conscious part of the whole. Lady Evelyn could not help her faith, it was given to her without asking and it paralleled her life unpremeditated, unplanned. It was sepa-rate and part of her roles as traveller, writer and mother; her social position, her aristocratic breeding and contacts. Where was Lady Evelyn's Islam? So deep that when it surfaced it surprised her. When the Pope asked, her reply rose sincere, a reflex, the truth summoned forward by the authority of a man of God. 'I am a Muslim.' And where had that come from? From her childhood in Algiers and Cairo, the kindly servants who bowed to Allah alone and not to her parents, the murmur of their prayers, the sound of the azan floating through the window. Little girl, loved as one of them. Carried and fed, clutching the black veil of her nanny because they were leaving the house, the warm calloused hand nursing insect bites and bruises, holding up her chin to look into her eyes, voice soothing to her ears. All that she had absorbed. But her experience was not unusual for a colonial child. As a teenager, she had written in a poem, 'I felt His Presence within and around'. But this in itself was not an explanation either. Perhaps it was, as she described, the *weird cadence* of the muezzin's cry. Perhaps that sound went in and lodged itself years after she came home, her home, here, the unmistakable mauve mountains and glens, grouse and salmon, leaves turning colour, the thrill of the hunt, the smells of fear, blood and the bellows of the stags – these were hers too, her ancestry, her robust health and independence – her toughness, Scottishness and sense of entitlement – all together, one and the same.

'I can't go on,' said Moni, stopping. 'I need the toilet'.

The others stopped too. 'What toilet?' said Iman. 'We're in the middle of nowhere.' This was no tourist destination; there was neither phone signal nor picnic bench.

'Squat behind a bush,' said Salma.

'I can't.'

'What do you mean you can't?'

'I've never done that, I don't know how.'

'There is nothing to it,' said Iman.

'Even if you turn around now,' reasoned Salma, 'you won't make it in time. It's four miles back to the car.'

Moni had no choice. 'I can't believe I'm doing this,' she said, heading into the bracken.

Iman rolled her eyes at Salma. They looked the other way.

When Moni reappeared, she was distressed. 'I made a mess. It would have been easier with a skirt.' The bottom of one trouser leg was wet.

'How on earth did you do that?' said Iman.

'Never mind,' said Salma. 'It will dry. Don't worry about it.' She started to walk, expecting the others to fall in step.

'Salma, I can't go on,' said Moni. 'Not like this. I will wait here for you. I don't feel clean. I don't feel right.'

'Wash it then,' said Salma. 'From the stream.'

'That's what I want to do,' said Moni, 'but I need my own time. I don't want you hovering over me, impatient. You go on and I will head back and meet you at the car.'

Salma was disappointed in her and for her. Moni had come so far, walked for hours, overcoming her early reluctance and weakness. She had tried her best. Iman was willing to argue with her, but it was no use. Salma handed her the car keys and the two kept on walking.

They walked faster, believing they were two thirds of the way. They stepped over puddles and passed a bridge made up of only two wires, one high up to hold on to and another one to slide the feet along. 'You use this bridge at your own risk', the sign said. Thankfully, they did not need to cross but just to keep walking and walking. The grave would be up on a hillock to their left.

The path rose up and suddenly there was a dip, the glen spread out beneath them. About a kilometre ahead, a jeep was blocking the road, stationary but pointing towards them. Two men in hunting gear were leaning on the bumper. 'They can see us,' said Iman and that situation lasted a good ten minutes, the men becoming clearer as they approached them. One of them was holding a greyhound on a leash. The other was eating an apple. Closer still, they noticed there was also a puppy, a spaniel, frisking around the men and the jeep.

The dogs barked as Salma and Iman approached. The encounter could not be avoided, but that they were heading for the grave did not elicit surprise. 'Another mile,' said the man who was crunching the apple. 'When you see the shooting lodge ahead of you, the grave would be up to your left.' Iman cooed over the puppy. She knelt to stroke it, declaring that she had fallen in love with it, making the men smile. Salma reminded Iman that they must keep going. Iman, standing up, did not hide the fact that she was reluctant to leave.

The path twisted and, looking back, they could no longer see the men with their car. They speculated about them. So, they were the deer hunters, but what were they doing just standing there with a jeep? Were they waiting for a signal about the whereabouts of the deer? Were they already done for the day? Their hunting clothes had made them look as if they were from another century, but it was because they belonged to a different tradition, a way of life that Salma and Iman would never know. And yet Lady Evelyn had known this life, was part of it. Worlds intersecting, overlapping.

Above them, the clouds separated and a shaft of sunlight touched the mountains like in religious paintings.

Iman started talking about a sign she had seen near the car park. 'A hostel, and the sign said, "help needed".'

Salma didn't reply.

Iman went on, 'I want to go back and ask about this position. Maybe it would include lodging too. My things are in the car. I could just stay on.'

Salma felt the same sense of rejection as before. So, Iman hadn't changed completely, hadn't put away her reluctance to return with her to the city. Better humour her this time. Let her ask and, nine out of ten, it would come to nothing. 'Sure, no harm trying. You can ring the doorbell and enquire when we get back,' she said.

'Those two men could give me a ride back in their car. It would save time.'

'What a crazy idea!'

'I can say the Fatiha for Lady Evelyn from here, I'm close enough. It's just as good as reaching the grave.'

They argued back and forth, but Salma felt calm, a little detached. She did not want to squander her energy, she did not want to tarnish the journey. No ugly words or recriminations. No tears. If Iman already felt as if she had reached her destination, Salma couldn't force her to keep going. They would all meet later at the car.

So, Salma walked alone, the wind stinging her eyes. Up here in the mountains, it was already autumn. She was by herself and it felt as if it were a weaker position. From the beginning, she had been the one who had cared the most about visiting the grave. The others were never as keen; she was leading them, but they did not want to be led, or perhaps there were places to which you could not lead others, at least not the whole way. Perhaps she was being unfair. Moni and Iman had done their best. She walked faster but was suddenly vulnerable to anxieties. What if she got lost? What if she got hurt all alone in the middle of nowhere? The more she walked, the more she doubted herself. What if she had already passed the grave?

The road went on, the views of mountains and gullies, brambles and bracken, burns flowing, marshes that were in every shade of brown. The last stretch would always be the most difficult, the longest, accompanied by silence, too late for enthusiasm, too late for change of any kind. She must keep going.

She was tired too, she had to admit. Her knees were beginning to ache, her back a little stiff. She did not want to stop and stretch, nor eat a snack. She did not want to risk losing momentum, giving up like the others had given up. Come on, come on, you are nearly there, one last push. It would have been better if David had come with her. He would not have left her alone. He would have stayed with her until the very end. She should have thought of this – a trip for the two of them, a couple. Instead of the whole trouble with the women's group, instead of Moni and Iman. She missed him and suddenly she could make Glenuaig Lodge in the distance and soon, very soon, there would be the grave up on the hill.

Up on the left, she spotted the two gravestones, the taller one that belonged to Toby Sladen, Lady Evelyn's grandson, and then the shorter, older, broken one. It was a steep climb and she scrambled through stalks and brambles. She had made it, she had found it and here she was.

'Lady Evelyn Cobbold, 1867–1963, Daughter of the 7th Earl of Dunmore, Widow of John Dupuis Cobbold.'

Salma sat near the grave, catching her breath. When she could speak, she greeted Lady Evelyn, knowing that her presence could be sensed, maybe even her prayers could be heard. She called her by her Muslim name – Zainab. Your state is my future, Zainab, one day I will follow to where you are, and I will know what you now know. Motionless after hours of walking, Salma could feel the wind cool against her face and parched lips, the muscles of her thighs stretching. Here she was at last looking down at the bronze plaque, the photo of which had caused such offence and made the women in the group stay away. Certainly, someone had tried to cross the words out, clawed at the flat bronze with a rock or a knife, fuelled by outrage. Lady Evelyn had requested the original Arabic verse, but her exact wishes could not be fulfilled and instead an English translation was used. Words that could be read by anyone walking past, understood and objected to. *Allah is the light* . . .

The clouds shifted and a shaft of sun touched the bronze, blurring the words and the grooves that had been scraped in over them. Salma blinked, her eyes dazzled. Strange that now, instead of the words, she could see her own smoky reflection. It was blurry at first, but when she took a deep breath and wiped her eyes, she could see more clearly. It was not the Salma of today, weary and scruffy, instead it was her future, all she had ever done layered and marked over her features.

She did not recoil in horror, nor smile with joy. The future was stories repeating themselves. The future was a more pungent, more bitter extension of the present. A fresh mix of desires fulfilled, and others thwarted, the improbable and the inevitable. She will earn more, enjoy her work and her youngest son will graduate from medical school. She will dance at her daughter's wedding, carry a grandchild, book tickets for her and David to go on pilgrimage to Mecca.

Hints of her friends' futures floated towards her too, the bronze plaque a screen, a whirlpool of images, translucent as a mirage. Moni succeeds, against the odds, in getting Murtada to return from Saudi Arabia. They have another baby, a bright wilful little girl who sparkles their life until Murtada announces that he is returning to Sudan and he wants his family with him. No, says Moni again, I will not leave this country. Adam, Adam, Adam, Moni says, and her future is a more complex negotiation than the present. Iman's English improves. She works and can bring her mother over from Syria for a visit. But her greatest material success comes in middle age with the widower she lands as a husband, a house whose mortgage has been paid off.

Then the images were of Salma again. The positive medical test, the hushed voices and days in hospital. For her to be buried in her beloved Egypt would be too costly, too inconvenient, she was destined to stay put. Loved until the very end, her husband devoted, her children gathered around her.

She covered her face with her hands. The future was not meant to be seen. This was not why she had come, not to see the end but to save the present. Not to learn the obvious lesson that there was less time left. Is that all you will give me,

Lady Evelyn? Is this how you receive your sister, Zainab? I want to know how I can go on. How I can keep going without taking a fall, without giving up or making a fool of myself. You were lonely too, you were tired, help me. I came here for rejuvenation, a recipe for patience, a cure for disenchantment, the will to keep going, keep going, without wandering astray. I came to get the secret of keeping restlessness at bay, to learn how to feel settled. I came to see you, not to see myself.

She staggered down the slope; where was the strength now to walk six miles back to the car? A shot rang out. Close enough to make her freeze. She stepped away from the path and crouched down next to the rocks. She could now hear what must be the faint gallop of the wounded deer, the last sprints before the final collapse. Flooded with fatigue, she stretched out on the grass and looked up at the sky. She watched the cloud formations. Peace. The kind without thoughts or voices, neither images nor words.

She continued lying until the ground became uncomfortable for her back, the grass damp through her clothes. She pushed herself up and received the shot that was intended for her.

'I died,' she said to Moni and Iman in the car park. 'Then I felt better for it. It was easy to walk back.'

They had heard the gunshots and were relieved that she was here in the car, that she was safe, sane and strong. They were relieved that she would now be able to drive them back home.

Iman sat in the front seat next to her. Her queries about the 'help wanted' sign at the hostel had come to nothing but making the attempt had felt like the first small step towards independence. She could be herself without hating the femininity she had been born with. She could still learn even if she hadn't finished school. She could be Salma's best friend and nobody's pet.

Moni, clean now, was comfortable and soothed, ready to go back. She had walked much further than she could ever have imagined, exceeded her own limits. Given another chance, perhaps, just perhaps, she would do it all over again and succeed. She handed Salma a bottle of water.

'Did you remember to take a selfie at the grave?' asked Iman.

'No. And no one can ever prove that you two weren't there with me.'

This made them all laugh, and Moni said the prayer for the return journey.

Author's Note

In my favourite verses of the Qur'an, a woman reads out loud, to a gathering of men, or mostly men, a letter she has just received. The woman is Bilqis, the Queen of Sheba; she is addressing her royal court and the letter she holds in her hand was written by King Solomon and delivered by his special messenger, the Hoopoe bird. Bilqis reads the letter without omitting the heading. 'Nobles,' she says. 'A distinguished letter has been delivered to me. It is from Solomon and it says, In the name of Allah, the Beneficent, the Merciful, do not rise against me and come to me in submission to God.' In the background, the Hoopoe hovers, awaiting the answer it will carry back, Bilqis's response.

It was the Hoopoe who had first alerted Solomon to the existence of Bilqis. More than a courier, it is King Solomon's intimate, a scout and an explorer, a fearless traveller and a trustworthy source. In Sheba, the Hoopoe had found a woman sitting on a magnificent throne, ruling a prosperous nation. But she and her people worship the sun instead of God, the Hoopoe tells Solomon. 'Should they not bow down to Allah who brings to light what is hidden in the heavens and earth and knows what you conceal and reveal?' This verse is one of fifteen instances in the Qur'an when the reciter is required to stop reading and respond to the words by bowing down in prostration. It is always a stirring experience. Instead of continuing to read, there is a pause, a space to interact, a physical reply to the Hoopoe's rhetorical question. The only species of bird mentioned in the Qur'an, the Hoopoe has opinions, insight and a voice that rings eternally in the sacred text.

The 12th century Persian poet, Attar, places the Hoopoe at the centre of his masterpiece *The Conference of the Birds*. In this allegorical tale, the birds of the world gather together and, led by the Hoopoe, decide to embark on a journey to seek their king. Attar's Hoopoe is grand and confident, in line with the Sufi tradition which casts the bird as a spiritual guide and metaphor for the perfect man. Its golden crest is a crown bestowed on him as a reward for the correspondence he had carried back and forth between Bilqis and Solomon. Its double row of orange feathers tipped with black is the gown of the learned seeker. 'I am in tune with the Great Almighty,' Attar's Hoopoe says to the gathered birds, 'schooled in the ways of great mysteries.' The birds confer and make excuses not to embark on the journey. It is too dangerous, and they are held back by their weaknesses and avarice, their pride and ambitions. Then there is false humility and misguided longings: the parrot would rather sit tight in a corner of its cage and the peacock is content with thoughts of Heaven. The Hoopoe urges them to set out, 'Cast off the shame of narcissism . . . Surrender your ego and step into the Path, cross that threshold dancing.'

Salma, Moni and Iman in *Bird Summons* are also weighed

down by their egos, though it may not seem apparent to them at first and there is enough justification for them to feel complacent in their positions. I wanted to explore the extent to which a journey could change them. The Hoopoe in the novel comes with stories. Stories by the Sufi mystic poet Rumi and the Sanskrit animal fables of *Kalila and Dimna*. Having now reached the Scottish Highlands, the Hoopoe is also well versed in the fables of selkies and shape-shifters that originate from the folk tales of Aberdeenshire and the surrounding areas. He is familiar with *The Pilgrim's Progress* and the fantasy worlds of George MacDonald. For the women in *Bird Summons,* the Hoopoe is a spiritual teacher who imparts ancient wisdom and guidance. But his powers are limited. The women must make their own choices. Away from the city – with its restrictions, formality and rituals, both religious and secular – the spiritual freedom that the women encounter is vast and beyond control.

Acknowledgements

My gratitude to my wonderful editor, Jennifer Kerslake, for the emails that made me happy as well as the times I was challenged.

Thanks to Arzu Tahsin, Matthew Cowdery and everyone at Weidenfeld & Nicolson who has made this book possible.

Continued thanks to Stephanie Cabot, my agent for over twenty years.

Thank you to Vimbai Shire and Ellen Goodson Coughtrey for invaluable feedback on the first draft.

And to Todd McEwen and Lucy Ellmann for believing in this novel, for their help and understanding.

I am grateful to William Facey and to Angus Sladen for permission to quote, in Chapter 4 and elsewhere, from *Pilgrimage to Mecca* by Lady Evelyn Cobbold. And to Anthony Cobbold for help with information about reaching her grave.

For the Hoopoe's stories, I am mainly grateful to the following sources:

– *Aberdeenshire Folk Tales* by Grace Banks & Sheena Blackhall

– *Rumi's Tales of Mystic Meaning* by Reynold A. Nicholson

– *The Un-discovered Islands: An Archipelago of Myths and Mysteries, Phantoms and Fakes* by Malachy Tallack

– *Kalila wa Dimna: Fables of Friendship and Betrayal* by Ramsay Wood with an Introduction by Doris Lessing

– I very much appreciated Sholeh Wolpé's modern and accessible translation of Attar's *The Conference of the Birds* and the detailed notes in Peter Avery's translation.

Thank you, Nadir, for walking by my side to Lady Evelyn's grave.

Help us make the next generation of readers

We – both author and publisher – hope you enjoyed this book. We believe that you can become a reader at any time in your life, but we'd love your help to give the next generation a head start.

Did you know that 9% of children don't have a book of their own in their home, rising to 13% in disadvantaged families*? We'd like to try to change that by asking you to consider the role you could play in helping to build readers of the future.

We'd love you to think of sharing, borrowing, reading, buying or talking about a book with a child in your life and spreading the love of reading. We want to make sure the next generation continue to have access to books, wherever they come from.

And if you would like to consider donating to charities that help fund literacy projects, find out more at www.literacytrust.org.uk and www.booktrust.org.uk.

Thank you.